TAIL OF THE DRAGON

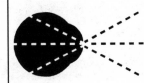

This Large Print Book carries the
Seal of Approval of N.A.V.H.

A ZODIAC MYSTERY

TAIL OF THE DRAGON

CONNIE DI MARCO

WHEELER PUBLISHING
A part of Gale, a Cengage Company

GALE
A Cengage Company

Farmington Hills, Mich • San Francisco • New York • Waterville, Maine
Meriden, Conn • Mason, Ohio • Chicago

Copyright © 2018 by Connie di Marco.
Wheeler Publishing, a part of Gale, a Cengage Company.

Wheeler Publishing Large Print Cozy Mystery.
The text of this Large Print edition is unabridged.
Other aspects of the book may vary from the original edition.
Set in 16 pt. Plantin.

LIBRARY OF CONGRESS CIP DATA ON FILE.
CATALOGUING IN PUBLICATION FOR THIS BOOK
IS AVAILABLE FROM THE LIBRARY OF CONGRESS

ISBN-13: 978-1-4328-5890-2 (softcover)

Published in 2019 by arrangement with Midnight, Ink, an imprint of Llewelyn Publications, Woodbury, MN 55125-2989 USA

Printed in Mexico
1 2 3 4 5 6 7 22 21 20 19 18

This book is dedicated to
Onofrio Picone
(1908–1991)
Grazie a te, tutto era possibile.

ACKNOWLEDGMENTS

Many thanks to Paige Wheeler of Creative Media Agency, Inc. for her hard work, good advice, and expertise, and to Terri Bischoff, Sandy Sullivan, Jake-Ryan Kent, and the entire team at Midnight Ink for welcoming the Zodiac Mysteries to their home.

Special thanks as well to my writers' group and first readers — Kim Fay, Laurie Stevens, Cheryl Brughelli, Don Fedosiuk, and Paula Freedman — for their critiques and encouragement. I would be remiss if I didn't give a big thank you to Llewellyn Publications for all the wonderful astrology books they've published over the years. Without that esoteric knowledge, this series would never have been created.

Last, but certainly not least, thanks to my family and my wonderful husband for their tolerance in living with a woman who is constantly thinking about murder.

Canyons of steel had plunged the street below into a false early darkness. Sunday afternoon, bleak and gray, downtown deserted and misty. The attorney worked alone in his office, a halogen lamp casting a bright pool of light on the papers spread across the desk. His brow furrowed in concentration as he studied the documents, considering which would be needed for the court hearing later in the week. A file box filled with reams of paper rested on the floor next to his chair.

He grasped another handful of documents and flipped through the pages, mentally cursing his associate who should have already completed this task. He closed his eyes for a moment and took a deep breath in an effort to control his temper. His doctor had warned him about his blood pressure. Lazy damn incompetents, he thought. All of them. Did he really have to do this scut work himself?

He heard the ping of the elevator doors in the corridor but ignored the sound, certain it was the weekend cleaning staff. He wanted no interruptions and planned to finish his review within the hour. He glanced up in irritation as the door swung open.

"What the hell do you want now?" he barked. Not waiting for an answer, he swiveled in his chair and leaned forward, flipping up the lid of the nearest file box.

A blinding light filled his sight as sharp metal was thrust into his neck. His attacker stepped back. Arterial blood sprayed the wall. His hand reached for the wound. His mouth opened but he could not speak. Twitching uncontrollably, he slumped forward onto the desk, the complexities of trial strategy no longer on his mind.

ONE

Revenge is a dish best served cold, or so it's been said in many cultures and various ways. I'm not sure I agree. I've always imagined that impulse arising from a hot cauldron of bubbling poisonous hatred, an anger nurtured and folded in upon itself for so long its force is a volcanic eruption. Hot, Plutonian, exploding from the depths of the psyche.

If I want to be honest, I'd have to admit to falling prey to the desire for revenge upon mine enemies as well, however transitory those adversaries might be. Lord knows I have my share of Pluto-ruled Scorpio in my chart, but in the final analysis, I am a Sagittarian, able to *eventually* rise above all those deep and murky impulses, however painful that process might be. And like a good little girl, I give myself a whacking self-righteous pat on the back for doing so.

My name is Julia Bonatti — Julia Elizabeth Bonatti — and I'm an astrologer. I study natal charts. I contemplate character. I analyze things to death and always wonder what makes people tick. What drives a person to an act of revenge? And how to spot that in a natal chart? After all, revenge isn't a planet or a house or an aspect. It's not even an emotion like clear hatred. It's a reaction borne of perceived injury and humiliation.

Looking back now, little did I think my life could become forfeit to someone else's need for retaliation, for a transgression I never committed nor knew of, just because I was sticking my nose in the wrong place at the wrong time. As they say . . . no good deed . . .

Two

It was that very same good deed that found me clambering off the 38 Geary bus, dressed in my grown-up lady clothes at eight thirty on a chilly October morning. The coming week would find me at a law firm where I had once worked. Almost three years ago, back in the days before I built my clientele and found a measure of independence.

Independence does have a downside though. It's called *no steady income.* Well, that's not quite fair. I have a decent income from my private clients and the astrological advice column I write for the *Chronicle,* but a serious car repair, a vet bill, and a dental bill had put a major crimp in my budget. So when David Meyers, my old boss and now a client, called and begged me — yes, he begged — to cover for his vacationing secretary for a week, I agreed. Not without trepidation. I had no intention of returning to my old life of working nine to five, but I liked David and he'd been a good friend at a time when I needed one. He'd hired me when the death of my fiancé had sucked my life into a black hole, and the job, as tedious as it was, had given me sanctuary and a little bit of security during a long healing process. So I figured I owed him. That was the other reason I agreed. I just hoped Muriel, his secretary, had no intention of extending her vacation.

The bus pulled away in a blast of exhaust fumes and the wind whipped dead leaves along the gutters of the street. I pulled up the collar of my coat and craned my neck, staring up at the shiny steel megalith at 44 Montgomery. I sighed. Just a week. *I can do this,* I mumbled to myself and joined the throngs of office workers crossing the street. I stepped into the revolving door and entered the lobby. A central concierge desk was decorated with an autumn display of chrysanthemums, gourds, and dried flowers. A sign announced a pumpkin-carving contest, all entries to be submitted by Thursday at five o'clock.

I headed for the elevator bank, hit the button for the 41st floor, and squeezed to the rear. David's firm, Meyers, Dade & Schultz, LLP, had grown a bit in the last few years and now occupied the entire 40th floor and half of the 41st. The other half of the 41st floor was sealed off; it had once been occupied by a now-defunct mortgage brokerage, and I was sure David planned to expand and occupy the entire floor. The elevator whizzed past the first twenty floors, the digital display showing XXs. I've always felt a degree of discomfort at that digital display. What would happen if the doors opened on such a floor? Would we enter another dimension, Rod Serling hovering in a darkened corner? Or face a blank brick wall? I would definitely suffer an extreme claustrophobic meltdown. Best not to think about all that. My imagination sometimes gets the better of me.

The elevator made several stops between the 21st and 40th floors and by the time it reached the 41st, I was the lone passenger. I stepped off, turned the corner, and walked the long carpeted corridor to the double doors of David's private office. As I passed the employee lounge, my nose twitched at the aroma of freshly brewed coffee. I pushed open one of the doors and entered David's reception area. As the senior litigation partner of the firm, he enjoyed a private suite — a waiting room lined with oak paneling, built-in bookshelves, and plush carpeting, as well as a corner office. A small tapestry-covered sofa and two chairs stood across from Muriel's secretarial desk. Several lamps on low tables around the room provided lighting. I could hear David's voice droning into a Dictaphone in the inner office. The overall effect was hushed and restful. Good for nervous clients, but a few days of this and they'd find me snoring over my keyboard. I hung my coat in a small closet concealed by the paneling and tapped on the inner door.

David was seated behind an executive-sized mahogany desk piled high with files and loose papers. The surrounding floor was littered in the same fashion. "Julia, hi! Come on in." My ex-boss is in his mid-fifties, with a round face and ruddy complexion. Today he wore a blue shirt, open at the neck, and a gray sweater-vest. He'd loosened his tie and shed his suit jacket, now thrown over one of the two leather wing chairs in front of his desk. Three half-filled cups of coffee from prior days sat on the desk blotter, two of them showing the first signs of new life forms. David held a jelly donut in one hand and an open file in the other. A dribble of jam spotted his chin.

I pointed to his chin. He laughed. "Excuse me. Terrible table manners. How are you, by the way?" Before I could respond, he continued. "I so appreciate your coming in this week. I'm always lost when Muriel's gone. I can never find a thing." He waved the jelly donut in a semi-circle, vaguely indicating the mounds of surrounding paper.

I resisted the temptation to rush at his donut with a napkin. "Anything I can do now?"

He smiled, his face lighting up. "No, no. I'm fine. I may have some letters in a little bit. Get yourself settled. Would you like a donut?" He gestured toward a half-open box on a side table.

"Thanks, I'm fine." I stood. "You know, it must be synchronicity because I was about to call you."

"Really?"

"Yes. Remember we talked about setting up a reading? I've been expecting you to call."

David stared at me in silence for a moment. "Oh, I'm sorry. You're right. I forgot."

I waited a moment to see if he'd have any further comment. "Everything going okay at work? At the firm?"

He nodded. "Sure. Everything's fine."

I wasn't so certain, given what I knew about David's chart. But if he wasn't interested in hearing what I had to say, what more could I do? He began to ruffle through a stack of papers, donut still in hand, nodding distractedly. I headed back to the outer office, shutting the door behind me.

I sat in Muriel's chair and adjusted it higher, then flipped on the computer. I glanced around. The desk held an old-fashioned Rolodex, a phone with several buttons, a pottery urn full of pens and pencils, and a small clock. Two photos in silver frames sat in a place of honor on the desk. One was of a large taffy-colored Persian cat and the other of a young couple posing with a boy in his early teens and a girl of maybe nine or ten. I hadn't seen Muriel since I left the firm, but I remembered her as a quiet, attractive woman in her fifties, her dark hair sprinkled with gray. The family picture must be her nephew, his wife, and their two kids. I stashed my purse in the roomy bottom drawer of the desk, next to a pair of well-worn flats, a box of crackers, and two containers of dry soup. I dug the crackers and soup out and moved them to an upper drawer. High-pitched voices filtered down the corridor from the other offices in the litigation section, the only department on this floor. Ever nosy, I stepped out to the corridor and sauntered in that direction.

A female voice, dripping with barely controlled annoyance, said, "I left that on your desk yesterday."

A higher-pitched voice tinged with authority responded, "That can't be possible. I would have seen it!"

"Would you like me to come in there and find it for you?"

Four litigation attorneys — Jack Harding, Ira Walstone, Roger Wilkinson, and Nora Layton — had offices around a central area. They shared two secretaries. One very small office was set aside for Suzanne, the lone paralegal. The demanding voice had to be Nora's.

A painfully thin man leaned against the wall of the corridor outside the door to the attorneys' offices. He was dressed in jeans, black leather chaps, and a red and black bulky jacket. He held a motorcycle helmet sporting red and yellow flames in the crook of his arm. His straw-colored hair was shaggy and hung in ragged strands around a long sallow face. He didn't smile as I walked toward him.

"That *might* be a help if it were on my desk," Nora's voice replied.

I turned the corner. A young woman with cropped hair, dyed green, sat at the first

19

desk. Her head was down. *"Bitch,"* she mumbled under her breath. I wondered if her hair color was permanent or just an early Halloween statement. A plastic skull draped with tiny flashing orange bulbs took up a corner of her desk.

She jumped when she realized I was standing in front of her. "Oh!" She recovered quickly. "Can I help you?" Another woman, older and heavyset, with straight black hair to her collar, occupied the second desk. She glanced up at me briefly and then returned to her work.

I wanted to laugh but not within earshot of Nora's office. Instead, I smiled conspiratorially and held out my hand. "Hi. I'm Julia. I'm filling in for Muriel for a week while she's on vacation. I thought I'd come down and introduce myself. I used to work here a few years ago."

The green-haired woman visibly relaxed and smiled. She stood and accepted my handshake. "Nice to meet you. I'm Dani. Dani Nichols." Her hands were tattooed with flowers and sported a lot of silver. Her clothing was dark, her makeup even darker, and an iridescent titanium ring flashed at one nostril. Several more earrings on each ear climbed to the top of her ear lobes. She was a few inches shorter than I. Her baggy shirt was cinched with a wide belt and her black pants were tucked into heavy boots. Her eyes drifted to the doorway where the biker in leathers was waiting. "Oh, Billy! I'm sorry. I forgot you were still here. They decided to file that with the court tomorrow. Can you come back same time?"

"Sure." Billy nodded sullenly and turned toward the elevators, his leathers creaking as he walked.

Dani turned back to me. "That's Billy, one of the guys from our attorney service. He does our court runs most days. I should have introduced you; you might need to send something to court."

"I hope not. It's been a while and I'm pretty rusty."

Dani nodded. "I hear you. Necessary evil if you want a paycheck."

Besides the two secretarial desks, the area was crammed with several filing cabinets and stacked boxes. The door farthest from the entrance was shut, as though its occupant hadn't yet arrived. It was the large corner office, and I was sure it belonged to Jack Harding, the most senior member of the group after David.

I glanced into Nora's office. She was seated at her desk with a phone to her ear. She'd swiveled in her chair and was looking out the window at a view of other high-rises. She swung back quickly and slammed the phone into its cradle. "Dani, you still have my file with the handwritten notes? I asked you to keep it in here!"

Dani took a deep breath and looked at me as if to say, *Give me patience.*

Nora rose from her chair and moved to the doorway. She hesitated when she saw me at Dani's desk. "Oh, I didn't . . ."

During the time I'd worked at David's firm, I'd never dealt directly with Nora. She had joined just as I was leaving. Her look swept over my outfit, probably tallying the cost of my clothing to the last penny. She smiled suddenly, a smile that did nothing to warm her eyes. Unsure who I was — another attorney, a client — she wanted to remain within bounds. After an uncomfortable beat, I extended my hand. "You're Nora, right? I'm Julia. I'm filling in for Muriel for a week."

Nora's eyes glazed over. "Oh, yes, nice to meet you." She shook my hand limply. I was no longer an object of interest.

I turned to Dani. "If you're busy and need help, just call me. You know where I am."

"Thanks, but I try to stay out of the way of the big guy."

"David?" I smiled. "He's not that bad. In

fact, he's a very nice guy. And I love the skull." I said, referring to her office decoration.

"Dani, I really could use your help *now.*" Nora retreated to her office.

"Yes, ma'am." Dani grimaced at me and made an obscene gesture at Nora's back with her tongue. I beat a retreat rather than be caught laughing.

On the way back, I made a stop at the staff lounge to grab a cup of coffee. An overhead cabinet held mugs decorated with the firm logo, but the little coffee maker took me a moment to figure out. I sighed. Computerized coffee. I lifted its hood and popped a small plastic pod in the slot. The machine began to spit out a dark brew. When it gave its last burp, I slid the cup out. My hand jerked involuntarily as a high-pitched keening sound reached my ears. The mug slipped from my hand, spewing coffee into the sink. Someone was screaming.

THREE

The cry had come from the litigation section. Coffee forgotten, I ran back down the hall and sensed rather than heard David's footsteps behind me. Inside the central room, the door to Jack Harding's office stood open. Dani was standing next to her desk, staring at the open door. A man I recognized as Roger Wilkinson came to his doorway, a puzzled look on his face. I maneuvered around them and stepped through the door to Jack's office. A girl, not much more than high school age, her blonde hair in a ponytail, stood frozen in the center of the room. A sickly odor filled the air. Jack's body was slumped over the desk, a letter opener jutting from his neck. Scattered papers were pinned beneath him. Blood spatter marked the framed diplomas on the wall. Jack Harding was very dead.

The only sound now was the quiet moaning of the young woman. The files she'd been delivering had fallen to the floor. I fought against the feeling welling up from my insides and grasped her shoulders, turning her around to lead her out of the room. David stepped back from the doorway as I led her out. Nora and Roger and the two secretaries, now pressing in to see, made way for us.

"Yvonne," David said, "are you all right?" The copy clerk raised her eyes to him and opened her mouth but couldn't speak. David's face was pale. He took one step inside the corner office, then backed out. "I'll call the police." He turned to face the others. "We should all get out of here and wait in the lounge."

"What?" Roger said. "I can't possibly . . ."

"I'm sorry. I want everyone out."

"Is he dead?"

"Yes."

Yvonne's weight pressed against me. She was threatening to sink to the floor. Dani rushed forward and together we half-walked the girl down the hall to the small couch in the staff lounge. We helped her into a sitting position and covered her with a blanket from the emergency supply cabinet.

"She's in shock." Dani placed a hand on Yvonne's forehead. "We might need paramedics too."

"Good idea." I hurried after David. He'd picked up Muriel's phone and was describing our plight to the 911 operator. I whispered, "Paramedics too." He nodded in response. He relayed the request and replaced the phone in its cradle. He turned to me. "What the hell, Julia . . ."

We heard a shout from the corridor. "What's going on? Where is everybody?"

David groaned. "That's Ira. Let's get back." Roger was explaining the discovery of Jack's body to the new arrival as we entered the lounge.

Ira's gray hair straggled over his collar and a smudge of blue ink marred the pocket of his shirt. He turned and stared at Yvonne. "What's wrong with her?" No one answered.

"We need to lock the litigation section." David slipped a single key on a small metal ring out of his pocket. He handed it to me. "Julia, go lock the main door. Then call down to the reception desk and tell them to advise everyone in the firm that this floor is off limits." He turned to the others. "Anyone expecting a client to arrive?" He was greeted with silence. "Okay, good. Then we'll all stay here while we wait for the police."

"I need my purse and things," Nora whined. "Dani, can you gather up my things? I can't possibly go in there now."

Dani stared at her boss. *"You* can't go back to your office, but it's okay for *me?"* She shook her head and sighed.

"What's the matter, Nora? Since when are you so sensitive?" Ira snickered. Nora narrowed her eyes, skewering him with a look that could have shriveled a wild boar.

David ignored the exchange. "Your personal belongings are safe in there. You can get them later. I don't want anyone touching a thing until the police arrive."

I took the key from David's hand and walked the length of the corridor. My knees were wobbling and my hands were shaking so badly I could hardly fit the key into the lock. When Jack Harding was alive, I'd made sure to avoid him. Now I had absolutely no intention of opening that other door and going near his body. I managed to get the department door locked on the third try and returned to the lounge.

Yvonne's complexion had taken on a gray sheen. I sat next to her and took her hand. "You're safe. You won't be left alone. I promise." Yvonne turned to face me and nodded silently. Dani perched on the edge of the couch next to the young girl and put an arm around her shoulder.

Nora was pacing back and forth in front of one of the windows. "Somebody give me a cigarette," she demanded. "I feel sick." She sat down at the opposite end of the sofa from Yvonne, holding her head between her hands.

"No smoking here, Nora," Roger remarked in a judgmental tone. He pursed his lips. "Although you do have the distinction of being the last of the dinosaurs, someone who still smokes at the office."

"Oh, give me a break. Who would care? Dani . . . ?"

"What?"

"Do you have a smoke?"

"Yeah." Dani reached into her pants pocket and passed a cigarette and lighter to Nora. She smiled at Roger. "I guess Nora's not the last."

"David, this is ridiculous," Ira grumbled. "You're treating us like criminals."

"No, I'm not," David replied. "All of you need to settle down. It's very important we stay together and don't touch anything in Jack's office or the central room. You can stay here or you're welcome to use my office. But we wait."

Roger had slumped into a plastic chair, his legs stretched in front of him. He was immaculately dressed in a gray suit, coordinated shirt, and a striped tie. His dark hair was touched with silver. He looked less upset than annoyed. Karen, the other secretary, sat at a table near the coffee machine fidgeting with her hair. Her complexion was pasty, the color of uncooked dough.

I caught Ira staring at me. "Who do we have here?" he asked with a suggestive smile.

"This is Julia," David answered. "You remember her, don't you?"

"Obviously not well enough," he leered, exposing a mouthful of stained teeth. I ignored him.

"Why don't you just shut it, Ira," Nora huffed. She began to pace again, then stopped and turned to Dani. "Where's Suzanne? Why isn't she here?"

"She isn't in," Dani responded. "Look, I don't know about anybody else, but I need coffee. I'll make a few cups. I'm sure we can all use some."

The young copy girl started to rock back and forth and cry in spite of Dani's moral support. Ira glanced at her. "Can *someone* get her to be quiet?"

Dani frowned. "Can someone grow you a heart? She just found Jack dead, for chrissakes." Ira's head jerked back as if Dani had slapped his face. Nora observed the exchange between the two and smiled coldly.

The elevator doors dinged and we heard a commotion in the hallway. David left the lounge and walked toward the elevator bank. We heard him greeting the new arrivals. He reappeared in the doorway followed by two men. The older detective was short and stout with fair hair. The younger man wore a brown tweed jacket and dark rimmed eyeglasses. He looked like he'd been abducted from a high school chemistry class.

The shorter man spoke. "Good morning. I'm Sergeant Ralph Sullivan. This is Officer Nick Ray. We're with the Homicide Division of the San Francisco Police Department." They held up their badges with the seven-pointed star of the SFPD. "We'll talk to each of you individually and take a more formal statement within the next few days. Please be sure you are available to us if need be." The sergeant turned to David. "I understand everyone here works on the 41st floor?"

"Yes," David replied. "It's only the litigation section on this floor. The rest of our offices are on the 40th. I've asked the reception desk to keep anyone from coming up on the elevator. The man who . . ." David took a deep breath and tried to calm himself. "My partner, Jack Harding . . . he's been murdered." David's complexion paled. He turned to me. "Julia, you have the key?" I passed it back to him. He turned away and led the detectives down the hallway to Jack's office, returning a few minutes later. "The detectives will take each of you into my office to take your statements. I'm closing the firm early and I want everyone to leave here as soon as we're done. You'll be allowed to collect your personal belongings under supervision and if you'd like help getting home, I'd be happy to call a taxi service." He looked around the room. "Could someone notify the answering service? Julia, if you don't mind, I could use your help for a short while until all this is done."

Karen looked up quickly. "I can stay and help too."

"Thanks, I appreciate that, Karen, but I think we'll be fine," David replied.

"Okay then." She smiled, patting her forehead with a napkin. I wondered if she was actually taking everything in.

Sergeant Sullivan reappeared in the doorway. "I'll speak with whoever discovered the body first and then each of you one by one. After that, you're free to go. My officers will assist you in removing any personal items."

Yvonne attempted to stand. "That would be me. I found him." Dani helped her to her feet and watched silently as Yvonne was escorted down the hall to David's office.

When they'd cleared the doorway, Nora said, "Christ, what a mess. I'd say Jack got exactly what was coming to him." Roger laughed mirthlessly in response.

I caught David's eye. He returned my look with something that said, *Later.*

FOUR

Two hours passed before we were free to go. David and I headed for the elevators but were brought to a halt as men from the Coroner's Office struggled to maneuver a gurney into the corridor. The shape of a human arm bulged from the side of a zippered black body bag. My breath caught in my throat. David reached out to halt my steps as the men continued toward the service elevator at the end of the elevator bank. David was tense and silent. We rode down to the street level and, pushing through the crowd, reached the sidewalk.

"Julia, I'm so sorry," he said. "I never should have asked you to come here."

I shook my head. "It's not your fault, David. How could you have known something like this would happen? I'm just glad I *was* here today, if only for your sake."

"Let's find a place to sit. Maybe get something to eat."

I groaned. "I'm not sure I can." My stomach was churning from the coffee I'd managed to swallow an hour before.

"Well, have something with me. A cup of tea at least." We crossed the street and turned up the hill on Sutter.

I did my best to walk next to him on the crowded sidewalk, but I was jostled continuously as people hurried past us. "Where are we going?"

"I'm thinking the Rose and Thistle. It's quiet and we can talk there." David sighed again. "Best of all, they serve liquor and I could use a stiff drink right about now."

Being at the firm again, walking these streets, was stirring old memories, memories from a few years earlier. Michael and I had become engaged as soon as I finished work on my masters in anthropology. He was heading out of the country for a month on a dig. I anxiously awaited his return. He did return, only to be killed by a hit-and-run driver on his way to meet me that very day. When I was finally able to get my bearings, I took the job at David's firm. When I wasn't at my job, I was a lost soul, wandering through the city at all hours. One day, in North Beach, I discovered an occult shop called the Mystic Eye. I became fascinated by the astrology books the shop offered, and the owner, Gale Hymson, encouraged my interest. We eventually became close friends. That period of my life was a painful time, but one I can now look back on if not with fondness, at least with gratitude. It was a time of healing and recovery.

David and I entered a restaurant under a red awning. A black-clad hostess stepped forward to greet us. "Hello, Mr. Meyers, how are you today?"

David struggled to smile. "Fine, thank you. Could we have a booth at the back, a quiet spot?"

"Of course." The woman turned, and, weaving around linen-covered tables, led us through the elegant dining area to the rear. The walls were covered in a pale taupe fabric. Small sconces lit each booth. I slid into my seat and sank into the upholstered depths of the banquette. Leaning back, I tried to ease the tension in my neck. A waiter arrived immediately with two menus. David ordered a Scotch and soda and looked questioningly at me.

"Just water please," I said. I wasn't sure I could eat and tried to push the image of Jack's body out of my mind. I turned back to David. "Did Jack have any family?"

David shook his head. "Not really. His parents died years ago and he's divorced.

Never had children. He does have a sister in the city, but for some reason I don't think they were on good terms."

"Where did he live?"

"He has . . . had a condo somewhere in North Beach. Filbert, I think."

I know North Beach well. I grew up there, and my grandmother, Gloria, who raised me after my parents' death, still lives in Castle Alley. North Beach is a stone's throw away from Montgomery Street and the financial district.

David sighed. "I guess we'll have to get access somehow and make sure he wasn't keeping any office files at home."

"Look, I have to ask. What was all that vitriol in the lounge upstairs?"

"Huh?" David replied, just as the waiter returned with his Scotch. He took a sip. "You mean Nora?"

"Yes, and Roger had a strange response to the situation."

David frowned. "They were just being nasty. Frankly . . . well . . ." He hesitated. "Jack wasn't well liked, as you can imagine. Not by the staff and not by his colleagues. There's that and then there was a rumor floating around . . . don't know if it's true or not, that Jack was having an affair with Ira's wife. Frankly, I don't know and I don't want to know, but if it did happen, I think it was a while back."

I watched as David took another sip of his drink. "Meaning Ira was someone with a motive to kill Jack?"

"That's ridiculous of course."

"It's not ridiculous, David. Somebody killed him." I looked up to see our waiter standing next to the table with a basket of warm rolls in his hands. He'd overheard my comment and attempted to cover his reaction. "Would you like to hear our specials today?" I nodded and smiled in response as he recited the menu. The restaurant was beginning to fill with a lunch crowd and had become noisier. I was grateful we were at the quiet end of the room.

"I'll have the salmon and baked potato." David turned to me. "What would you like, Julia?"

I ordered a spinach salad with mushrooms and feta cheese. My appetite had returned. I took one of the warm rolls and broke it open, buttering it generously. Our waiter nodded and moved away, casting a last dubious glance at me.

"Where were we?" David asked. "Oh, yes, Ira's wife." He shrugged. "I doubt Ira particularly cared if his wife was carrying on with Jack or anybody else. She . . . uh . . .

it's been rumored she has a drinking problem and their marriage is pretty much . . . nonexistent."

"You should mention this to Sullivan."

David grimaced. "I don't know. It feels like I'm just gossiping. Maybe someone else will tell him about all that."

"You can always give him a call. I have his cell number. He wrote it on the back of the card he gave me." I took a large bite of my buttery roll. "What about Jack's ex-wife? You said he was divorced? Is she around?"

"Yes. Hilary. Hilary Greene. She uses her maiden name now. Hilary got the house in the Marina after the divorce. I believe Jack made alimony payments for several years. And I heard she opened an art gallery, of all things."

"A gallery, huh?" I thought of my friend Gale, who besides her venture with the Mystic Eye had become involved in the art world over the past year. Perhaps she knew of Hilary Greene. "Where's her gallery?"

"Someone told me. Can't think who it was now. Oh, it's where Fillmore starts to climb. In fact, it's on Fillmore. I remember now. I was taking to Suzanne — Suzanne Simms, our paralegal — about it. She and Hilary know each other. They went to school together."

"And Jack's sister?"

"She's here in the city, out in the Sunset. The police were going to get her address from Human Resources. I really should try to contact her myself, tonight or tomorrow." David swirled his glass around on the table. "There's something else . . ."

I waited. He seemed nervous. "What is it?"

"I . . . uh . . ." David rubbed his forehead. "I had a bit of an ulterior motive in asking you to be here this week."

"What do you mean?"

"Well, it's as I said. Muriel wanted to take this week off. I could have called an agency or asked for someone from the 40th floor to fill in. I don't really go to court very much anymore. I can always assign one of the other attorneys . . . but I thought, given your talents . . . you're very perceptive, and your intuition about people . . . well, I thought you'd be a good person to do some snooping, maybe pick up gossip or offer some insights."

He was looking more nervous by the minute. And he was making *me* nervous. Given the events of the morning, I wasn't in great shape to begin with. "David . . . get to the point."

He took a deep breath. "A few people at

the firm have received death threats."

"*Whaat?*" I almost choked on my hunk of buttered roll. "What kind of threats?"

He hurried to explain. "I thought if you were here, you maybe could —"

"And you didn't think it was necessary to tell me this?" I squeaked. Hadn't I just questioned him about the firm?

"I know. I'm sorry. I really am. I was just waiting for an opportune moment, but . . . That's why I feel so bad now."

"Was Jack one of those people?"

David nodded.

"I hope you told the police."

"I made a report at the time, or rather the people who got those nasty things did. They came to me about it, so I made sure there was something official on file."

"I meant today. Did you tell Sergeant Sullivan about this?"

"Yes. Of course," David replied in a defensive tone. "Three people got them. All in litigation. Jack was the first, then Ira, and then Suzanne. They were found in their office mail, in a plain envelope with just a name on the front. No postmark, no indication of where they came from."

"What did they say?"

"One said, *'You will pay for what you've done.'* Another was *'Prepare to die.'* The third one . . ." David's hands were shaking. "I don't remember right now." He took a long sip of his drink. "They were put together with letters cut out of magazines. The police have them now. No fingerprints, no indication how they got into the firm. No one in reception remembered receiving them. I should have taken it more seriously, Julia. If I had, Jack might still be alive."

"No. That's crazy. You can't beat yourself up. You did what you thought was right at the time." *Except not telling me about it.* "How does the mail come in?"

"We have a service that picks up from the post office and delivers. Hand deliveries come through the main reception on the 40th floor. They're all *supposed* to be logged in. But there's nothing to indicate these envelopes arrived that way."

"What makes you think there were only three?"

David looked up suddenly. "What do you mean?"

"I mean," I said, leaning across the table, "maybe other people received weird threats and didn't say anything."

David looked puzzled. "But why wouldn't they?"

I shrugged. "Maybe they're too freaked out. Maybe they laughed and dismissed it.

Who knows?"

"Oh . . . this is going to sound pretty stupid, but I honestly never thought about that. But what could I do? I couldn't just casually ask everyone who works at the firm, 'By the way, has your life been threatened?' Wouldn't that be just dandy for office morale!"

"I see your point." The waiter arrived with a tray and deftly placed our dishes on the table. I sprinkled salt and a few drops of dressing over my salad. "Is the mailroom locked?"

"It is now. It wasn't before. Three people work there. There's Steve and Joey. They're full-time, and Monica. She's a college student who comes in during the afternoons to help them out. We never used to lock that room. It's right off the lobby on the 40th floor, and everyone in the firm has always had access to it, plus a lot of the copy services and delivery people have been allowed in there to carry in boxes and whatnot." David shook a napkin out and placed it on his lap. "That's all changed now. No one is allowed in except those three people. Messengers have to wait in the lobby until someone from the mailroom can meet them. No one from the outside or inside, for that matter, has any access now. There haven't been any more of those letters since."

"What about the three who work there? What do you think of them?"

"They're great, they're all great. The two guys have worked here for a long time, Monica for a couple of years. I can't imagine any of them doing anything like that. Besides, the police questioned them at the time." David rubbed his hands over his temples. "Julia, listen, I still feel bad about dragging you into this mess. Maybe you should reconsider. I think it'd be better if you didn't come back tomorrow."

"What are you talking about?" I bristled. "If the people who regularly work here can come in, then I can show up too. Nothing's going to happen to me."

David looked exhausted from the shock of the morning's events. "You know, I should have called you for a reading when this first happened. You were right. Could I impose on you now?"

"Of course. When?"

"How 'bout this afternoon?"

His request took me by surprise, but under the circumstances I could certainly understand. I knew he was heading toward a difficult time. I mentally reviewed the work piled up on my desk but decided everything was under control and a few things could wait. "Okay. How about five o'clock? That'll give me some time to get home and have a look at your chart."

David had been as hard-nosed and un-metaphysical as anyone could be when I first met him. He used to laugh at my pursuits. That had all changed when his college-aged son dropped out of school. He and his wife Caroline were beside themselves. They'd groomed their son for law school and were upset by his rebellion. I'd volunteered to have a look at the boy's chart and offered the opinion that his true talent was music. It wasn't at all what they'd wanted to hear, but they finally allowed their son to transfer to a well-known music school and, since then, their son had been performing and working steadily, and was quite happy. David and Caroline eventually became believers in the benefits of astrology.

"Can I at least drive you home?" he asked.

"Oh, no. Not necessary. Thanks, though." I knew David was heading up to Russian Hill, so 30th Avenue would be out of his way. "There's something I'd like to do, now that I'm downtown and have a little time."

"Julia, my apologies. I've been thoughtless. I've been so wrapped up in my own problems, I haven't even had a chance to ask how you're doing." I knew he was referring to Michael even though he didn't say it.

"I'm okay. Really." I hesitated. "I'd like to say I never have any bad moments or bad dreams, but . . . there are actually days now when I don't think about all of that. Then sometimes a memory comes up and it still feels like a knife in my heart." David was silent. "But, all in all, I'm doing well. I have good friends. I'm very busy and happy with the work I have, so there are blessings I'm grateful for."

"The police never found the driver?"

I grimaced. "Nope."

"I'm sorry . . . I don't mean to bring up the past."

"It's a natural question. Anybody would want some kind of resolution. Especially me."

"Are you seeing anyone now?" David asked.

I laughed. "No. Although I can admit to a couple of dismal dates. A well-meaning friend and my grandmother twisted my arm." Our waiter arrived to take our dishes away.

"Sure you won't change your mind about

that ride?"

"No, really. I'll see you at five."

FIVE

At the corner of Montgomery and Sutter, David headed back to the office building to retrieve his car and I turned in the other direction, toward North Beach and the Mystic Eye. I was hoping to catch Gale at the shop. Gale's first career had been in real estate — she was very good at it and had made quite a lot of money. Then she branched out and started her first business venture with the Mystic Eye. Since then, her shop has become the most popular metaphysical store in the city. The Eye carries a wide range of books on occult subjects, jewelry, accessories, Tarot cards, candles, herbs, and gifts. Something for every taste and belief. Gale isn't much of a believer in the occult, but it's thanks to her I've collected an impressive astrological library.

Tonight she was hosting an exhibition for a new artist at the Fort Mason Center, a group of buildings at the water's edge in the Marina District with a long and interesting history. The original fortifications date back to 1776, and after the great quake of 1906, the tidal cove was reclaimed and the boxy buildings that stand today were erected. Fort Mason is hardly an architectural *wow,* but it's a national landmark, now put to good use for nonprofit businesses, galleries, and theatres. I had promised to attend, and hoped to catch up with Gale to see if she needed any help preparing for the evening's event.

The streets of the financial district were virtually deserted now that the lunch rush was over. An elderly black man stood at the corner playing a saxophone, his case open to accept donations. The wind had abated and his doleful notes echoed off the buildings. I rummaged in my purse and dropped a couple of dollars in his case. He nodded and continued to play, his music trailing me as I walked on.

The intersection of Broadway and Columbus is the heart of North Beach. The neighborhood isn't a beach, but nothing in the city is very far from the ocean or the bay. Italian immigrants coming west settled here and created a unique neighborhood, now a major tourist stop full of clubs, cafes, and restaurants. I hurried across the busy intersection to reach the Mystic Eye. I spotted our friend Cheryl in one of the display windows, arranging gargoyles, Tarot cards, books, and crystal balls against an artful backdrop of draped velvet. Cheryl manages the shop and can be found there most days, especially when Gale is busy with other things. I tapped on the glass. She looked up and waved. I waved back and entered the store.

The aroma of sandalwood filled the shop. A small fountain gurgled and heavy drapes muted the noise of the traffic. The Mystic Eye was an oasis of calm in the hubbub of the city.

"Julia! Hi. Didn't know you were coming by today." Cheryl extricated herself from the window platform and climbed down on a short step stool. "What are you up to?"

"Well . . . you remember this is the week I promised David, my old boss, I'd fill in."

"Oh, that's right. I forgot."

"Dere she is!" A booming voice came from the back of the shop. "A sight for sore eyes!"

It was Nikolai, a friend and one of the Eye's loyal customers, who was known primarily for his regular appearances on a community access station exorcising demons from the bodies of attractive young women.

Charging down the aisle, Nikolai grabbed my hand and kissed it. "You look vonderful." A crafty look came into his eyes. "A new man?"

I shook my head.

"You sure? I could svear. But dat's good news. I still have a chance."

"You're such a flirt, Nikolai! What are you doing here?" I asked.

"I vant to check the space out. You know I'm doing a presentation here on Halloween, at the open house."

"Oh, I didn't know. What sort of presentation?" I'd heard Gale was throwing a party late Saturday afternoon at the shop with snacks and music, and that she'd encouraged guests to attend in costume. "I know Zora will be here for psychic readings and Jonathan will be doing Tarot."

"Yes, yes." Nikolai waved dismissively. "All dat's nice, but I'm planning someting very special. You'll see. It's a surprise, I not telling anyone."

I glanced at Cheryl, who widened her eyes to indicate her trepidation over Nikolai's plan.

He bowed. "Excuse please, darling ladies. I must go now. I will see you both Saturday."

As soon as the door closed behind him, I turned to Cheryl. "You have no idea what he's going to do?"

"Nope. Gale just threw up her hands. She loves Nikolai. I mean, how bad can it be?"

"Nothing wrong with an exorcism on Halloween," I replied drily.

"Come on outside." Cheryl grabbed my arm. "I'm still fussing with that window. Let's see what it looks like from the sidewalk." We stepped outside and took a critical look. "What do you think?" Cheryl asked.

"I . . ." I felt a tickle run up my spine. I had the distinct impression we were being watched. I turned quickly, having half caught a reflection of movement in the glass. But when I looked across the street, no one stood out. I shook myself. Nerves. The sidewalk was crowded with pedestrians shopping at the outdoor Chinese market and passing the Wah Fong Hotel. No one had taken the slightest notice of us.

"What's wrong?" Cheryl asked.

"Uh . . . nothing. I was imagining things. I just had a strange feeling." Cheryl turned to follow my gaze. "It's not important."

"Well?" she said impatiently. "What do you think of the window?"

I gave her my full attention. "It looks

51

fantastic."

"Come on inside. I want to show you something. I have an idea and I'd like your opinion." We stepped into the shop and Cheryl headed down the aisle, past the display cases of jewelry and rows of bookshelves and into the storeroom. She pulled a large cardboard box from a shelf. "I want to do a sort of pagan Halloween or Samhain theme in the windows. Gale reminded me we had these Venetian masks back here." Cheryl pulled off the top of the box. Inside were six bundles, all wrapped in white cloth. She unfolded the first and held up a gold-painted female face draped in black lace, with a headdress of long feathers. "What do you think?"

"Wow! Is that the real thing?"

Cheryl smiled. "All the way from Venezia. One of Gale's trips there." She placed the first mask on the shelf and reached for another one. Once again she unwrapped the cloth and held the mask up for me. A face in cured brown leather and horns, neither human nor animal, stared back at me. I shivered involuntarily. Something about the mask reminded me of Jack Harding. "What do you think?"

"Definitely creepy."

"Maybe I can use these against the backdrop of velvet with those big jack-o'-lanterns. They have small bulbs inside, so I can light them up at night. I really want the windows to look dramatic. Hey, want a coffee? It's quiet right now."

I nodded and followed Cheryl to the tiny lunch room. She filled the electric kettle with water and plugged it in. "You know, I love interior decorating magazines, and when I was a kid, I used to fall in love with department store windows."

I laughed. "With your nose pressed against the glass, I'll bet."

"That was me. I thought a job like that would be wonderful. And now I have one!" Cheryl's face was alight.

It was nice to see my friend so happy. Her divorce from her cheating ex-husband had gone through a few months earlier, and Gale had helped her buy an apartment near the Bay with her settlement. "How's the new house coming along?" I asked.

"It's coming. Slowly. I'm just kind of afraid to spend money right now. I still feel like I'm getting used to everything, being on my own and a homeowner and all. I'm scared to charge anything or go into debt, so I've been collecting things from garage sales and thrift shops. But it's very homey. At least I think so. I want you and Gale to come to dinner some night. Would you like that?"

"I'd love to, and I'll bring a housewarming present too. Let me know what kinds of things you can use, okay?"

Cheryl poured boiling water through the coffee filter. The aroma of rich ground beans filled the air. As if she could read my mind, she said, "I got this blend from Giovanni's over on Green Street. He has the best."

"Oh, before I forget, are you free Thursday night?" I inquired. "We're getting together for Gloria's birthday. Gale's invited too, as soon as I can reach her. Kuan's made a reservation at the Asia Inn."

"I'd love to. Yes, I'll come. Your grandmother's such a sweetheart and I still haven't met Kuan. I just keep hearing about him. What can I get her for a present?"

"Don't buy a thing, just bring yourself. And you'll love Kuan." Kuan Lee is my grandparents' old friend who lives in the first floor apartment of my grandmother's house in Castle Alley. He practices Chinese medicine and acupuncture, and I've benefitted from his talents many times. I think of him as my surrogate grandfather.

"Speaking of getting together, you haven't forgotten about Gale's art show tonight?"

"No." I cringed. "Are you kidding me? She'd never forgive me."

"Me neither. I'm closing the shop at six so I have enough time to go home and get all dolled up." Cheryl pulled a pitcher of half-and-half out of the tiny refrigerator and passed it across the table. "So what are you up to today?"

I sighed. "Well . . . it's been a pretty chaotic morning." I filled her in on the discovery of Jack Harding's body at the firm.

"You are kidding me!"

"I wish I were."

Cheryl squinted her eyes. "Didn't you once tell me about him? What an ass he was? And how awful he was to everyone? Is that the same guy?"

"One and the same."

"Somebody really didn't like him." She took a sip of her coffee. "Will your name be in the papers again?"

"Oh, I didn't even think about that." Cheryl was referring to my fifteen minutes of fame last year when I'd been credited with rescuing an elderly woman from an abusive religious cult. "I certainly hope not. And I really doubt it, but it does bring up another issue. David's going to have to think about the press and damage control."

"Yeah, I agree. An attorney murdered in

his office wouldn't exactly engender client trust, now would it?"

"I'll have to talk to him about that. He's stopping by my apartment later today for a reading."

Cheryl sipped her coffee. "Speaking of later, you'll get to meet Luca tonight." Luca Russoli was the artist whose show Gale was arranging. He'd arrived on the San Francisco art scene thanks, in large part, to Gale's connections and public relations savoir-faire. Gale told me they had been introduced at a dinner party given by a local neurologist who fancied himself a collector and she'd decided to take Luca under her wing. I waited. There was something Cheryl wasn't saying.

"Have you met him?" I asked her.

Cheryl pursed her lips. "Yes."

"When? Where?"

"I dropped some things off at Gale's condo the other night and he was there."

"Okay. What are you not saying?"

"Oh," Cheryl groaned. "Please don't repeat this to Gale?"

"No. I won't say anything. You didn't like him?"

Cheryl waggled her head. "It's not that. He's good-looking and he's very charming and everything, but . . ." She trailed off.

"Something gave you the willies?"

"I guess he's just a little too smooth for my taste." She looked up suddenly. "Don't say it. I know I'm certainly no judge, not after the turd I was married to."

"Well, it's different when it's someone you're not attracted to, isn't it? You can listen to your instincts better."

"Please don't say anything to Gale. I don't want her to be mad at me. There's nothing so awful as a friend who doesn't like your latest love interest."

"Ah, so it's love, is it?"

"I hope not."

"I have great faith in Gale. She's a smart cookie and can definitely take care of herself."

"Not like me, you mean?"

"No." I reached across the table and took her hand. "That's not what I meant at all."

Cheryl smiled suddenly. "I have to show you this." She opened a drawer and pulled out her purse. She rummaged inside and found a small paperback book and handed it to me.

"What's this?" The cover was a simple sketch of a lone candle.

"It's a book on candle-burning rituals by Raymond Buckland. He's very famous, you know. I bought a red male-figure candle and

I'm going to give it a shot, see if I can attract a passionate man." Cheryl glanced at me to make sure I wasn't rolling my eyes. "That's what I need in my life right now, some passion! And maybe you do too."

I sighed. "I'm just not ready yet. Don't get me wrong, there's nothing wrong with passion, but I'm too busy with everything else I'm doing now."

"Well, maybe it's something to think about. Who knows? Maybe some tall dark handsome thing will walk into the Eye one day and sweep me off my feet." Cheryl stirred her coffee. "Of course with my luck, he'll be short, squat, and ugly, like my ex."

Six

I said goodbye to Cheryl and left the Eye, crossing the street to cut through the Stockton tunnel. If I hurried, I'd be able to catch the next bus at the corner of Bush and get home in time to prepare for David's reading. At the best of times and the sunniest of days, the tunnel is dank, dirty, and filled with exhaust fumes. Two-way traffic whizzed by as I entered the pedestrian walkway. Halfway through, the same feeling stole over me that I'd had outside the Eye. Someone was watching, following.

The concrete columns of the tunnel stretched into the distance, an alcove between each where anyone could hide and never be seen by a passing car or pedestrian. I turned and looked back. No one. I was alone. Why couldn't I shake this feeling? Was it just the gloomy tunnel or was I more shaken from the events of the morning than I realized? I continued walking, determined not to look behind me again. I moved as fast as I could, hoping to reach Bush Street and the sunlight. I heard footsteps and turned to look. A shadow, highlighted by the light pouring into the far end of the tunnel. A man. He slipped into a crevice between the columns. My heart beat faster. I wasn't imagining things. Someone *was* there.

Suddenly terrified, I felt a cold sweat start to form on my forehead. Breathless and almost running, I finally reached the end of the tunnel. I turned back once again, certain I was now in a safe zone. A bulky shadow emerged and shuffled along the walkway. A homeless man. Probably more scared of me than I was of him. I breathed a sigh of relief. My heart slowly returned to its normal rhythm.

A bus was lumbering up the hill. I ran to the corner and climbed aboard with the other passengers, snagging a seat by the window before the bus lurched into forward motion. Half an hour and several stops later, I exited at 30th Avenue and walked the block and a half to my apartment, a small flat on the second floor of a duplex.

I love my neighborhood. It's not fancy, strictly working to middle-class, but on the other side of California Street is Seacliff, an exclusive and pricey area that edges out along the cliffs over the Golden Gate straits. Those homes are in the multi-millions, but the land isn't solid and one mansion actually collapsed into the sea after a winter of heavy rains. My little building is built on bedrock, which helps me sleep a lot better at night.

Wizard greeted me at the front door, his bell tinkling. I picked him up, hugged him, and carried him up the stairs, rubbing his favorite spot on the top of his head. "Did you miss me?" He yowled in response.

Wizard is completely black, with green eyes, and weighs about twenty pounds. He's as gorgeous as an ocelot, and he's used to having me around much of the day. I knew he'd been confused that morning when he saw me leaving, all dressed up, at an ungodly hour. I opened the pouch of kitty treats and dropped two on his plate. Then I hung my coat in the hallway closet and dumped my purse in the office. My answering machine was blinking. I remembered that Jane, a new client, was scheduled for the following week, but I needed to reschedule Celine. I wouldn't be able to fit her in this week at all. Howard, a regular client, lives in Los Angeles and I could handle his reading by phone sometime this weekend or next week.

There were three messages, all from Celine. She was a young mother who had given birth to twins six months earlier. She was currently suffering through a Saturn transit to her Moon. Not an easy transit by any means, but certainly not the worst. She'd visualized motherhood as something out of a glossy baby food commercial, and she wasn't doing well reconciling dirty diapers, rash-pocked bums, and complete exhaustion with her vision. I felt slightly guilty about putting her off, but she'd been to see me twice already about the same transit, and any advice I would give her now would be the same as I gave her then. She had perhaps a week and a half to go until she was out of the woods. I found her number and dialed it. It rang four times and I waited for her voicemail, hoping to leave a message. No such luck. Celine picked up at the last moment.

"Oh, Julia, where have you been? This Saturn transit is just awful!" I could hear one of the twins wailing in the background. "Can I come see you tomorrow?"

"I'm so sorry. I can't do it. Something's come up and I'm totally booked this week." Working nine-to-five wasn't going to leave me enough time for my clients.

"Oh, I know how busy you are. But I need

62

another pep talk. I'm exhausted, I'm depressed, and I've started to talk baby talk to my husband. I'm in trouble! Is there any way to stuff these monsters back in?"

"I don't think so." I laughed. "Look, I'm happy to see you next week, but I don't think there's anything new I can say. You're going through a lonely time right now, but it'll be over soon."

"I don't care. Just talking to you about all this stuff helps me so much!"

"Okay. Next Monday then." I crossed my fingers, hoping that nothing would go wrong and my agreement to work at the firm would be over. Under the circumstances, I didn't feel I could bail out on David now. "How about noon? Can you get some help with the babies?"

"Yes, I can ask my mom. She'll come over if I need her. I just need a break so bad. I feel so damn isolated."

"I guarantee you'll be fine. Keep your chin up and we'll have a good session next Monday."

"Okay, thanks, Julia." She sounded somewhat brighter with my encouragement. "I'll see you then." I suspected Celine would dial another astrologer or psychic to get her through the week as soon as we hung up. So be it. I turned on the computer and opened my astro program to view the Meyers family's charts.

Under the circumstances, it wouldn't take a genius to figure out what was on David's mind — Jack's murder, the death threats, maybe even the stability of his firm. I checked the current transiting planets against his natal chart and then checked his solar arcs and progressions. There it was. I remembered seeing this coming a year ago, but I hadn't wanted to bring it up ahead of time. Transiting Pluto in Capricorn was moving through David's sixth house and conjuncting his natal Saturn. Neptune by transit was approaching his Moon and Mars in Pisces in the eighth. He was definitely under a great deal of pressure, perhaps even betrayal, in his career life. His health could be affected because of the sixth house transit. I printed out a color-coded triwheel chart showing the natal positions in the inner circle and the transiting and progressed planets in the outer circles. Then I lit a cone of incense and placed it in the belly of my bronze Buddha on the hallway table. My little ritual before a client arrives. I'm convinced my Buddha protects my home and hearth. No sooner had I done this than the doorbell rang. I hurried down the stairs and opened the door.

"Julia, I really appreciate your time." David had changed into a pair of casual slacks and a windbreaker.

"Come on up." I ushered him into the office, where he sat in the client chair next to the desk. "First of all, before we start, how's your health? Have you had a thorough checkup recently?"

"What? Oh yes, just two weeks ago. I'm fine and Caroline's fine."

"Good. I wanted to eliminate that possibility." I shifted the monitor toward him and pointed out the relevant transits. "You have some tough things going on right now." I explained the transits in as simple a manner as possible. "Your tenth house cusp is Aries and that's ruled by Mars. The tenth is all about your public standing, your career, your firm. Neptune is transiting your natal Mars and Moon. Neptune transits are associated with strange nebulous occurrences, things that are hard to get a handle on, perhaps even sabotage of some sort. The combination of Pluto moving through the sixth house and the Neptune connection to the Moon makes me think that possibly a woman, even a woman at the firm, might be involved." I hesitated. "I did see these coming up last year and planned to call you. In light of what's happened, I should have touched base with you sooner. I hope you'll forgive my editing. I didn't want you to worry ahead of time."

David waved away my apology. "Could you have predicted a murder?"

I shook my head. "I don't think it would have even occurred to me. Sabotage, slander, secret enemies perhaps, but not murder. Of course, I don't have everyone's birth information and haven't seen Jack's chart, so I don't know. But murder . . . Did these threats first appear about three weeks ago?"

"Yes. How did you know?"

"Well, that's when Mars —"

"Oh, never mind," he laughed. "I should have known. When the first threat came to my attention, I guess I dismissed it, but when the second one arrived, I called one of my old friends from law school. He does criminal work, and he put me in touch with someone in the District Attorney's Office as well as the police."

"What did they suggest?"

"That it's a crime if we could find out who sent them. But I assumed it was just some crank who had no intention of acting on the threats. I considered maybe the intent was to unnerve people or harass them. They could be completely unrelated to Jack's murder."

I didn't want to say anything, but personally I thought that was too much of a coincidence. "The sixth house is what we used to call the house of 'servants,' or, in modern terms, 'employees.' It's also the area of life related to the work you do on a daily basis, unlike your career, which would be more of a tenth house arena. The moon is a female symbol. So that whole Moon-Neptune thing could represent a woman or manifest through a woman."

"I hope you're wrong, Julia. I hope it's not internal. That would put a whole new slant on it. Are you saying it could even be an *attorney* who's sent these threats?"

"Possibly." I sighed. "I agree it's a dark problem, but I also think it'll come to a head within a week. Both these transits will have reached those exact positions and moved on by then."

David stared at the computer printout. "You're saying things haven't come to a head?"

"Not yet." I shivered involuntarily as a chill passed through the room.

SEVEN

After David left, I rummaged around in the kitchen to see what I had to eat. I don't keep a lot of food at the best of times, but my grandmother, Gloria, who's a fabulous cook, is always packing up containers for me. Those were in the freezer and I didn't want to spend time thawing them out. The pièce de resistance in my refrigerator was a large hunk of sharp cheddar cheese. I dug a box of crackers out of the cupboard, and yes, I had yellow mustard. Just the kind of nutritious snack I craved. I sliced the cheese, laid it on the crackers, and liberally squirted mustard over everything. I managed to pop one bite in my mouth before the phone rang.

"Julia?" It was my grandmother. "I tried your cell but you didn't answer."

"Oh, I had a client here. Sorry. I had to turn it off."

"I just saw the news on TV. There was a

murder at David's firm?"

Oh no. Jack's murder had hit the news. "Yes. I meant to call you this afternoon. I'm sorry."

"But weren't you there today? You said you were going to fill in at the firm!" I could hear the first hints of panic in Gloria's voice.

"I was there, but it actually must have happened some time over the weekend. I'm fine. There's no need to worry. David closed the office and I left early."

"Well, I hope he plans to keep it closed! You're not going back there, are you?"

"I don't know what's going to happen tomorrow. I'll go back in the morning, but the office may not stay open. I really don't want you worrying about me. Please."

My grandmother sighed. "Well, I do, dear. That's my job." I smiled in spite of myself. I wanted to reach through the phone line and give her a great big hug. "Stay in touch this week, will you?"

"Of course, and I'll see you Thursday night."

"Kuan says he's planning a special treat for me but he won't tell me what it is."

I knew whatever party he organized would be perfect. "Well," I teased, "you'll just have to wait and see."

"I'm not very good at that. I get so impatient."

"He'd be so upset if you spoiled his surprise."

"I know," she grumbled. "Make sure you call me this week. I don't like to think you could be in any danger, darling."

"Nothing's going to happen to me. I'll be very safe there."

"You better be. Otherwise I'll go right down the street and give David Meyers a piece of my mind."

I sighed and replaced the phone. I hated to think of Gloria worrying about me. She deserved a peaceful life. So did I, come to think of it.

The doorbell rang. My first thought was that David had left something behind. I hurried down the stairs to the front door. I hesitated as I saw a woman's figure through the glass. Maggie! It was Maggie.

I threw the door open and we hugged. Michael's sister and I have gotten along famously from the first moment we met. Maggie probably understands better than anyone how I feel since Michael's death, and even though we don't stay in touch as much as we used to, every time we meet it's as though no time has elapsed at all.

I stepped back and took a good look at

her. She wasn't smiling. "Maggie? What is it?"

"Can I come in?"

"Of course. Yes." She was quiet as we climbed the stairs. She headed straight for the kitchen and sat down at the table. I joined her. "What's wrong?"

"Something's come up."

"About . . ."

"Yes." She didn't have to say it. I knew she meant Michael.

"What's happened?" Part of me hoped against hope that we might find an answer some day about the hit-and-run. Another part of me just wanted the sadness and unknowingness to go away.

"Let me try to tell you in some kind of order." She took a deep breath. "Do you remember the elderly man who used to live across the street from Michael's old apartment?"

I nodded. I did remember. Michael's apartment at 45th and Taraval was just a few blocks from my old place in the Sunset District. "Michael and I used to see him when he walked his dog. And then" — I shrugged — "there was a time when we didn't see him as much."

"Well, I think what happened was his son took the dog because it became too much

71

for the old guy. But the dad didn't want to leave his home so the family arranged some care and a companion for him." I waited, not sure what Maggie's story had to do with Michael. "Apparently, the old man was always taking pictures. He wasn't any kind of a real photographer, but he liked to do that. He was always fooling around with his camera."

"Yes, I remember now. He'd even take pictures of the flowers in his yard."

"He died a couple of weeks ago. And his son and his daughter-in-law are putting the house up for sale. They've been there every day, moving stuff out and selling a few things to the neighbors. The thing is . . . they found a box of photos. The father had an old-fashioned camera that he used, and then he'd —"

"Maggie . . ." I couldn't imagine where she was going with this story.

"They found a photo of Michael. On the street. Just as that car hit him."

I gasped and covered my mouth. My heart was racing wildly. "He saw. He saw who hit Michael?"

"He must have. He must have tried to take a picture of what happened from his window."

"Why didn't he ever say anything?"

Maggie shook her head. "I don't know. I really don't. Maybe he didn't want to get involved. Maybe he was afraid he'd have to testify."

As much as I dreaded looking at what Maggie had described, I still needed to see the photo. "Do you have it with you?"

"I don't. The old man's son and his wife knew what it was. They didn't know Michael, but they knew there'd been a hit-and-run in the neighborhood and that someone had died, so they turned it over to the police."

"Have you seen it?"

"Yes, they showed it to me and my mother. She's hysterical right now." Celia, Michael's mother, had been nothing but cold to me since his death. She wasn't on firm ground to begin with, but after the accident, in her convoluted logic, she blamed me for her loss. If Michael hadn't been in such a hurry to meet me, he would have been more careful, he wouldn't have been killed.

"I can imagine." I didn't envy Maggie the emotional turmoil she must be dealing with.

"I told you before, Julia, she's made a shrine of Michael's room and I'm so worried about her. She never wants to go out or do anything. Once in a while I manage to drag her to a restaurant for brunch or something, but even her old friends have given up calling her."

"What can they tell from the photo?"

"Not much. Michael is lying on his side on the street, and . . ." Maggie's voice shook. "And you can just see the edge of the car. It's dark or black and there's a bit of a bumper and the corner of the right rear tire. The police think the driver must have panicked and taken off. The old guy might have been looking out his window when it happened and just snapped it really quick. They're going to try to get as much information from it as they can, but they don't really hold out much hope."

"Who's in charge of this?"

"Actually, a retired detective has volunteered to work on it. The case was never closed, but this is the first thing they've had to go on at all. I can get you the name of the detective in charge downtown, and maybe he'll give you more information. I'll let him know you might want to talk to him."

"Thanks, Maggie." My heart sank. In all this time, no witnesses to the accident had come forward. One woman at the end of the block remembered a dark vehicle traveling fast, but she couldn't swear it had anything at all to do with the car that had hit Michael. "We shouldn't get our hopes up."

"I want some answers, Julia!" Maggie's voice had risen. "And I'm sure you do too. It's not right. What this has done to our family, to me, to you. All our lives have been changed because of this. I want to see someone pay for what they did."

I nodded. "I do too. It won't change anything. It won't bring him back. But you're right. We've all gone through so much . . ."

"I have to go." Maggie stood suddenly and I realized she hadn't even taken her coat off. "I'm staying at my mom's for a little while. I'm so worried about her. I don't like the thought of her being all alone in that big house."

"Okay. Stay in touch and let me know what you find out?"

"I will." Maggie leaned toward me and I put my arms around her, holding her tight. I felt her chest rise, a quiet sob. "I'm sorry to arrive on your doorstep like this, but I had to tell you face to face."

"I'm glad you did, Maggie. I'm glad you did. And maybe we'll learn more."

Maggie pulled away. I could see tears forming in her eyes as she rushed down the stairs.

EIGHT

I slumped down on a kitchen chair. I was stunned by Maggie's news and needed to sort out my feelings. In a very strange way I derived some comfort from the fact that a clue existed, however small. That maybe there was a logic to this crime. That someone out there, someone older, experienced, with resources, would be working on a case that had undoubtedly been shifted to a back burner. I had no doubt the police wanted to catch the driver who had struck Michael, but in spite of their best efforts there was so little to go on. Maggie was upset, but I hoped the possibility of solving Michael's murder would give us all some measure of peace. The phone rang and I grabbed the extension in the kitchen.

"Don't tell me you forgot about the show tonight? I thought you were coming early to give me moral support?"

It was Gale. I took a deep breath. "Of

course I didn't forget! I did leave you a message asking what time you wanted me there."

"You sound funny. What's wrong?"

There was no way I could recount the swarm of emotions I was feeling after Maggie's visit. Especially right now. "Nothing. I'm fine."

"Well, just get down here. I'm having a nervous breakdown. Cheryl's not here yet either."

Gale hosts her events at her own expense, a fact which makes me gag, since I have never been tempted to spend a dime on any of the work she so proudly hypes. But the artists are happy and Gale takes a cut. A win-win situation for all. Her hysteria on the phone probably meant the catering company hadn't brought the correct wine or the color of the filters on the dramatic overhead lighting was wrong. I needed to hustle down there and be sure I was dressed to the nines.

"I'm on my way." I crossed my fingers behind my back and determined to push all thoughts of Maggie's photo out of my mind. I had to get through the evening, but most of all, I didn't want to rain on Gale's parade.

"Just get here," she hissed. "Please . . . I'm nervous and I need you." She hung up.

I stripped my clothes off in the bedroom and hurried down the hall to the storage closet. Gloria had been a seamstress most of her life and eventually opened her own shop. When she retired and sold her business, she gave me tons of clothing and sample outfits in my size, for which I'm very grateful. I could never have afforded these fashions. I pushed a few items out of the way and found a dark green cocktail dress with long sleeves. Considering how chilly and damp it would be near the water, the dress and its wrap would be perfect.

I slipped it on and found a pair of bronzy-green strappy sandals. Most days it's a struggle to make my thick, unruly hair look presentable and I invariably end up pulling it back in a clasp. Tonight required a little more work. I brushed it up into a twist and pinned it, a few strands straggling down. I pulled a few more strands out to make it look intentional and added a pair of long jeweled earrings. I found a beaded evening purse and transferred a twenty-dollar bill, keys, cell phone, driver's license, eyeliner, and a small container of blush into it. I was ready; that is if I didn't kill myself in these shoes. I could save time by slapping some makeup on in the car while stopped at traffic lights. Always adds that extra panache. I have a theory that the less time you spend getting ready, the better you look. I clip-clopped down the back stairs into the garage. My faithful red Geo started right up and the gas tank was even full. A good omen. I hit the control for the garage door and backed out into the street.

I followed the winding road through the Presidio and rolled down my car window to breathe the pungent fragrance of eucalyptus and pine. The Presidio is pristine land along the edge of the peninsula with buildings and military officers' homes erected in the 1940s. For many years, these structures had remained vacant and untouched, a time capsule, a small town where all the residents had disappeared. Real estate developers salivated over these acres for years, but now, controlled by a trust, the buildings have been restored and leased. Hopefully the trust will be able to hold out forever.

I exited at Marina Drive before the road continued on toward the Golden Gate Bridge. I veered into the Fort Mason Center and grabbed a ticket from the dispenser at the kiosk. Other events were in progress here as well and parking looked scarce. I finally found a spot at the rear of the last building and backed in, my car facing an unused pier. Water lapped quietly around the pilings and seagulls shrieked overhead, occasionally dive-bombing for crumbs.

Fog, like cotton batting, had settled over the spires of the Bridge in the distance, biding its time before creeping ashore. I leaned back in the car seat for a moment and closed my eyes, savoring the smell of moldering ancient wood and sea. I personally thought Gale was a little nuts to be getting so involved in the art scene, but it seemed to make her happy and I had girlfriend duty, so I finally roused myself, strappy sandals and all, and walked carefully on cobblestones around to the front entrance, where a caterer's truck was parked. I climbed the wooden steps to the long loading dock.

Inside the building, two men stood on ladders, calling orders to others who were moving about the floor. White drapes covered six large pieces of what I could only assume were sculptures. The workmen were struggling to place spotlights, aiming them at the artwork from angles that would create the best effect. I approached one of the draped sculptures and was in the process of lifting up the sheet to see what the surprise would be when Gale spotted me.

"Oh, Julia, I'm so glad you're here. Isn't this exciting?" she breathed happily. Tall and glamorous, tonight Gale was wearing a slinky deep-red number with a garnet necklace that set off her dark hair beautifully.

Even though I always find these events a little tiresome and pompous and was sure this one would be no different, loyalty to my friend dictated keeping my mouth shut. "Hmm," I replied noncommittally. I didn't know how far her flirtation with Luca had gone, but I planned to find out. "What can I do?"

"The catering truck just pulled up. I want you to supervise and let them know where to set up the tables for the wine and champagne and the hors d'oeuvres, okay? I want the tables at the other end of the space so people have to pass by the sculptures to get their free drinks and eats."

At the mention of the possibility of food, my stomach rumbled. With the exception of a cracker and a bit of cheese, I hadn't eaten since lunch.

"Will do," I replied as Gale hurried away. I spotted a young guy wearing a white jacket and black pants. He had an earring in one ear and a haircut that caused his white-blond hair to stand up in spiky bursts. I waved to him and headed in his direction.

"Are you the forward scout?"

"Yeah, the rest of the guys are outside

81

unloading the truck."

I extended my hand. "My name's Julia. What's yours?"

"Eddie. Eddie McNamara."

"Are you the bartender?"

"Naw, he'll be here in a little bit after we set up the bar. I just work for the catering company. Parties in Motion. I'm really an artist."

"Oh?"

"Yeah. Is this an art show?" He sounded impressed.

"I guess so. You'll have to tell me what you think of it later, okay?"

"Deal. Where do you want the tables set up?"

I pointed to the other end of the space. "At that end, facing the sculptures."

"Okay." Eddie walked back out to the loading dock and started waving his arms at six people carrying in long tables and various containers. They looked like they knew more about what was happening than I did, so I left them to do their thing, telling Eddie I'd check everything in a little while.

I wandered over to the other end of the space where Gale was directing the draping of deep purple- and plum-colored sheets of fabric around the white walls.

"Hey, what do you think?"

82

"Impressive. I really like that color!"

"It'll work, I think."

"Anything else I can do, other than check on the caterers in a little bit?"

"No. Oh wait, yeah, one more thing. In the trunk of my car are some standalone signs that say 'Reserved Parking.' Can you put them in the parking spaces at the front that are closest to the entrance?"

"You got it."

"You're a doll. And I promise not to run you ragged."

By the time I found Gale's keys, found her car, which I then decided to drive to the front of the building, and hauled out all the signs and placed them where she'd indicated, I remembered the caterers. I pulled her car around to the side of the building and went back up the wooden stairs to the entrance. Eddie and crew had done a very thorough job. The portable bar was set up in the corner with two long tables hugging the walls on either side. Red and white wines and champagnes of various kinds were available. Trays were arranged on three levels and the tables groaned with the weight of tiny quiches, smoked salmon, cheeses, crackers, bruschetta, and fruit. Gourds and dried flowers decorated the spaces between the food. The effect was very chi-chi and colorful. No wonder my stomach was nagging me. I decided to help myself to two little quiches, then rearranged the rest of the tray so the deletions didn't show. The white-jacketed men and women bustled around making last minute touches as the catering truck pulled slowly away from the bay to park in the rear and await the end of the evening.

"Julia!" Cheryl was standing in the doorway. She stepped inside and surveyed the large room. "Looks wonderful. Where's Gale?"

"She's . . . uh . . . well, she was with the lighting people, but now I don't see her." I took a peek at my cell phone. It was eight o'clock and the first guests were due to arrive in half an hour. "I think everything's handled, but let's check with her." We found Gale in the ladies room, freshening her makeup with the contents of her purse scattered over the countertop.

"There you are!" She turned and beamed at us, a mascara wand in her hand. "Cheryl, you look gorgeous. Doesn't she?" Gale asked me.

"She does," I agreed. Cheryl is a petite blonde and tonight she was wearing a short cocktail length dress in a pale ivory color. "Where did you ever find that?" I asked her.

"On sale at Macy's," Cheryl replied. "Unlike you, I don't have a closet of designer clothes. I'm jealous. I wish your grandmother would take me under her wing."

"I'll have a word with her. Oh, speaking of Gloria" — I turned to Gale — "are you free Thursday evening? We're getting together for her birthday. You're invited if you'd like to join us."

"Thursday? Oh, I would. I'd love to, but I've made plans with Luca."

Cheryl raised her eyebrows. I caught it, but Gale had turned away.

"Too bad. She'd love to see you." I slipped Gale's keys back into her evening purse.

"Julia, come closer, sweetie. You need more makeup," Gale declared.

"No I don't."

"Cheryl, you look fine." Gale turned back to me. "Julia, just sit, okay?"

I allowed myself to be lined and brushed a bit more, with some lip gloss added. I'm really impatient when it comes to sitting still for this stuff and can't ever stand to be in a beauty salon.

"You have such a great face for makeup. You should wear more. And these colors work with that fabulous hair of yours. I can't believe it's natural. There are women who would kill for that color."

"Trust me, it's natural. I couldn't be bothered changing it," I mumbled as Gale added color to my lips. I personally subscribe to the less-is-more school of thought with makeup but refrained from saying anything.

"How does it look out there?"

"Good. The caterers are completely set up. There wasn't much I needed to do. The parking signs are all out. The guest book is on a table near the door. The sculptures are still covered with drapes. Do you want those taken off?"

"No, not yet. My plan is to introduce Luca at the appropriate moment and then, with a bit of fanfare, the workmen will raise the drapes by the attached cables and the spots will highlight the sculptures."

"I don't know where you find the time or energy to do this stuff."

"Oh, it's fun. I enjoy it. I can't wait for you to meet Luca."

"Mmm . . ."

"What does that mean? 'Mmm'?" Gale bristled. "Don't tell me you don't like him already?"

"I'll know better after you find out his birth date and birth time, okay?" I hazarded a glance at Cheryl as she fluffed her hair in a mirror.

"I will, I swear, Julia. I really will find out."

"I'll hold you to that." The last time Gale had been romantically involved, it was with a painter who'd claimed to be an orphan and had no idea of his birth time. He'd told her his birth date was January 12th, which would have made him a Capricorn, but I didn't buy it and just knew he was lying in general. Turned out he had a wife and three kids in Albuquerque, which Gale discovered when she checked the outrageous long-distance charges on her home phone.

"We're not going to talk about him, remember?" Gale said, getting my drift. "No more Capricorns, I swear."

"I'm sure he even lied about that."

"Fortunately, we'll never know, and he's out of my life now. In fact, he better never show his face in San Francisco for that matter."

Cheryl checked her watch. "It's getting late. I think we should get out there."

"You two are the best! Thanks for being here tonight." Gale hugged us both, patted her hair, and headed out the door to the big room.

Cheryl followed her, and I took a moment to rinse my hands at the sink. I reached for the door handle, but as I did, the door swung back and nearly hit me in the face. I stepped back quickly. A thin blonde woman wearing an opalescent blue dress charged through the door. It was Nora Layton from David's firm. I started to say hello, but Nora looked right through me. Ignoring the fact that she'd almost broken my nose, she marched into the first stall and slammed the door. Charming.

I tucked my evening purse under my arm and left the restroom. It was a quarter past eight and Cheryl was at the food table sampling each of the tasties. I joined her. "I'm absolutely starving," she said. "I didn't have time to eat anything today."

"Me neither. Well, other than a salad at lunch and some crackers." I filled a small plate with a few delicacies and asked for a glass of white wine. "I'm not sure if there's anything we can really do here tonight."

Cheryl popped a piece of sushi into her mouth. "We're here for moral support, that's all. And, who knows, maybe I'll meet a fascinating man." She glanced around to make sure no one was watching and licked a few grains of rice from her finger. "Maybe I'll meet a fascinating *wealthy* man!"

"Good luck," I replied as she moved away to circle the room.

Within a half hour, the gallery was packed with guests. I helped myself to more food and nursed a second glass of wine. At one point, I spotted Nora across the room. She was sipping champagne and talking to, of all people, Roger Wilkinson from the firm. She must have forgiven him for his earlier comment about smoking and dinosaurs. Had they come together? Roger's eyes were darting around the room as if he wished to escape his present company and attach himself to someone more important. Looking at them now, it was unnerving to think that only that morning we'd spent hours cooped up together after the discovery of Jack's body.

NINE

At nine thirty exactly, Gale stepped to the center of the room and, clinking a spoon on a crystal glass, caught everyone's attention. "My dears, I'm so glad you could all be here this evening." Her glance took in the entire gathering. "I've arranged this event so you could have a very special preview of the fantastic work of Luca Russoli. Luca is Milanese and has been working in Europe on his latest sculptures. I'm proud to present him and his work to you this evening." Gale held out her hand, beckoning Luca, who stood on the sidelines, to join her. Built much like a square box wearing a tux, he joined her in the center of the room. "Everyone . . . may I present the work of Luca Russoli . . ."

At this point the ceiling spots trained on the covered sculptures brightened, and the thin, taut cables lifted the drapes up toward the rafters. This magic trick was greeted by a round of applause from the eighty or so guests, who then began to walk around and examine each monolith. A growing murmur filled the space as the guests relaxed and resumed their chatter.

The evening was a huge success. Gale buzzed around, smiling and greeting the well-dressed and well-heeled patrons who were sipping alcohol and balancing hors d'oeuvres on tiny napkins. Hopefully many would spend lots of money on Luca's art, with a commission for Gale, of course.

I found myself standing next to a piece that looked like a cross between the Willendorf goddess and Big Foot. A silver-haired gentleman holding a wine glass identical to mine walked around the piece, studying it, then turned to me.

"His rendering is quite extraordinary, particularly in this medium, don't you think?"

I smiled, temporarily at a loss for words. I wracked my brain for something intelligent to say, but failed. I could have sworn the stranger read my mind.

"Or perhaps you disagree?" he questioned, raising his eyebrows. Fine lines were etched around his deep blue eyes.

"My knowledge is limited." Since I couldn't figure out what any of the pieces were about or what this particular one was supposed to represent, I decided to keep my mouth shut. In spite of his years, this man was very attractive. I wondered who he was.

A bespectacled younger man in a black suit approached and cleared his throat. "Sir, you asked me to remind you . . ."

"Oh, of course." The older man nodded. He turned back. "Forgive me, my dear. It has been a genuine pleasure, Ms. . . ."

"Bonatti. Julia Bonatti."

"What a lovely name."

"And yours?"

"Henry Gooding." He smiled and turned away, heading for the exit with the younger man following a few feet behind. As he passed Roger Wilkinson, Gooding nodded to him. Roger's face brightened. He moved forward a step as if to speak, but Gooding walked past him.

"Julia . . . Julia," Gale called out happily as she maneuvered through the crowd. "Where did you get to?" She leaned closer. "I can't believe you. How did you manage to meet Henry Gooding?"

"Oh . . . we just struck up a conversation."

"I'll bet you don't even know who he is."

"You're right about that. Who is he?"

"He's only the richest widower in San

Francisco. Made a fortune in import-export. And he's a big collector. In fact, it was Henry who urged me to show Luca's work." I had a momentary twinge of guilt about my lack of enthusiasm for the monolith.

Then Gale looked over my shoulder and flashed a brilliant smile. "Julia, I'd like you to meet Luca. Luca, this is my dear friend Julia Bonatti."

"*Piacere*," the Cro-Magnon growled deep in his throat.

Gale shot me a look that said *Behave yourself,* and then Luca turned on a three-hundred-watt smile and took my hand in his, bowing his head slightly. I was waiting for his heels to click together. I made sure I kept my expression pleasant.

"Gale has spoken very highly of you . . ." I began. Gale was standing close to me and I could feel the pressure of her shoe on the side of mine. "Of your work. This is very impressive."

"Oh, I do not know." He spoke slowly, in halting English. "I am not completely happy with many of my pieces."

"You must be a perfectionist."

"Ahh . . . yes, you do understand . . . so many people do not." He had turned up the volume and his charm felt like an oil slick.

Cheryl was observing us from across the

room, and Gale was staring at me in a pursed lips/constipated smile kind of way. I knew she knew what I was thinking. I didn't dare grab a third glass of wine from the tray the waiter waved under my nose since I might have said something to blow my perfect behavior. I smiled at Gale and she relaxed.

"Julia, I'll give you a call this week. Let's get together for lunch, okay?"

That was code for *I can't wait to talk to you and chew your ear off about my latest obsession.*

"Let's do that," I said. Gale, now smiling widely, tucked Luca's arm under hers in a proprietorial sort of way and pivoted to greet a group of people who were standing behind us.

The long day had taken its toll and the wine had made me very sleepy. I meandered around some more, nodding vacantly at people I didn't know, and managed to kill another three-quarters of an hour. I feel my aloneness most keenly at events like this. It was time to leave. I found Cheryl and said good night. No one would miss me now and I had done my bit. I walked to the bar, left my wine glass on the top, and came eye to eye with Eddie of the spiky blond hair. He was busy reorganizing trays and cleaning up the debris.

"Are you leaving already?" He looked disappointed.

"Yes."

"Well, I'm sorry you're going."

Was he trying to pick me up? "What did you think of the artwork, Eddie?"

"Well, I don't know much about sculpting."

"Me neither. I'm just bored out of my skull. I'm here for a friend and I know a lot less than you."

"Actually, these pieces aren't bad," he said thoughtfully. "I'm just surprised anyone outside of California or the west would choose to work in that particular type of stone."

"Why? Not popular?"

Eddie shrugged. "No, just not readily available anywhere else. If I'm not mistaken, it's either Utah alabaster or some sort of alabaster from Central Mexico, but I could be wrong. It's beautiful, but not that much used in Europe."

"That is interesting. What kind of work do you do?"

"I work in various media, oils . . . acrylics."

"Ah, sounds interesting." I had exhausted my commentary and my feet were killing me. Just then, one of the men in catering jackets behind the table called Eddie's name and he turned, winked once, and rushed off.

In a moment I was through the huge doorway to the loading dock, then clumping down the stairs and through the fog to my car. The parking lot stretched out into utter darkness as if sliding into the black waters of the bay. No delineation marked the end of the tarmac. The headlands on the far side of the straits loomed a darker gray against the night sky, bare rounded peaks that resembled a great sleeping beast. Shivering against the chill, I hurried to my car, kicked off my heels, and fastened my seat belt. I cranked up the heater and waited for my feet to warm, then pulled out slowly, following the path that would take me out to Marina Drive.

As I passed the end of the loading dock outside the exhibit space, my headlights raked over two figures standing far away from the brightly lit doorway. I slowed down to get a better look. One was a large man in a tux, the other, a blonde woman. It was Luca. And the woman was Nora Layton.

Judging by their body language, they were arguing, although I couldn't hear a sound. I hit the brakes and turned off my headlights.

What possible connection could there be between Nora and Luca? I rolled down my window, hoping to catch their voices. Too late. Luca turned away suddenly, and just as suddenly, Nora grabbed his arm. He pulled away violently, causing her to stumble. She regained her composure and turned, walking toward the entrance doors into the brightly lit gallery. Luca was alone. As if he could sense my gaze, he turned and looked in my direction. I was sure he couldn't see me in the darkness, but nonetheless, I slid down in my seat. A moment later, he too returned to the gathering.

I flicked on my headlights and handed some cash to the attendant at the parking booth. I pulled out to Marina Drive and mulled over the scene I'd just witnessed. I would definitely have to mention it to Gale. I hoped she'd have an explanation.

My route home was deserted and free of traffic. The streets were shiny with the moisture of fog. The wind had picked up, blowing mist from the lip of the Bay across the Marina Green. I followed the road west as it wound its way toward the Bridge and took the turnoff to the Presidio. My high beams picked out clumps of brush, wildflowers, and tree trunks. At Park Presidio, city lights illuminated the streets once more.

I reached 30th Avenue and pulled up to my building. The best thing about my neighborhood is the fog that rolls in every afternoon, summer or winter, and the foghorns that lull me to sleep at night.

I hit the garage door opener, pulled in, and waited for the automatic door to close behind me. Exhausted, I grabbed my shoes and purse, exited through the back door of the garage, and picked my way carefully up the wooden stairway to the kitchen door in my bare feet. Inside, I stripped off my evening dress, hung it in the closet, pulled the hairpins out of my hair, washed my face, and slid under the comforter. Wizard climbed onto the bed and curled into a ball next to me. The foghorns and Wizard's deep-throated purring lulled me into unconsciousness.

TEN

To say that a gray pall had settled over the offices of Meyers, Dade & Schultz would be an understatement. Despite the presence of a skeleton crew, the office was officially closed. The litigation department had various court deadlines to meet and David hadn't seen the sense in asking for continuances only to have time crunches later on. He'd hoped for some semblance of normality, but silence enveloped the hallways, broken only by the ding of the elevator doors opening and closing and a few whispered conversations.

I arrived at quarter to nine and, after settling in, headed down the hallway to see what was going on in the other offices. Yellow tape was stretched across Jack's office door. Nora Layton was nowhere to be seen. Roger was rifling through papers laid out on his credenza, and Dani was typing madly, transcribing from a tape. She looked up with a glazed expression and rolled her eyes to indicate both boredom and burden. Karen Jansen, seated at the desk behind Dani, smiled and rose from her chair. I was taken aback by her friendliness, but perhaps she hadn't been at her best when I'd arrived the day before.

"I'm surprised you came back," Karen said.

"It's horrible, I agree, but what can any of us do? If I didn't need the money, maybe I wouldn't have returned."

"Did someone tell me you used to work here before?"

"Yes. Maybe Dani." I nodded my head toward Dani, who was still typing furiously and ignoring us.

"When was that?"

"Oh, about two years ago now, I guess, a little more. I didn't work here for very long, but it's a nice place, so when they called me to fill in, I agreed."

"I see." At that, she turned abruptly and walked away. I glanced at Dani, who shrugged and raised her eyebrows in an expression that seemed to say *It takes all kinds.* I moved closer to her desk. She stopped typing and looked up.

"Dani, I was wondering if Suzanne had come in." If, as David had said, Suzanne

Simms, the paralegal, had been one of the three recipients of the death threats, I wanted to talk to her.

Dani hesitated. "Uh, no, she isn't in. She was out yesterday too, probably sick, I guess. I imagine she'll be in later. She hasn't called me or anything to say she wouldn't be." Dani looked at me quizzically.

"Okay . . . thanks." I made a quick excuse. "David had a question for her. Maybe if you hear from her, you could let me know?"

"Sure, I will." Dani smiled and returned to her typing. I walked back down the hall to David's office. As soon as I stepped into the reception area, the door was flung open. David stood on the threshold talking over his shoulder to someone I couldn't see.

"Julia, there you are. Come on in." I stepped inside and came face to face with a tall, dark-haired man. I resisted the urge to pat my hair.

"Julia, I'd like you to meet Adam. Adam Schaeffer."

"Hello, Adam." I offered my hand. His was warm and strong. I liked his handshake. It's a prejudice of mine, but I can't stand anyone with a damp, limp hand. He had a nice smile too. A really nice smile. A strong jaw and just enough irregularities to his face that you might not call him handsome, exactly. Was it my imagination or did he hold my hand a moment too long?

"Julia?"

"Yes. Julia Bonatti."

"Very glad to meet you." He was dressed in a suit that was well cut but not flashy. Who was he? An attorney? Somehow I didn't think so. David indicated the two wing chairs in front of his desk.

"Have a seat. Both of you." David turned to me. "Adam works for Sinclair Investigations, our regular investigators. He's handled a few jobs for us in the past and he's been assigned to us for the time being. He's going to organize some security for the firm and interface with the police investigation . . ."

"I actually asked to be assigned," Adam said. "I know this firm a bit and really like working with David. Plus I have a good relationship with a lot of people at the police department, so I think I can be of some help."

Adam had a grace of movement, yet didn't appear arrogant or smooth. A few strands of gray at his temples kept him from looking too boyish.

". . . and Julia is here out of pity for me," David was saying. "I've asked her to fill in for Muriel, but now I think I've dragged her into a dangerous situation."

"Let me be the judge of that, David," I said.

"Oh, and before it slips my mind . . ." David opened a side drawer in his desk. "You'll need this." He handed me a bright new key on a small ring. "This is an extra one you can keep while you're working here. It'll open our stairway doors and all the offices."

"Thanks," I said, pocketing it.

Adam shifted in his seat. "David has a good point. Office gossip and intrigue is one thing, even cranks sending death threats, but there's been a murder here. It's nothing to fool with. You could be nosing around in the wrong place and become a target yourself."

"If I feel it's too much, I'll back out. But for now, everyone who absolutely has to be here has shown up, so why shouldn't I?" I neglected to mention that Suzanne hadn't yet put in an appearance and I did really want to talk to her.

"Hopefully the police will come up with some answers soon, but everyone needs to be careful," David replied. "Once the immediate work is handled, I may keep the office closed until things get resolved. I'm not sure yet. We'll see how it goes."

Adam said, "We can provide top notch-people, twenty-four hours a day if you feel it's necessary. Believe me, no one will gain entrance to this floor or to the 40th floor without a good reason."

I thought that sounded just great, but if the murderer was already in the firm, as I suspected, it wouldn't do much good. I could be wrong. I'm only an astrologer. I decided not to voice my opinion then and there.

Adam pulled a small notebook from his jacket pocket. "Any important court cases going on right now?"

"Well, the most pressing is a case we got from Public Counsel. You know, they take cases where the client is without funds to speak of and often refer them to large firms like ours. And we do the work on a pro bono basis. It's a tax write-off for us, and a good way to train less-experienced attorneys. The clients get legal help they could never afford otherwise." David leaned forward. "Now, this case . . . they're a nice enough couple. Apartment managers. They live in the building that they manage. They suffered damages from a leaky roof, as did a lot of other tenants in the building. The owners refused to repair the roof. Then the managers were subjected to all sorts of insults by the owners. Their complaints about the roof and

104

other things were ignored, and finally they were fired. They have two small children. Suddenly they were out of work and out of a home."

"Who owns the building?"

"Two brothers . . . the Farradays. Real scumbags. They do business under the name Deklon Management. We're claiming constructive eviction on our clients' behalf, as well as wrongful termination."

"Any possibility the threats you got are from the brothers? To upset the applecart before trial?" Adam asked.

David heaved a sigh. "Anything's possible. As I told you, only Jack, Ira, and Suzanne received those disgusting letters." He glanced at me. "As far as we know. But what if there are more to come? Part of me wants to believe it's just the work of some nut case and the threats have absolutely nothing to do with Jack's death."

"Are you supervising this case?" Adam asked.

"No. Jack was, but Nora Layton was doing pretty much all of the work."

While I'd never been the object of Jack Harding's worst behavior, I had been a witness to his screaming fits and his threats. "David, he treated people terribly," I said. "I know it's none of my business, but I don't know how you were able to stand having him as a partner."

"I know. He was a son of a bitch. But he had an incredible memory for details. He was never a particularly winning personality in front of a jury, but we won a lot of cases based on his hard work."

"Listen." Adam stood. "I need to get busy and make sure my people are set up and apprised of everything. I'll see you both later."

Once Adam left the room, David turned to me. "Don't get me wrong, Julia — I'm glad you're here. I need someone around I can trust. I don't want you to actually do anything except keep your eyes and ears open, as before. Let me, Adam, or the police know about anything suspicious or anything out of the ordinary. I need your insight and your intuition. That's something that you're good at, and . . ." David trailed off. "I guess . . . well, I'm just grateful to have someone here who's a friend."

"You've got it."

"Oh Christ, I can hardly believe this." He put his head in his hands and took a deep breath.

We heard a tap on the door. David looked up as a woman entered. Her hair was a frizzy mop pulled back with a rhinestone clip. She wore Birkenstocks and a long gypsy dress in a paisley print. She sauntered toward David's desk. "We need to talk."

"I know," he replied. "Julia, this is Beth, our Marketing Director."

"Hello," I said.

Beth looked at me as if I had no business being seated in David's office. She plopped into the wing chair that Adam had just vacated.

"Julia's helping me out this week while Muriel's away," David offered.

Beth didn't give me a moment of her attention. "My phone's been ringing off the hook. The papers have gotten hold of this and we have to do some damage control. Somehow, someone accessed the police report and the press knows the murder happened here in the office. A few of the attorneys have gotten calls from Jack's clients, who are extremely upset."

David groaned. "Well, we knew this would happen. I want your response to be 'no comment, pending the police investigation.' And send an email — mark it urgent — saying that no one, and I mean *no one,* is to talk to anyone from the press. Take messages and don't call anyone back. Is that clear?"

"Perfectly," Beth replied. Her body language was in contrast to the urgency of the situation. "I'll tell my assistant to take care of it."

"No. You. Please don't leave it to anyone else. I want everyone made aware. Anyone spills anything to any reporter and I'll have their head on a plate."

"Of course," Beth replied lazily, moving out of her chair toward the door. "No worries, I'll make sure everyone knows."

David sighed when the door closed behind the woman. He turned to me. "I asked her to come in today to handle the press queries." He shook his head. "I don't know why we hired her. I try to like her but I just don't. Her whole attitude is *So what.* I keep trying to give her the benefit of the doubt."

"I'd really like to have a look at the personnel files, David. With your permission, of course."

David's brow furrowed. "Why do you need those?"

"I'm certain someone here is either involved or knows more than they're saying. I want to gather everyone's birth dates and run some charts."

"Okay. Fine with me. Anything you can think of would be a help."

I headed back to my desk. The first thing I needed was a parking card so I wouldn't have to depend on city buses to come downtown. I dialed the Human Resources office on the 40th floor, hoping someone would be in.

"This is Manda. May I help you?" Manda had an ingratiating nasal voice.

"Hi, Manda. I'm Julia, working in David Meyers' office this week. Mr. Meyers would like to have the personnel files for all the attorneys and staff in the litigation department sent up. Could you get them together and bring them up to his office?" I wasn't sure, but I was willing to bet that any answers lay right here, in this department. Only rarely was there much interaction between different sections of the firm. It was the best place to start.

There was a long moment of silence on the phone. "It'll take quite a while to gather those files and I can't possibly do it. They told me I had to go home." Manda sounded like something quite sour was caught inside her nose.

"Manda, David Meyers would like those files on his desk immediately." I was enjoying my little moment of power. I thanked her in the sweetest of tones and hung up. Let's see if Manda can get a move on, I thought.

Exactly fifteen minutes later, a rail-thin,

overly made-up woman in her thirties entered from the hallway, pushing a small cart and heaving great sighs. Her face was narrow, with close-set eyes and thick hair teased into a flip. I was sure she was someone who had perfected the art of whining. She looked me up and down, unsure if I was a person who warranted subservience or hostility. I enjoyed watching the conflict on her face.

"Thank you so much for being prompt. You can leave them right here."

"I thought Mr. Meyers wanted these?" she complained.

"He does. However, he'd like you to leave them right here on my desk." Another minute and I might just growl and snarl at her. Was this woman bringing out the worst in me or what? I had a vision of ripping the tiny pearl earrings out of her ears and watching blood drip down her pink sweater set.

"Well, these files are completely confidential, you know . . ." Thinking for a moment she might have the upper hand.

"I am well aware these are confidential, and Mr. Meyers is also well aware that these files are confidential. I would appreciate your putting them right here, right now, on my desk." I took a deep breath. "Thank you."

"Fine . . . all right!" With a frown, she lifted the files from her cart and dumped them on my desk. "We'll need them back, you know."

"Oh, and I'll also need some sort of a temporary parking card. Could you take care of that today too?" I walked her to the door and held it open, watching her roll her cart to the end of the hallway. Then I closed the office door very firmly.

I returned to the desk, grateful the office was quiet. In keeping with David's request, I had set my voicemail and email to an automatic response, putting off any incoming queries. I sorted through the file folders, starting with Jack Harding. There were the usual withholding forms, bar association receipts, emergency information about next of kin. His sister, Sarah Larkin, lived at 3104 Ulloa in the Sunset District. I made a note of the address and the phone number. Then I went through the rest of the files, noting each person's birth date, birth place, former employment, and anything else that might be fruitful. Without the time of birth, I could only set up solar charts, but the signs and angles between the planets and major transits would still tell me a great deal about each person.

Jack's next birthday would have been December 18th. Transiting Pluto, a planet that ushers in major life changes, had passed over his Sun several years earlier. Possibly his divorce? I noted the birth dates and birth places of Ira Walstone, Roger Wilkinson, and Nora Layton, then moved on to Suzanne Simms, Dani Nichols, and Karen Jansen. The personnel files contained letters, resumes, and applications for employment, as well as beneficiary forms for life insurance, 401K information, and annual reviews. David had mentioned that Jack and Ira had made lateral moves to David's firm at the same time and brought Suzanne with them. Ira's wife was Rita Walstone, and they had two grown children. Nora had been with David's firm for approximately three years and named a sister in Wisconsin as her next of kin.

The attorneys' files included claims for prescriptions and other medical expenses. That surprised me. Medical information is strictly confidential, but Nora Layton's file for the preceding year caught my eye. There was a long list of laboratory and prescription charges from the Bay Area Life Services Group. All had occurred within a four month period from June through October of the prior year. I had heard of this group. It was a private organization that catered to a lot of different medical issues: eating disorders, drug rehab, liposuction, cosmetic surgery, and psychotherapy. I dialed Manda's extension. She didn't sound very happy to hear from me again.

"Manda, I have a question for you. Some of these files contain information for medical claims."

"Yes?"

"I thought those were confidential."

"It is, but the attorneys have an additional insurance policy, kind of an executive care type of thing, that picks up charges that the regular insurance doesn't cover. The staff isn't covered by it, just the attorneys. So we submit whatever isn't covered by the regular policy to another company."

"I see. Thanks. I'll get these back to you in a little while." Unfortunately, nothing indicated what type of treatment Nora had received.

It was getting close to lunchtime and I thought it might be useful to coax Dani away from the office. Possibly she'd open up a bit outside the firm. I walked down the hall to her desk and found her busily organizing exhibits to various documents, debris and paper strewn over the top of her desk.

"How about a bite to eat, Dani? Are you free?"

"I'd love to. Just gotta double check these exhibits are in the right order."

"I can wait. In fact, I'll give you a hand."

"You'd think just once these guys could get something ready before the last minute?" Dani grumbled. "I swear they think their words exit their mouths and land on the judge's lap with no process in between." She handed me a stack of copies to be served on opposing counsel. "These are just gonna be mailed. Can you stuff the envelopes?"

"Sure, no problem." I slipped each set into pre-labeled large envelopes.

I sealed the last envelope and Dani said, "Okay, these are all perfect. I'll scan and e-file after lunch. I'm absolutely starving. I only have an hour though. I've got to finish this and leave by six o'clock. I've got a rehearsal at six thirty."

"A rehearsal?"

"Yeah. I didn't mention it, but that's my real career. I play bass. We've got a gig in North Beach. A place called Stoned on Thursday nights. Hey, why don't you stop by?"

My ears had gone up. "Maybe I will. I'd love to." There was no way Dani could know, but Stoned is a club owned by my good friend Googie from the neighborhood. We had known each other since elementary school. "I'll just go grab my purse. Be right back." I walked quickly down the hall toward David's office and pushed the door open. Nora Layton stood next to my desk and the personnel files.

"Nora!"

"Oh, there you are. I was just looking for David. Has he gone to lunch?"

"Yes, he has." I studiously avoided looking at the stack of files on my desk. "I'll have him call you when he returns?"

"Thanks." Nora nodded and brushed past me on her way to the door.

I breathed a sigh of relief as soon as she was gone. I scribbled a note to David and stuck it on his phone. Then I picked up the notes I had made from the files, tucked them into my purse, and locked the outside door to David's reception area. I wondered how much Nora had seen.

ELEVEN

Billy, in his leathers, was waiting at the end of the corridor, his flaming red and yellow helmet clutched to his chest. Karen stood next to him. Heads together, they seemed to be conferring quietly. When they heard the door close behind me, they straightened up and turned to stare. Then Karen moved toward the elevator bank and Billy looked down at the floor as I passed him, avoiding my eyes.

In the central room, Dani was busy bundling her court documents together with rubber bands. She was the last one left in the section. She gestured to Billy and he stepped into the room. "Here you go, Billy. All set for the judge."

Billy's expression was sullen, but he nodded.

Dani sighed and turned to me. "Electronic filing's supposed to be so easy, but it doubles the work with these old judges who insist on having paper copies delivered. There were nineteen exhibits and every page had to be consecutively numbered. What a damn pain." Her desk was littered with envelopes and exhibit tabs. "I'll clean up later. Let's go. I'm starving." She grabbed her purse and we took the elevator down to the lobby. She suggested a fast-food Middle Eastern restaurant on Kearny. I knew the place. A little heavy on olive oil but the food was great. Once seated at the restaurant, our plates arrived quickly. Dani had ordered a giant falafel and I got the hummus plate with stuffed grape leaves.

"So, tell me about your gig."

Dani made an effort to speak but only managed a mumble. After a few moments, she swallowed her bite. "We're so excited we're playing at Stoned. Do you know the place?" She wiped drips from her mouth.

"Sure. That's a great place to play."

"Oh, yeah, this is big exposure for us. We're all really jazzed about it. We'll be there the next four Thursday nights. Of course, there's not a lot of money in it, not when we split it four ways, but it's still a great place to be heard. I hope you can come."

"I'd love to. I have a dinner to go to that night, but I'll definitely try to stop in and have a drink. Break a leg, huh?"

"Thanks. So Julia, is all this stuff creeping you out or what?"

"That's a good way to put it."

"You probably didn't have to come in if you didn't want to. I'm sure they'd understand if you didn't want to stay."

"It's okay. Really. I said I would, and I'd like to keep on good terms with the firm for future temp jobs, you know?" *Hopefully not.* "What about you? Are you worried?"

"Me? No way." Dani continued to munch on her sizeable lunch and then said, "Well, yes, I guess it is kind of scary, although I don't really think anybody's after *me.* I mean, why should they be?"

I scooped a glob of hummus with a tiny piece of bread and popped it into my mouth. "Tell me, what's with Karen? She seemed really distant initially, and then, today, she's overly friendly."

"She's weird, Julia. Don't pay any attention to her." I kept my mouth shut, hoping Dani would be motivated to gossip more. "She can't possibly have a life. I mean, she's the first one here in the morning. Even if I get here as early as eight, she's already at her desk when *I* get in." Dani took another huge bite of her falafel, liquid dripping onto her plate. "And did you see that bilious green sweater she has on today? No taste either. I swear, she wears that thing days on end. Maybe she never changes her clothes, but if she doesn't wear something different soon, I'm gonna burn it."

"I thought she was married . . . or married in the past?" I hoped I wasn't giving away my perusal of the personnel files.

Dani shrugged. "She's either divorced or her husband died, I can't remember which, but she's definitely an odd one. Never ever talks about anything personal and when you ask her a direct question, she smiles and her eyes kind of glaze over."

"Maybe she's just really private."

Dani didn't need much encouragement to warm to her subject. "I mean, she's so weird, working for Jack didn't even bother her. And he was a real bastard around the office."

"She never complained about him to you?"

"No. And that *is* really weird, 'cause nobody could stand working for him. That's why they hired her from outside. But, hey, if she doesn't want to get personal with anyone, that's fine with me. I don't really care. I was just asking to be polite, you know? Probably goes home and talks to her cat for all I know."

I wondered what Dani would have to say about my conversations with Wizard, if she only knew. Maybe I'd be relegated to the same category as Karen. "I have yet to meet Suzanne. Do you know where she is?"

"Home, I guess. In all the confusion yesterday, I forgot about her. She called in after we spoke this morning, said she was still sick. Plans on coming in tomorrow."

"Does she live in the city?"

"Yeah, out in the Laurel Heights area, I think. She has a flat she shares with a roommate."

"Did you tell her about Jack and what happened?"

"I started to, but she already knew. Somebody told her."

"I wonder who?"

"Could've been anybody. She might have called Ira or Nora directly. She was doing some work for both of them."

"I heard Jack had an ex-wife the police want to talk to."

"I'm sure they do, and a girlfriend too." Dani smirked through a mouthful of food.

"Oh? Really? So who's the girlfriend?"

"Suzanne."

I was stunned. "Whaaat? How do you know?"

"Had to be. She was always following him

around, working on special projects over the weekend. Can you believe it? Now, man, I think that's truly weird. The guy's a putz. I cannot imagine any woman being attracted to him."

"How many people knew about this?"

"If I know, I'm sure they all did. I mean, I don't know for certain, but I'm pretty sure." Dani took a last bite of her falafel. "You wouldn't believe some of the things that go on around here."

"Oh yeah? Like what?" This was getting interesting.

"Well . . . Ira's a perv, that's for sure. He's come close to a sexual harassment charge. He was writing gross notes and leaving them under one of the secretary's keyboards when she was away from her desk. He was slipping down to the 40th floor and didn't think anyone would notice. She was sure it was Ira but couldn't really prove it. He's just lucky the woman didn't want to make it public."

"Would he have been fired?"

"I think they would have had to, or at least fined him big time. Has to be a zero tolerance policy about that stuff." She looked up quickly. "Which is a good thing, I think. Jerk denied it, of course." She popped half a grape leaf into her mouth. "Believe me, if the clients knew half of what went on around here, they'd run screaming to another firm. Roger, he's another slippery character. His business reimbursements aren't for lunches or dinners with potential clients. They're all his dates, and he's charging the firm for them. Some ethics, huh?"

I'd have to remember to mention these confidences to David. I knew he didn't involve himself in personnel issues and was probably clueless about the shenanigans among the attorneys. "So, this thing with Jack must have really hit Suzanne hard?"

"I imagine. She didn't sound too good."

Twelve

We returned to the office and Dani went straight to her desk to clear up the mess from the morning's court filing. I walked down the hall and stepped through the door to David's office. He must have come back from lunch because the door was now unlocked. I hung up my coat, shoved my purse under the desk, and picked up the phone. Time to do a little checking of references.

Dani had begun her employment at Meyers, Dade & Schultz two years earlier. It was her first job in the legal world. She'd done bookkeeping and clerical work for Greensafe, a private environmental group that was well known in San Francisco. She listed her occupation as musician slash secretary. Karen's employment had started slightly more than one year ago. She was the most recently hired. Mendelson & Mendelson had been her former employer for two years.

Her birthplace was St. Paul, and her next of kin was a cousin named William. Her references from Mendelson were easy enough to check. They were just up the street at 650 California.

When I reached the office supervisor at Greensafe, I told her I was with the firm of Arps, Skadley & Biggerton — it was the first combination of unreal names that came into my head — and that I was verifying employment for Dani Nichols regarding her application for a job with our company. The supervisor was a woman named Mildred Hadley, who remembered Dani very well.

"Yes, that's right. Dani worked for us up until two years ago. And before that, she did clerical and bookkeeping work for a small contractor, electrical, I think. I'm not sure where she went after she left here. If you need the exact dates I can check, but it'll take a day or so to retrieve our files. We're still in the process of converting them electronically."

"No, that's okay," I said. "I'm sure the dates she gave us are accurate. There's no need."

"If you change your mind, just give me a call. She was a dear. I was really sorry when she left. She was accurate and fast and a very hard worker."

"That's good to hear. She seems like a very nice person," I purred.

"I know we're only supposed to tell potential new employers certain information, but I know you'll be really happy if you hire her. I don't blame her for leaving. She wanted a chance to make more money, you know."

I thanked Mildred Hadley profusely and told her I was glad to get the information. I was sure things would work out, blah blah and more blah as we hung up.

Next up was Karen Jansen. I wasn't sure what I was looking for, but if I kept sifting through things, maybe some lie, some little fib, some something, would lead me in the right direction. Whoever had killed Jack had access to the firm or was connected to the firm in some way. The answers were here, I felt sure. David's transits confirmed it. And the best place to start checking was the past.

The Human Resources Director at Mendelson was a man named Ronald Givens. I gave him the same story, that I was calling from the firm of Arps, Skadley & Biggerly — or was it Arps, Biggerly & Skadington? Didn't matter. He didn't question the idiocy of the names either. He confirmed that Karen Jansen had indeed been employed at Mendelson & Mendelson. She'd worked there for one year. I made noises about that not being a great deal of legal experience and he informed me that her reviews at Mendelson were quite positive. I asked him if she'd listed a prior legal reference.

"Hold on, I'll pull her file. It's just in the next room. It'll take a few minutes. Can I call you back?"

Ooops. "No, I'll hold, if you don't mind. I'd like to finish this. I plan to leave the office early today."

He came back on the line a few minutes later. "Well, actually, she didn't have any prior legal experience, but she picked things up pretty quickly."

"Oh?"

"She's from the Midwest. So we were her first employer when she relocated to San Francisco. Before that she worked for a company that went out of business, so I guess their address and phone number wouldn't do you any good."

"No. That's all right. I appreciate the information. I was more interested in checking her legal references. Thanks all the same."

"No trouble."

We hung up. So much for that. In spite of laws that restricted employers from providing any information other than the date of hire and date of termination, it was amazing how chatty company reps could get. By now, I was really itching to set up the charts at home.

There's an astrological theory that a strong Pluto or Mars connection can always be found between the charts of a victim and a killer. I'd read one or two studies on the subject and the theory made sense. This could be true even when the two people were strangers to each other. Following that line of logic, some strong connection must exist between Jack's chart and the murderer's, and hopefully it would jump out at me. I was wondering if there was any further need for me to stay at the office for the rest of the day. I got up from the desk and stuck my head in David's office.

"Julia, come on in. I just called Sarah Larkin, Jack's sister. I wanted to touch base with her to see if I could do anything to help her out."

"Did the police get out to see her yesterday?"

"Yes, I'm sure. She certainly knew what had happened. Here . . ." David rummaged through odd bits of paper on his desk. "I'm sure I have it somewhere." I watched him lift up files and sift through paper to no avail. "I'm lost without Muriel. Ah, found it. I'm wondering if I could ask you to do something today."

"Sure, what is it?"

"Would you be willing to talk to her?"

"Oh." David's request surprised me. "All right, if you think it would give us some information."

"I'm thinking she may know things we could have no way of knowing."

"Did she give you a hint of that?"

David grimaced. "No. That's why I thought you might glean more. She wasn't exactly grief-stricken, if you follow me." He passed over a slip of paper with Sarah Larkin's address.

"That bad, huh?

David shot me a dark look. "Let's just say there was no love lost and leave it at that. Good luck."

THIRTEEN

I shut down my computer, slipped on my coat, and grabbed my purse. Carrying the stack of personnel files, I took the elevator to the 40th floor, wandering the deserted hallways until I found the Human Resources office. Manda was at the front desk scrutinizing her manicure. She didn't look happy to see me, but, to give her credit, she wordlessly handed me a small white rectangular card with tiny numbers in the corner for access to underground parking.

I started to turn away, then hesitated. "I thought you were being sent home."

"That's what I thought too." Manda's mouth twisted. "But then Beth, my boss, told me I had to handle all the phone calls."

"I see." I made a mental note to let David know his orders were being ignored, and then I thanked her and dumped the personnel files on her desk. She flashed a tight smile and returned to studying her nails for minute flaws.

Once outside the building, I caught a bus at the corner of Pine. This time of day there were few passengers, and within twenty minutes I was deposited on the corner a block from my apartment. I hurried down the hill, crossed Clement Street, and reached my building. Incoming fog had blocked the sun and a stiff gust of wind carried the smell of the sea. I let myself in, found my car keys, and refilled Wizard's bowl with some dry nuggets. I called to him but I didn't hear his bell. He was nowhere to be found. I finally peeked out the kitchen window and spotted him splayed out on the roof of my neighbor's one-story cottage, one of his favorite napping spots.

Most of the houses on the Avenues are duplexes or single family homes built in the 1930s and 1940s, but some of the tiny cottages erected as shelters after the big quake are still scattered throughout the area. My duplex had just such houses on either side. Wizard loved that he could scoot out through his kitty door and jump onto my neighbor's roof from our landing. He lifted his head, stared at me lazily, yawned, and curled into a fetal position. "Okay, if that's what you want," I replied. I let myself out the kitchen door, locked up, and went down the back stairs to the garage.

I followed the curve from Sutro Heights down to the Great Highway. Here, the road runs parallel to Ocean Beach. Sheets of sand had blown across the highway and formed dunes that every so often were high enough to block the ocean view. Waves crashed against the concrete abutment, sending saltwater spray across my windshield. I closed the car window, cranked the radio up, and sang along with an oldies rock song.

My musical tastes are wildly eclectic — rock, jazz on a tenor sax, Bulgarian women singing a cappella, hypnotic Native American flutes, sea chanties, and all sorts of genuine tribal and ethnic music. I have a collection of CDs recorded live by my fellow grad students in their travels from Guatemala to Chinese Turkestan. The stranger and more exotic, the better. Bear in mind, I'm incredibly ignorant musically. I can't read music and can't sing worth a damn. I couldn't tell a B flat from a C sharp. But at that moment, with no one listening, I could happily sing along at the top of my lungs.

South of Golden Gate Park, I turned east on Ulloa away from the roiling Pacific. I slowed after crossing 34th and spotted

Sarah Larkin's address on the opposite side of the street. The house was a two-story stucco-fronted duplex. In this part of the city, very few houses boast a front yard; concrete stretches to the front stairs and garages open directly onto the wide sidewalks. The wind off the ocean picked up, blowing east. Particles of dust and beach sand hit my face as I climbed out of the car. Keeping my head down for protection, I hurried across the street.

Up close, pale pink paint, blasted by constant wind and sand, was peeling off the wooden framing on the sides of the house. Even the front stucco facing showed splotchy wear and tear from the elements. Two dark green garbage cans with ancient spills were the only decoration at the front. One was empty with its lid hanging open, the other, blown over by the wind, was on its side, crusted debris stuck to its bottom. I guessed no one had bothered to take them in after garbage pickup day. Maybe no one ever took them in. I climbed the long stairway to the front doors, where a sign indicated numbers 3102-3104. At least here, in the shelter of the entryway, there was respite from the wind. I pressed the buzzer to the door on the right. After a moment a woman called out, "Who is it?"

"Hi. My name is Julia Bonatti. I've come from Meyers, Dade & Schultz."

The door was quickly yanked open by a woman in her late forties. Her face was round and slightly puffy. She wore no makeup and was dressed in a nondescript brown jumper over a black sweatshirt. Her long hair, streaked with gray, was combed back behind her ears.

She peered at me. "For God's sake. What now? I told him I didn't want anything from him or his damn law firm." Her eyes were thin, puffy slits.

"I . . . uh . . . I understand. But that's not really why I'm here."

"Oh, really? And why *are* you here?" Her weight shifted and she placed a hand on her hip, her body betraying her belligerent mood.

"I'd just like to talk to you about your brother. I was hoping maybe you could help us in finding his murderer."

"His murderer . . . I'd give his murderer a prize if I knew who he was," she sneered. She looked me up and down and finally made the decision to talk to me, even if it was only because I offered a sounding board for her bitterness. "Come on in," she said resignedly.

I stepped into a hallway leading to a living

133

room at the front of the house, with kitchen and bedrooms toward the rear. She motioned me through the opposite archway into the dining area. A large oak table that had seen better days dominated the room. Its finish was dull, chips and gouges marring its surface. The table held several piles of both dirty and clean unfolded laundry. I suspected the piles were a permanent fixture rather than a work in progress. Three mismatched wooden chairs in various stages of peeling paint stood around the table. The walls, a color best described as landlord beige, were devoid of decoration.

"Pull up a chair," she said. I sat down and Sarah lowered herself slowly onto another chair. "What do you want to know?"

"I gather you and your brother weren't close, but I am sorry for your loss."

"Don't be. Wasn't a loss. Believe me." Sarah began to busy herself folding one piece of laundry at a time. "I haven't talked to him for years. Since my son died." She reached for a fresh garment from the pile of laundry. "I blame Jack for that."

"Oh, I'm so sorry. I didn't know." A familiar pain flickered in my chest. My loss seemed small in comparison. Sarah Larkin had suffered the most painful blow of all. "But why do you blame Jack?"

"Nicky was sixteen when he died. He had a drug problem. He got mixed up with the wrong kids and they were into some heavy stuff. I tried everything I knew to get him to clean up. He went in and out of rehab trying to quit." She fell silent for a moment. "I found out about a private place, out of the city, where he could stay in a really good situation and get therapy. I was sure if he had one more chance . . . a good chance, he might make it." Her voice trailed off. "I begged Jack for the money. I'd never asked him for a thing in my life. Never. But I begged for that."

"He refused?"

"Said he didn't see why he should pay for rehab or counseling. The other places hadn't done Nick any good, so what difference did it make?" She sighed. "Nicky was a good kid, but there's so much stuff around, how do any of these kids steer clear of it?" She looked at me, her eyes betraying a deep well of pain. "Jack never really loved anyone in his life. How could he possibly understand what it's like to love a child?"

"You hated him for that."

"Oh, yes. And I enjoyed hating him. Still do. I wanted somebody to blame after Nick's death, but the fact remains, my own brother wouldn't spend a penny to help his sister's only son. I didn't have anyone else to ask. My husband was killed in a car accident when Nick was seven. Our parents are dead, and Jack had plenty of money. Big, successful lawyer . . . but he didn't give a damn about me or Nick. Yeah, I hated him. I still hate his guts. I don't care if he's dead. I only wish he had suffered more." Sarah's face closed down as she continued to fold laundry. "So, that's it. That's my story. I get disability now. It's hard for me to work and I got nobody left."

I felt the room closing in on me. My chest tightened and it took me a moment to get my breath. Her bitterness seemed to suck the very air out of the room. "What about other people? Was there anyone who hated him enough to kill him?"

Sarah Larkin snickered mirthlessly. "Probably anybody who knew him. I don't know. Try his ex-wife. Try his business partners. Trust me, he was anything but a nice guy."

"Look, I am sorry I bothered you." I gathered my purse and rummaged in it for my car keys. "I thought it might be worth a try."

She didn't answer but rose to walk me to the door. "Hey, David Meyers says I've got some money coming, is that true?"

"It looks that way. We're checking now to

see if Jack left a will, but under California law, without a will, his next of kin would inherit everything. And that's you."

"What do you know," she mused. "How much do you think it is?"

"I have no way of knowing, but I'm sure his condo must be worth well over a million. More if he had a life insurance policy."

She smiled with a sad look in her eyes. "What good's it gonna do me now? You know how much I asked him for when Nicky was sick?"

I shook my head.

"Ten thousand." She watched me silently as I descended the windblown steps from her door to my car.

FOURTEEN

Shivering, I climbed in, turned the key in the ignition, and cranked up the heater. I wasn't sure if I was cold from the proximity to the ocean or my time with Sarah. The wind had done its best to stand my hair on end. I shook it out, then smoothed it with my fingers and pulled it back into the clasp again. I couldn't decide where to go next. There was really no point in returning downtown.

I had managed to push Maggie's visit the night before out of my mind, but now it all came flooding back. I certainly understood her anger, but I was more concerned by how fragile she had seemed. I wasn't far away from her apartment. I checked my watch. It was just possible she was home or close by. She answered on the second ring.

"Julia! You must be a mind reader. I was just thinking about calling you. Are you home?"

"No. I'm in the Sunset on Ulloa. I thought I might catch you."

"I'm at the market on Taraval, picking up a few things for my mother. Can you meet me?" Maggie hesitated. "There's something I can show you."

My breath caught. "Is it . . . ?"

"Yes. I've got a copy of the photo. The doctor gave my mom a prescription for a sedative and she's resting now, so I have a few minutes."

My heart was pounding. "I'll meet you at the coffee shop on the corner." Maggie agreed and I started the car, driving away from the ocean. Taraval and 46th was just a few blocks away. It's easy to find your way in the Sunset District; the streets are alphabetical if you don't count Lincoln running along the south side of Golden Gate Park. They begin with Irving and end at Yorba. Taraval falls between Santiago and Ulloa.

Maggie was waiting inside the coffee shop at a small table when I got there. She looked up and smiled as I came through the door, then moved her purse to another chair. Wordlessly, she pushed a cappuccino across the table.

"You're a doll. How did you know I needed this?"

"I figured." She reached into her purse

and passed the photo to me.

For a moment, I couldn't take a breath. The photo was slightly blurry. Michael lay on his side, and only the lower part of his body and his legs were visible. He might have been knocked unconscious. At least I hoped so. It was as Maggie had said: a glimpse of a tire, the edge of a chrome bumper, and a dark or black vehicle. Some self-protective part of my brain distanced me from the vision of Michael either dead or dying. I felt nothing. In truth, I'd imagined worse, much worse. I passed the snapshot back to Maggie. "What are the police doing?"

"You mean the retired detective? I don't know. I'm just glad the son didn't dump the old man's photos in the trash." Maggie took a sip of her cappuccino. "The old guy was elderly and maybe he was getting a little gaga taking pictures of birds and plants and stuff, but hey, maybe he was bored and lonely and just having fun. Most of the photos were junk, but there were piles of negatives. He had a Nikon, I think they said, with film, if you can believe that." She smiled for the first time. "I remember those. So, the detective promised to check all the negatives to see if there are any more that he might have taken."

I took a deep breath. "I see."

"Are you okay?"

I nodded. "Yes. Just trying to get my head around all of this. To think, all this time, somebody saw what happened."

"It just kills me that he didn't come forward and say something then. Maybe it would have been possible to catch whoever did this if he had."

"I know. Maybe. We don't know for sure — eyewitnesses are notoriously incorrect. Finding a better picture would be good. Whoever it was, I can't imagine how terrible it would be to know you killed someone, even accidentally. Hiding it all this time, what would that do to a person?"

"Torture them to the grave, I hope," Maggie said grimly.

"Who's the detective in charge? Do you think I could talk to him?"

"I don't see why not." Maggie rummaged in her purse. "Here's one of his cards. Give him a call. Listen, I have to run. I'd love to stay and chat, but I don't want to leave my mother alone for too long."

"I'm so sorry, Maggie. It's not fair that this falls on your shoulders."

"What's fair got to do with it?" she answered. "I'm taking my vacation time now so I can stay with her. I've got to go back to work next week." Maggie worked as an administrative assistant at Cal State San Francisco, where Michael and I had both attended classes. She'd been enrolled there too, but after Michael's death she dropped her classes and took a full-time job at the university.

"Maggie, have you thought any more about returning to school and getting your degree?" I asked now.

She sighed heavily. "I have. I should. I don't know. Somehow it all seems too much. And what difference would a degree make?"

It was yet another example of how all our lives had changed with Michael's death, but it was a shame Maggie might realize one day that her life hadn't moved on. "You'll be glad you finished someday," I told her. "You never know. You could stay at your mom's house for free and wouldn't have to worry about food or a roof over your head. And it could lead to some better opportunities."

"You're right. I know you're right. I've been feeling like my life's on a loop these days."

"Think about it. I don't mean to nag you, but you're young, too young not to be venturing out."

"I'll think about it." Maggie smiled and grasped my hand. "Have to go."

I slurped the last of my cappuccino and followed her out to the sidewalk. We hugged and she headed to her car. The sun had disappeared behind steely clouds and the wind whipped fiercely from the west. The day had grown bitter and cold. I watched Maggie until she drove away and then returned to my car. I climbed in and shivered until the heater warmed up the interior.

I felt adrift. My normal working life had been disrupted, and Jack's murder had disrupted my temporary working life. I needed to think about something else, otherwise I'd spend the rest of the day being haunted by that photo.

FIFTEEN

I had to admit to curiosity about Hilary Greene, Jack's ex-wife. David hadn't asked me to speak with her, not directly, but I thought it might be a good idea. Jack may not have been in her life for several years, but that didn't mean she hadn't been in contact with him. David had said her gallery was on upper Fillmore. I realized I should have thought ahead and asked him its name, or at least looked it up. But it couldn't be that hard to locate. I decided to risk the traffic and followed Ulloa until it hit 19th Avenue. It was bumper to bumper with lights at every block. After twenty minutes, the traffic flow finally picked up. I took the road through Golden Gate Park over to Geary and down to Fillmore. Once there, I started searching for a parking space. Here, the sun had given up its valiant fight against the fog, just as it had in the Sunset District.

Parking in this neighborhood is always difficult and the afternoon tow-away zones certainly don't help. It was close to four o'clock now, the danger zone for being ticketed or towed. I cruised slowly down the block, turned right toward the Pacific Medical Center at the top of the hill, and came around the block again. On my second pass I got lucky. A car was pulling out of a metered space on the right side. I flicked my turn signal and slowed down, moving as far over to the right as possible to allow other cars to pass.

The art gallery had to be somewhere in this four-block area between Pine and Clay Streets. A few blocks north, the elegant homes of Pacific Heights took over, and unless Hilary was running her business out of a basement, I had to be close. One block up, I noticed a sign done in gold lettering: *The Greene Room.* The façade was painted a deep greenish-black color. Window boxes below the two large windows at the front overflowed with trailing ivy and blossoms. I pushed open the beveled glass door and an old-fashioned bell rang. Inside, the floors were a pale, glossy hardwood. Upholstered chairs were placed strategically around the room. Paintings occupied most of the wall space, and small sculptures sat on pedestals.

I moved through the first room and then through an archway into a larger room. Spotlights took the place of daylight here and larger landscapes hung in ornate frames. A five-foot stone sculpture was on display in the center of the space. As I moved closer, a sense of *déjà vu* was hard to ignore. This piece was suspiciously similar to the ones I had seen the night before at Gale's art show. A small card indicated the artist's name.

"May I help you?"

I turned. A slender woman in her forties stood behind me in the archway, smiling. She wore a deep blue silk shirt and matching pants. Her hair was long, streaked with blonde, and pulled back into a bun at the nape of her neck. I'm a little over five seven, and as she approached I realized I had to look up to her, a thing I'm not at all used to doing. I found it slightly disconcerting.

"Uh. Yes, actually, you can." She continued to smile at me, but after my experience with Sarah Larkin, I wasn't sure how long I'd be welcome. "My name is Julia Bonatti. I'm working for David Meyers."

"Working for . . . are you an investigator?" Her brow furrowed.

"Oh, no, nothing like that. Well, maybe you could say I am . . . in a way. I hope you don't mind, but I'd like to talk to you about your ex-husband."

"Oh. Yes . . . Jack." She sighed, her face clouding. "David called me yesterday. It was very thoughtful of him. And I spoke to the police this morning."

"David wants to do everything he can to get this thing cleared up. You can imagine what it's doing to everyone who has to work there and the reputation of the firm."

"Would you like a cup of coffee? I was just about to close up. It's been a very quiet day."

"Yes, I'd love one." After the cappuccino Maggie had offered me, I'd really be buzzing.

"Come on in the back then." I followed her into a small kitchenette-storage room. Large crates were stacked against the walls and packing materials were strewn on the floor in the corner. A partial room divider separated the rest of the space from a heavy oak desk and a large filing cabinet. Hilary poured two cups of coffee from a pot on an electric warmer and carried a sugar bowl, creamer, and napkins to the small table.

"Cream? Sugar?"

"A little cream please, that's all." She handed me a large mug. I took a sip. It was delicious first-rate Italian coffee.

"Thank you. This is great."

"Oh, I'm glad you like it. I can't stand weak coffee." She passed a napkin across the table to me. "Now, how can I help you?"

"I just came from seeing Sarah Larkin."

"Oh my God. How is she these days?"

"Not good. Very bitter. She's very hateful toward Jack. And she still blames him for the death of her son."

"Nicky . . . yes." Hilary's face took on a faraway look. "Can't say I blame her. That was just awful. I only wish I'd known she needed that money. I would have given it to her in a second, no matter what Jack thought. I heard about it later from him, but it was after Nicky died." She was silent a moment. "I still can't believe it when I think about it. I was so furious with him. Ten thousand dollars was nothing to Jack."

"Would it have made a difference to her son, do you think?"

"Who knows?" She shrugged. "Maybe it would have, we'll never know. People relapse and OD all the time, but I thought it was a disgrace not to give her the money and at least try to give Nicky another chance."

"So he never told you she'd asked for the money?"

"Not at the time. And I guess she must have thought I'd agree with Jack even though we were on the verge of a separation. She never tried to contact me." Hilary dropped her gaze. "That just confirmed once more that I was making the right decision to get out from under his control. And make no mistake, Jack doesn't have relationships. He has control challenges . . . had . . . I just thank God I escaped."

"Why did you ever marry him?"

"Oh . . . I don't know . . . I was young and not very experienced. Jack wasn't the greatest-looking guy in the world, but he was older and he seemed so smart and sophisticated to me. I'd been married briefly before, but it didn't last very long because we were both really young. I think Jack appealed to me so much because he *was* older. He seemed solid. Maybe I was looking for security." I nodded at her encouragingly. "And he was sexy. It was something he just gave off, like a scent."

"How long were you together?"

"Ten years in all. Ten years too long."

"That bad, huh?"

"Well, let's put it this way. I grew up. I didn't need some guy, a powerful man, telling me what I could and couldn't do. I'm too independent and I didn't like being controlled." She laughed. "I was so naïve, it took me a while to realize that he *was* controlling me. I mistook everything for love and concern." She was silent for a moment. "I started to see things I didn't like. I guess I'm just a very ethical person and I really started to not respect Jack and the way he dealt with people. It was only a matter of time."

"Was it a bitter divorce?"

She shook her head. "No. Not really. Jack was angry, make no mistake. But I think he finally realized that he couldn't exert his will toward me any longer. The wiring had been torn out. When it finally came down to it, we worked out a settlement. But I would have walked without a dime if it had come to that. Maybe some people thought I was only after money, but that wasn't it at all."

"Are you happy now?"

She smiled and her face lit up. "Oh, yes, very. I have fun here. I love my clients. And I really like dealing with the artists. We have another big room in the back and we hold art classes there. Yes, I'd have to say I'm happy now and I'm doing okay financially." She shook her head. "It's horrible what happened to Jack. It really does give me the creeps, but in a way, I'm not surprised."

"What do you mean by that?"

"It's hard to explain. He was the kind of

man who, if you weren't strong enough to buck him, could demolish you. Somebody must have felt that killing him was the only way they could survive." She shuddered involuntarily. "There could have been lots of people who wished him dead. Still, I wouldn't have wished *that* on him." She sipped the last of her coffee and wiped a spot on the table with her napkin.

"I noticed a large sculpture in the back gallery . . ."

"Oh yes, that's quite impressive, isn't it?"

"Who's the artist?" I didn't mention that I'd already seen the name.

Hilary's eyes flickered slightly. She cleared her throat. "His name is Ragno. Len Ragno. I doubt you would have heard of him. Anyway, that piece just sold."

"Well, that's good news for the artist," I replied.

"Yes. He has a workshop near Sacramento and occasionally ships me something. He tends to work in stone. I think he's quite talented. He might catch on. Are you interested for yourself?"

"No, it's definitely beyond my budget, but I was curious. Thanks."

Len Ragno, huh? Well Sacramento was a long way from Milan and I knew absolutely nothing about sculpture, but I found the similarity to Luca's work a little too much of a coincidence. We said our goodbyes and Hilary let me out through the back of the gallery into the parking lot. I walked to the end of the alleyway and around the corner to my car. As I stood on the sidewalk searching for my keys, I realized I wasn't alone. I turned.

Henry Gooding stood next to me. "Ms. Bonatti, isn't it?" He was as perfectly turned out today as he had been the night before.

"Mr. . . . Gooding!"

"Ah, you remembered. I *am* flattered that a beautiful young woman would remember my name." The tiny lines around his eyes crinkled.

I smiled back. "Flattery comes easily, Mr. Gooding. What brings you to this area?"

"Oh, visiting an interesting shop I know well. The owner is a close friend and sometimes holds occasional pieces for me." He smiled. "A pleasure to meet you again so soon." He nodded and turned away, heading for The Greene Room. I heard the bell ring as he stepped inside.

What a small world, I thought. Do they all know each other? On the surface, Hilary Greene seemed a completely open and likeable woman, but as far as I knew, she could be a twenty-four-karat liar. Maybe five years away from Jack wasn't enough. Maybe she had a motive to commit murder after all.

Sixteen

I checked my watch. Almost five. Time to head home. I revved the engine and pulled an illegal U-turn at the end of the block to get back to California Street. Rush hour traffic had started, but within twenty minutes I was at my apartment. I parked in front and trudged up the stairs. Wizard's bell was tinkling as I turned the key in the lock. One light set on a timer burned in the living room. Wizard rushed to greet me and pushed heavily against my shins as I dumped my purse on the table. I reached down and picked him up.

He emitted a series of quacks, which I interpreted as *Why weren't you here to feed me on time?* He settled on his haunches on the kitchen floor while I opened a fresh can of salmon in gravy and plopped it in his dish. Then I stripped off my clothes and pulled on a pair of jeans and a warm sweater. I needed to spend some time on my newspaper column, even though I was really itching to set up charts for the people at the firm.

Obligations first. I settled into the office chair and flicked on the computer. Wizard, now sated, curled up in a ball in the chair normally reserved for clients. I clicked open my email and signed in. Samantha at the *Chronicle* had forwarded me forty-three *AskZodia* emails. I heaved a sigh. So many people asking for advice. I separated out the letters that asked no particular question and returned those to Sam. She'd respond, explaining that *AskZodia* received far more letters than it was possible to answer and refer the writers to other reputable astrologers. Then I separated the emails into male and female groups. With some, of course, the gender of the writer wasn't obvious, but I did the best I could. I further separated these into different age brackets.

Each week the paper published eight *AskZodia* questions and the astrological responses. My column had become extremely popular. Les, my editor and Samantha's boss, was making noises about running it on a daily basis. I hoped that decision wouldn't be made. It would be far more than I could handle, given my private clientele, but if so, I hoped Les would listen to my recommendations for other astrologers.

A few of the emails were quite intriguing. One woman wrote to ask about the dynamic between her brother, now deceased, and her mother. Her mother blamed herself for her son's death and was torturing herself with guilt. I could tell by the brother's chart, with strong Uranus and Mars aspects, that there was absolutely nothing her mother could have done to control her son. The mother had done the best she could and needed to let go.

I clicked on another.

Dear Zodia:
I've been happily married for twelve years. My wife is a wonderful woman and a loving wife and mother. For the past few months I've found myself attracted to another woman. I know I shouldn't be, but I can't help myself. It's become an obsession and I don't know what to do. I've never cheated on my wife but I find myself thinking about it all the time. I think this other woman is also attracted to me, but I'm not sure. I'm so confused, I don't know what's happening to me and I don't know what to do. My birthday is August 20, 1976

at 3:13 p.m. in San Diego. My wife's birthday is December 1, 1977.

— Confused

Dear Confused:

I'll be very direct. It's really not a choice between one woman or another. You are yearning. You are seeking an aspect of your own "anima" or female self. Neptune is currently opposing your natal Venus and you, believe me, are most likely projecting all sorts of qualities onto this other person, most of which you would ultimately discover are not real.

We experience great yearnings with Neptune transits and tend to believe that the answer is "somewhere else." Under transits of Neptune especially, it is not possible to see things clearly. You and your wife are quite compatible astrologically. It would be a shame to destroy your marriage for what may be no more than a passing wraith.

I recommend seeking professional help to discover what you are missing in your life and your love life. Often, the "other" that you are attracted to turns out to be much like the person you are currently with. There is an excellent book on this very subject: *Love Triangles* by Julia

Bonatti, published by Stargazer Press. This might be a start in helping you sort out your feelings.

— Zodia

Samantha would get a kick out of this response. Me, anonymously, plugging my own book, but I really did think it would be a help to the man. I worked my way through ten more emails and sent them back to Sam. I was ahead of my deadlines for the next two weeks, so the newspaper would have plenty of fodder for the column. Finally I breathed a sigh of relief. It had taken all my discipline to focus on my *AskZodia* work, given Maggie's news and the events at the law firm.

I spread the notes I'd made earlier in the day across the desk and plugged the details into my astro program, creating solar charts for each person in the litigation section. The answer lay, I was sure, with the people in Jack's life, those who dealt with him on a day-to-day basis and those who were most affected by his actions. I printed each one out to study more carefully. Unfortunately, I had no birth information for Hilary Greene or Sarah Larkin or Ira Walstone's wife, all connected to Jack in some fashion. Because of the Neptune transit to David's

Moon, I was still convinced that a female, perhaps even an employee, was involved somehow. The phone rang and I jumped involuntarily. My nerves were still on edge.

"Julia, it's me." It was Gale. "Have you seen the news?"

"No, I haven't." I hesitated. "Are you talking about the murder at the law firm?"

"Yeeees." Gale's tone took on a heightened sense of drama. "Isn't that where you used to work? I saw it on the news tonight. It sounds awful. Did you know him? This Harding guy, I mean?"

"I knew him slightly a couple of years ago, but not recently." I wasn't sure if I wanted to get into this with Gale right now. "Actually, I was there yesterday when they discovered his body."

"You were *there*?" Gale shrieked. "Why were you there?"

"David had asked me to fill in for a week. He asked me as a favor, really. It isn't what I want to be doing, but the money is welcome."

"You'll have to tell me all about it. Does Cheryl know? Why didn't she say anything last night at the art show?"

"I asked her not to. You had a lot on your plate and needed to focus on your event. Besides, I didn't want to bring it up. It was gruesome."

"And you were supposed to call me so we could natter or maybe grab a bite to eat."

"Oooh. I'm sorry. I'm a flake. I completely forgot. With everything that's been going on, it slipped my mind."

"What are you doing now?"

"I just finished some *AskZodia* emails and I'm looking at some other charts. I'm sorry. Maybe next week?"

"Hmph. Well, that's quite all right, my dear," Gale replied in mock-offended tones. "Luca is available. I can have dinner with *him*. Ciao."

"Wait, listen, I have a question for you. You remember that man I was talking to at the art show Monday night?" I quickly described Henry Gooding.

"Well, of course. Henry. Lovely man."

"What do you really know about him?"

"Not much. I know he's wealthy as hell and he spends a lot on art of all sorts. He's been a good customer."

"And there was someone else there at the art show that night that I know slightly."

"Who?"

"Roger Wilkinson. Do you know him?"

"Oh, sure. Roger has very good taste actually. Gay, of course."

"Really?"

"I'm sure. My gaydar is never wrong." Gale, suddenly interested, said, "You don't think he's having an affair with Henry Gooding, do you? Is that why you're asking?"

I groaned inwardly. "No, no, nothing like that. Just wondering if you had some little tidbits about Roger." I hesitated. "I did run into Henry Gooding today, though. Outside of Hilary Greene's gallery. You must know her."

"Oh, yes. Not well, but I've met her. What were you doing there?"

"Hilary is . . . was Jack Harding's ex-wife."

"No!"

"Yes. It is a small world, isn't it?"

"I'll say. I met her about a year ago, but I don't know anything about her past. As far as Roger is concerned, I wish I could oblige. I've seen him around at some cocktail parties here and there. Seems like there was something about him . . . someone made a joke once."

"Like what?"

"I don't really remember. Just seems . . ." Gale groaned in frustration. "I had the impression . . . wish I could remember, now. If I recall, it referred to some scandal. Someone made a joke and he was the butt of the joke. Maybe it'll come to me. Why?"

"Nothing, really. He's another of the attorneys at David's firm. I was just curious what you knew about him and how he came to be at Luca's show. He was there with a woman, Nora Layton. At least I think they came together."

"She wasn't on my list. Maybe she was his guest."

"Ah, okay. It's not a big deal. I'll give you a call later this week. Oh . . . before I forget or before you forget, what's Luca's birth date and time?"

"Oh damn, I forgot."

"Right."

"Don't give me a bad time. I'll get it."

"You better."

"And don't forget the open house and costume party at the Eye on Saturday night," Gale said. "I've rented some outfits, so you should come by to pick one out. Everyone will be there, some of our readers and a lot of our customers. The doors'll be open to everyone. I think you'll look very cute in the cat outfit."

"I'll be there. Wouldn't miss it for the world."

"Just keep in touch. Kisses. Bye."

SEVENTEEN

I heaved a sigh and finally settled down to the charts. Ira's natal Sun was in Cancer with Pluto transiting in opposition. A powerful transit. Mars was approaching that point. He could just as easily have been the murder victim, especially since his solar eighth house, the house of death, was involved.

Karen's birth date was November 8th. Her natal Sun in Scorpio was conjunct her South Node of the Moon. Not a positive placement at all. She'd have a very hard time not repeating outdated patterns. Pluto, Uranus, Mars, and the Moon were in a tight stellium. She must be in a permanent state of emotional turmoil. Suzanne's Venus was in Cancer, a real softie, but transiting Pluto was opposing that position too. Her love life was in turmoil. Perhaps there was a breakup with Jack prior to his death, if Dani's information was to be believed. Nora was a

Taurus, but the normal steadiness of Taurus was undermined by an opposition from Neptune and a square from Saturn forming a T-square. Definite daddy problems. Death of a father? So much overcompensation to prove she was really important.

Jack's physical appearance had indicated possibly Scorpio rising. This was guesswork, I knew, but if so, Pluto might have been crossing over his fourth house cusp, the point representing the beginning and the end of life. Did this signal his physical death? His Moon was close to a conjunction with Suzanne's Venus, and his Mars in Gemini was in the same sign and close degree of her natal Venus. Those chart correspondences would definitely indicate an attraction between them. If Dani was right and they were having an affair, it was a rocky one given Suzanne's transits.

I hadn't anticipated that one Pluto transit could be hitting the charts of so many in different ways, and all in one working environment, but it couldn't be ignored. I stood up and stretched and paced around the room. What conclusions could I come to? Dani was convinced Suzanne had been having an affair with Jack, but it might have broken up by the time of his murder. Or, the breakup had caused his murder and Suzanne was guilty. Nora Layton had all those telltale medical records in her personnel file and the hard Neptune aspect could indicate problems with drugs or alcohol.

I reached for the phone, then pulled my hand away. I badly wanted to talk to Maggie some more. If she was staying at her mother's house, I was hesitant to call. Celia's sharp tongue and cold attitude toward me was an atmosphere I did my best to avoid. It boggles my mind how successfully she nurses her antipathy. What energy the woman must have! I hated to admit it, but Celia's treatment was working. I never did want to approach her or have to deal with her. I finally decided to try Maggie's cell. It rang four times and then her outgoing message played.

"Hi Maggie, it's Julia. Just checking in with you to chat. I hope all's well. Call me when you can. Love you."

I was concerned about her. She had been hit with the sudden death of a sibling she was extremely close to. She had been doing well, but now this newly discovered photo had opened that wound again. All our lives had been irrevocably altered — Celia, Maggie, and I. But there was hope for Maggie. She was young. She had her whole life ahead of her. I didn't want to see her held back by the past any longer. There was a time coming that I had seen in her chart. Soon both Jupiter and Pluto would form supportive angles to the ruler of her ninth house, the house of higher education. I'd wait for those transits and broach the subject with her again. I didn't hold out a lot of hope for Celia.

I study Michael's chart often, trying to understand why his death came at that time. It's an absolute no-no for an astrologer to predict death, with good reason. We're not God. We have no right. Even so, the unvarnished truth is that we all have our theories on that subject. I've often thought that if my study of astrology had taken place sooner, while Michael was still alive, I would have been smart enough to have been forewarned, to save him. Looking back even now, nothing in Michael's chart indicated the event of that day. Even if I had been an expert in prediction at that time, I doubt I would have seen anything that would have led me to fear his death. I still study his chart, searching for some sign that, had I but seen it soon enough, might have saved his life.

I clipped the charts from the firm on the bulletin board to study later. I wasn't ready to call it a night, and Maggie's photo was haunting me. I slipped on my jacket, grabbed my purse, and, making sure Wizard was in, closed the kitty door.

I cut across the Park and followed 19th Avenue to Taraval. Michael's apartment had been above a small Realty office in the 3400 block near 45th Avenue. The building hadn't changed — still peach-colored with dark blue trim. I pulled over and parked across the street, staring up at the front arched window. It was dark now, but someone was home. Light emanated from an interior room. From this angle I could see a lamp, pictures on the opposite wall, and a section of the beamed ceiling. A woman with long dark hair approached the window and turned on the lamp. Her face was flooded with light before she turned away.

Strangers were living there now. Many times I've dreamed that I still live there. Dreams so vivid I felt confused when I woke up, as if my soul or my astral body still lingered in the old place. Every detail of that apartment was clear in my mind. The tiles above the stove, the cabinet that never shut properly, the bedroom window that always stuck. It was strange, but I'd never wondered what had happened to that apartment, who might have moved into Michael's place where we'd spent so many days and nights. I tried to recall some of the details of our daily life. Things we'd worried about at the time. Small problems that seemed to loom large. How narrow our vision was.

I sighed and turned the key in the ignition. That's when I noticed a van parked further up the street, light emanating from its open doors. Two men were stacking boxes on the sidewalk. Could one of them be the son of the elderly neighbor who had died? I turned the engine off and climbed out. I hesitated, but finally headed in their direction. When I neared the house, I looked to the top of the stairs. A woman stood by an open front door, and a FOR SALE sign was stuck on the postage-stamp-sized lawn. I reached the men just as they were turning back to climb the flight of stairs to the house.

"Excuse me," I said. One man continued up the stairs but the other stopped and turned back. "I understand your father died recently."

He looked puzzled but said, "Uh, yes, he did. A few weeks ago. Were you a friend of his?"

"I . . . I didn't know him very well, but we used to see him all the time walking his dog. I was sorry to hear about his death." I hesitated. "I used to live across the street." I pointed vaguely in the direction of Michael's old apartment. "I've been told you found some pictures."

The man took a step closer. "How did you . . . ?"

"It was my fiancé who was killed here."

The woman who'd been standing by the front door descended and stood next to her husband. I could see now they were older than they'd appeared at first. Perhaps early fifties. The man started to speak, but his wife interrupted him. "I'm so sorry," she said. She glanced at her husband. "We did. We found a very strange photo, but we contacted the police about it." Was there a slightly defensive tone in her voice?

"I know. His family told me." I neglected to say it was only Maggie. Why make things more complicated? "I just . . . I happened to be driving by and I saw your van. I thought I'd . . ." What did I think? I was burning with curiosity and unanswered questions but I didn't want to alienate these two.

"We knew about the accident, of course. Just terrible. My father-in-law talked about nothing else for a while. Of course, it was such a long time ago . . ."

Not for me. "Two years and ten months," I replied. This woman had never lost anyone close to her.

Her expression shifted. "Of course, I . . . I didn't mean to imply it wasn't important."

"Can you tell me . . . if you found any other photos?"

They both shook their heads. "No, we didn't. We didn't have time to go through all the negatives. We turned them over to the police, so perhaps there's something there they can work with."

"Do you have any idea why your father-in-law didn't come forward at the time?"

The woman took a deep breath. "I don't know," she finally stated flatly.

"Look, I'm not criticizing anyone. I'm not. I'm just wondering why, if he talked to you about being a witness to a hit-and-run, he didn't talk to the police. And I know they canvassed the neighborhood."

The woman's lips pursed. She was weighing her options. But her husband spoke. "I can't say for sure. He was certainly concerned about it. I just assumed he'd talked to the police. I asked him about it a few weeks later but he shut me out. Said he didn't want to think about it. He was upset. Maybe he felt he was getting old and vulnerable and something like that might happen to him too. He said he really didn't see or remember anything."

I stared at them. I was confused. "Any idea why he did an about-face like that?"

"Maybe he was getting a bit senile." The man shrugged. "Maybe he thought if he dwelled on it . . . I don't know. I can only guess."

The woman turned to her husband. "I told you what I thought at the time," she said sharply. "I thought he was frightened. I even wondered if he was scared of something. Or someone." She shook her head. "But I don't really know, either."

There was nothing more I could glean here. My presence was making them uncomfortable, almost as if I were accusing them of a crime. "Well, thank you. I appreciate your talking with me." They nodded in unison. Probably glad to see me go. "I'm very sorry for your loss."

"Thanks," the man said. They watched me for a few moments as I turned away and headed back to my car. I hadn't learned a thing.

My stomach started to rumble as I sat in traffic on 19th Avenue for the second time that day. I reached Irving and decided to stop for a sandwich in one of the small eateries there. I pulled into a parking lot behind a hole-in-the-wall restaurant that offered organic fixings on freshly baked bread and picked up a tomato-avocado-sprout sandwich to go. I was so hungry I ripped the paper off as soon as I returned to my car. It was delicious. I was just about to take the last bite when I glanced up at the building on the corner. A brightly lit sign announced *Deklon Management.*

I almost choked on the last bite. Deklon Management was the defendant in the case that David had mentioned. The case with the evicted apartment managers that was coming to trial. The company run by the two sleazy brothers.

I started the car, pulled out of the parking lot, and crossed a small side street to the rear of the Deklon building. The company was housed in a four-story building with large plate-glass windows at the rear. At this time of the evening, most of the neighboring businesses were closed, with the exception of a bookstore across the street and the sandwich shop I'd just visited. Other than a few cars, the lot was empty. The first level of the building housed a bank, and a bright light illuminated an ATM set into the wall at the back entrance. I remembered being at this very bank two years ago with Gale when she was applying for a business loan, and I knew the bank's offices took up the entire second floor. Which meant Deklon

Management occupied the third floor. Could Adam's first query in David's office have been the correct one? That the Farraday brothers were behind the death threats at David's firm? Would murder be out of the realm of possibility?

Bright lights illuminated the strip of windows on the fourth floor, revealing gym equipment. The workout club was new. Just as I was about to file it away and head home, a light flashed on in one of the windows on the third floor. Straining to see, I caught sight of a tall man in a dark suit who stood near the window. He was facing the interior of the office, talking and gesturing. No one I recognized. Then a woman appeared near the window. I noted the expensive suit and the woman's blonde hair. She turned to face the window. She reached up, and with one pull, closed the blinds, shutting out my view of the office. But not so quickly that I didn't recognize Nora Layton.

EIGHTEEN

Stunned, I continued to stare at the window in spite of the fact that now there was nothing to see. David had said that Nora was the one doing all the work preparing for the trial against Deklon Management. It was completely unethical for her to have any contact with them. The company would have attorneys who would hit the roof if they knew their client was talking directly to lawyers from the opposing side. I waited, wishing I could be a fly on the wall and hear their conversation. What Nora was doing was enough to get her fired if not disbarred. I couldn't help but wish there were some way to go up to that floor and listen at the door without being seen. Could she be handing them information, information about the firm's strategy for trial? What other reason would she have to be there at this time of night?

I had a full view of the building's brightly

lit lobby from my angle of observation. I balled up the wrappings from my sandwich and stuffed the paper into a bag. After a few minutes, the elevator doors at the lobby entrance opened and Nora stepped out. I slouched down in my seat until I was almost invisible and then rose slowly until I had a view of the parking lot through the steering wheel. Nora pushed through the double glass doors and stepped outside. She scanned the area, then turned to walk toward her car. I was glad I'd ducked. I took a chance and lifted my head a bit more. There was a small package tucked under her arm.

Curiosity got the better of me. I was leery of following her because the streets were somewhat deserted this time of night, but I decided to give it a try. Nora pulled out to the side street and stopped at a red light. I started my car and slowly inched out of the parking lot. She was still waiting at the red light as I pulled up at a discreet distance behind her. She turned left as the light turned green, and then turned again on Lincoln. She was heading downtown. I stayed several car lengths behind her as the traffic became heavier and faster moving. She must be going home. From the personnel files I knew she had a condo on the corner of Davis. These were pricey little places with a lot of glass that faced the Bay.

Sure enough, Nora led me through the Park and out to Geary Boulevard. I followed her at a distance over Nob Hill, and then down into the Embarcadero. She pulled into a parking entrance that serviced her building. As I drove by, I spotted her outstretched hand keying in a code at the gate to the underground garage. I'd have to tell David what I had seen. There couldn't be any reasonable explanation for her meeting with the Deklon people after hours.

Intending to head west, back to my neighborhood, on an impulse I turned the corner and followed Pine. I pulled into the front parking entrance of the firm on Montgomery Street and drove down to A-level, the first parking level. A glass wall with two entrance doors separated this lower lobby from the parking area. Inside, the elevator bank and the security desk, manned by two guards, were clearly visible.

I now had a parking card for the building that would allow me to park on levels B through D. This first level was used only for valet service. But the guards were stationed where they would see anyone driving into the building. A security camera was mounted at the entrance. Even though there were no cameras on the other parking levels, there would be a record of anyone using a parking card to go down to the lower levels. And even if someone entered the lobby after hours from the street, they'd still need to use their same security card to gain entrance. The police had seemed convinced this setup provided a foolproof way to check who'd entered the building on Sunday, the day they'd determined Jack was murdered. I wasn't so sure.

A few years before, I had attended a birthday party for one of the people in David's firm. We'd met for dinner at a restaurant on Sutter Street, around the corner. My car was here, and we'd walked to the restaurant. After dinner, one of the women, who was parked under the restaurant, offered me a lift back to my car. When she realized she hadn't validated her parking ticket at the dinner, instead of returning to the upstairs restaurant, she told me she knew another way out, an underground shortcut to get back to our building on Montgomery. If she knew about this tunnel, anyone familiar with these buildings could know it as well.

It would be easy enough to check if the shortcut still existed. I made a U-turn and drove back up the ramp onto the street. I turned right, and then right again on Sutter. The parking entrance to the Abbey Grill at 55 Sutter was still there. I pulled a ticket from the machine and drove down one level. I slowed my speed, making a circuit of the area and searching for the large steel doors leading into the truck tunnel. I found them wide open at the very rear of the building. I drove into the tunnel and saw a sign that read PEDESTRIANS USE AT YOUR OWN RISK. DELIVERIES FOR 44 MONTGOMERY—55 SUTTER STREET—350 MARKET STREET. There it was. Entry into any of those three buildings, one level below the guard station. So much for security.

I followed the concrete tunnel in the dark, only my headlights illuminating the way. I turned right, and after several more feet, came to a huge open door. The tunnel was pitch black, but the door was outlined from the low-level lighting inside the parking structure of 44 Montgomery. A chain suspended from two short standing pillars blocked the opening. I left the engine running, got out of the car, and dragged one of the pillars to the side until there was enough room to squeeze my small car through. Once inside, I dragged the pillar back until the chain was stretched across the opening again. I had entered the B-level parking area of the Montgomery Street building and circumvented the security camera and the guards on A-level. Anyone could gain access to this building, as long as the metal door to the truck tunnel was open.

The next hurdle would be to get to the 41st floor from here without being seen. A bank of elevators serviced levels B through D, arriving at A-level. If I took that route, I'd have to pass the security guards and sign in. Another option was to climb the forty-one flights of stairs. That would be a daunting prospect, but not outside the realm of possibility for an athletic person.

I drove slowly around the perimeter of the parking area until I spotted the freight elevator, the only one that ran from the parking levels to all the upper floors. It was a large undecorated utilitarian box with front and back doors for easy deliveries. Best of all, it was sitting right there with its doors open. I parked my car in a nook between two concrete columns and stepped into it. Hoping it didn't make a lot of noise, I pressed the button for the 41st floor. The doors closed and the elevator started a slow and jerking ascent. A digital readout of the floors flashed above the buttons. It didn't stop at A-level. I breathed a sigh of relief. Would the guards' console alert them that the elevator was moving? It was just possible they might not notice. And if they took no notice tonight, then surely they wouldn't have batted an eye on Sunday.

The doors opened on the 41st floor, revealing a dark corridor. Total silence. No hum of computers, copying equipment, or neon lights. I stepped out into the darkness. The elevator doors started to close. I had a moment of panic and stepped back inside, pulling out the emergency stop button. The doors opened again. In case the security desk had an override, I dropped my purse on the track of the doors to prevent them from closing completely. I wasn't sure if the stop button would signal the guard's desk or trigger an alarm, but I'd take my chances.

I tested the doorknob of the main door to the litigation attorneys' area. Locked. I went back to the elevator and slipped the key David had given me out of my purse. I unlocked the door, and once inside, the lights, keyed to movement, flickered on. Yellow police tape still stretched across the door to Jack's office. I knew I'd never have another opportunity like this and decided to make the best of it.

I started with Nora's office and quickly rummaged through each and every drawer. Her office was small, and on the whole, messy. Books and papers were balanced precariously on top of a bookcase. The credenza held folders that looked like working files, labeled by hand. The large desk drawer contained more files, marked with typed labels. I opened the two drawers of the credenza. They were filled with dark green hanging folders and seemed to be notes and drafts on various matters.

Just as I had decided there was nothing of interest in Nora's office, I hit pay dirt in the top narrow drawer of the desk. It was stuffed with bills, demand letters, threats from collection agencies, and the like. A few bottles of cosmetics rattled around inside the drawer. I sat down and turned on the desk lamp. Either Nora was in financial trouble or she just couldn't remember to write a check. She undoubtedly made a hefty salary at the firm, so where was her money going? I stepped back from the desk and pulled the drawer all the way out, pushing a clutter of pens, pencils, and paperclips out of the way. At the very back of the drawer was a small gold-plated cosmetic case. I clicked it open. It held a mirror on either side. A button caused one mirror to pop up, and behind it lay a small amount of white powder. I touched my index finger to the powder and rubbed a tiny amount on my gum, immediately feeling the numbing effect of cocaine. Nasty habit and maybe the reason she was so wound up.

I moved on to Ira's office next door. It rivaled Nora's for messiness. Every surface overflowed with stacks of files and documents. Boxes stood on every available floor surface, with only a narrow path to the chair. How could this kind of chaos ever generate client confidence? Ira's desk drawers contained nothing more interesting than an extra tie, a T-shirt, a very old apple, and two pairs of socks, one of which didn't look particularly fresh.

This snooping business was turning out to be pretty dull. Roger's office was next. His desk was extremely neat, as were his drawers and bookshelves. Pending work was stacked in organized piles on the top of the credenza, and absolutely nothing was out of place. The desk accessories were black leather: a rectangular box with a lid and handle, a blotter, and a calendar holder. The leather box held a newspaper article with a photograph of Roger accepting a Bar Association award for his community work. A letter from the *Bay Area Gazette* thanking him for his recent article was clipped to a small stack of reprints. I scanned it quickly. The article Roger had submitted featured insurance company abuses in the care of AIDS patients and displayed his professional photo. Times have thankfully changed, but if Roger was gay, as Gale thought, living an alternative lifestyle could still subject him to career discrimination. This was certainly a topical issue and maybe Roger's practice involved litigation against the insurance industry, but the *Gazette* was a publication aimed at the gay community. I folded up one of the reprints and stuffed it into my purse. I stepped out of Roger's office and stared at Jack's door. A shiver ran up my spine. I'd have to search there as well, but I cringed at the thought of his murder and the smell of death. I'd leave it for last.

Karen's desk was so neat that the metal paperclips were separated from plastic ones. I like organization, but this was ridiculous. A search of the bottom drawer netted only a pair of flats and a lime-green cardigan. Dani's desk contained the usual assortment of pens, sticky pads, paperclips, and other supplies. One lower drawer was stuffed with sheet music and flyers, and under that was a stun gun. She wasn't taking any chances, I guessed, but I wondered why she didn't keep it in her car or her purse. The odds of Dani being attacked in an office where she usually never worked late seemed slim. Of course, now that Jack had been killed here, maybe it was something I should consider.

The overhead lights flickered off. I moved away from the desk and waved my arms, but the neon lighting didn't respond. That's when I heard it. A rustling sound. I wasn't alone.

NINETEEN

I stopped breathing. Adrenaline coursed through my bloodstream. This was the very last thing I'd expected. I squeezed my eyes shut, trying to adjust to the dark, afraid to call out. No one, including me, was supposed to be here. I hadn't heard any sound when I was rummaging in the various offices. I did my best to quell my fear and tried to take a quiet breath. Feeling the edge of the desk, I inched my way toward the door to the corridor in hopes of reaching the elevator.

There was a rush of air, and a painful blow hit my side. I fell and felt the rough carpeting against my cheek. Clambering to my knees. I couldn't see a thing, but whoever had hit me was still in the room. I pressed my hands against the floor, getting ready to sprint for the elevators. I heard breathing but wasn't sure it wasn't my own ragged breath. I moved quickly toward where I was sure the door was, but I hit the wall. Reaching out, I felt for the door jamb. The door was shut. I'd left it open.

A piercing alarm began to sound. A loud intermittent buzzing from the elevator. Had one of the guards realized the freight elevator was no longer on a lower level? I grasped the knob and pulled the door open. I lunged into the dark hallway and ran past the bank of three elevators to the freight elevator, where I grabbed for my purse and half fell inside. I pushed the red button in and jammed my finger into the B-level button, praying the doors would close quickly and take me to safety. I heard a low growl that made my blood run cold. I braced myself for another onslaught in case my assailant leapt out of the dark. It was only a few seconds, but it felt more like minutes before the doors closed. As the elevator picked up speed heading down, I wiped perspiration from my forehead. The lighted buttons flashed through each floor . . . 39 . . . 31 . . . 28 . . . 21 and finally A . . . The elevator stopped on A level.

Two security guards stood poised in front of the open door. One man's hand was placed inside his jacket. I didn't want to think what he was holding. I did my best to wipe the panicked look off my face, but I was still reeling from the blow to my ribs. I took a deep breath and pulled myself up to my full height.

"Ma'am, what do you think you're doing?" the taller one said.

"Uh . . . I work on the 41st floor, and I left my wallet on my desk, so I just popped in to pick it up." I really was breathless and it was the only story I could think of quickly. "But somebody else is up there."

The two men exchanged glances. "Somebody else is up there?"

"Yes, and whoever it was hit me and knocked me over." My ribs were starting to ache.

"Yeah, well, you and this somebody else didn't exactly pop by the security desk and sign in, now did you?"

"Well, no . . . I guess I should have, but I thought . . ."

"Ma'am, step out of the elevator, please."

The guards moved back as I stepped out. They were clearly nervous.

"Look, I'm sorry . . . I didn't mean to cause you any trouble, but there really is somebody up there who shouldn't be there."

"Could we see some identification please?"

"Of course." I decided the best course of action was to give them what they wanted.

My hands were shaking but I managed to extract my wallet and license. "Here's my driver's license. I work for Meyers, Dade & Schultz. You can contact David Meyers. He'll vouch for me."

The older guard stepped over to the security console and consulted a clipboard. "I don't see your name on this list."

"I know. They probably didn't have a chance to add it. I just started today. I'm temporary, for a week."

"How did you get into the building, ma'am?"

"Aren't you going to go up to the 41st floor and see who's there?"

"Ma'am, how did you get into the building?"

"Well, actually, I was at the restaurant on Sutter Street, and I just drove underground through the truck tunnel. I'm parked on B-level."

The two guards exchanged looks. The older man said, "Didn't you close the steel door tonight?"

"Uh . . . no." The second man seemed defensive. "I thought you did it."

"Jeez." The older guard took a deep breath and squeezed his eyes shut in frustration. "For Chrissakes, go close it. Now." The chastened guard hurried away.

"Look, lady, I don't know if you know, but you certainly should. There's been a murder here. On that very floor. And the cops have been crawling all over this place. There's supposed to be a security guy monitoring those floors. I'll take you to your car and I want you to leave the building. And I'll have to report you being here."

"Don't worry, they'll tell you who I am. I'm sorry. I didn't mean to cause anyone any trouble." I tried my most contrite expression. "But you really should have a look upstairs."

"We just want you to leave. I don't want anything happening to you and we don't need any more trouble, okay?"

"Yes. Okay."

He motioned me back into the elevator and hit the button for B-level. He was silent as we descended.

"Now, where's your car?"

"Right around the corner here. On the other side of the column."

"Just get into your car and pull out of the building. It's almost time for us to shut the metal grate down."

"Metal grate?"

"Yeah, it's a big steel mesh that comes down and closes off the front entrance from the street. We don't shut it before ten o'clock in case anyone needs to drive in or out."

"What happens if someone wants to get in after that?"

"They hit their horn to alert us. We can open it electronically and see who's there and check their ID."

"I see. Well . . . thank you." I climbed into my Geo and smiled shakily once more to a very annoyed guard. I started the engine and drove up the ramp to A-level, passed under the uplifted gate arm, and took the ramp out to Montgomery Street. I was sure a bruise was forming on my side. Whoever attacked me could have been Jack's killer and I had more than likely surprised him . . . or her. Maybe the only reason I'd been able to escape was the alarm on the freight elevator. And whoever it was obviously had ways of getting into the building undetected. What about the security that Adam Schaeffer had promised? The guard's comment indicated that someone should have been on duty up there. And even if the guards did decide to check things out, I was sure the intruder would be gone, or hiding. And there were plenty of closets and storerooms to hide in.

I drove straight up and over Nob Hill and headed out to the Avenues. I was too tired to pull into the garage. I parked on the street and dropped the garage opener in my purse. As I climbed out of my car, something registered in my peripheral vision. Was it a shadow or movement in the doorway across the street? I locked the car and hurried up the front stairs to my doorway. The overhead light bulb was burned out and needed to be replaced. I was grateful for that, because now I wasn't visible in the dark entryway. I stayed completely still and scanned up and down the street to spot any sign of movement. A dark shape near the end of the block seemed to vanish into a crevice between two house fronts. I couldn't shake the uneasy feeling I was being watched.

TWENTY

A low-grade headache plagued me the next morning. I dimly remembered tossing and turning, unable to fall into a deep sleep. At one point, I dreamed about stars whirling above me, forming the shape of a dragon. The dragon's tail flickered back and forth. In my dream state, I was afraid. It came closer and closer to me with every pass. I woke up in the middle of the night, my heart pounding. I'm a big believer that dreams are the key to the unconscious. They are sending us messages we need to heed, if only we can interpret them. But it made no sense. I had no idea what the dragon signified.

At the office, I grabbed two ibuprofen tablets from the first aid kit in the lounge and washed them down with some coffee. I settled in and stashed my purse in Muriel's desk. Voices filtered from David's office. I was sure he wouldn't be seeing clients under the circumstances, so I felt safe knocking on the door and peeking in.

"Hi." David was seated behind his desk and Adam stood by the window looking down into the street.

"Come on in, Julia. How did you make out yesterday?"

I plopped down in one of the wing chairs and tried my best to marshal my thoughts. "Well, you were right. Sarah Larkin had anything but sisterly love for her brother. And that's putting it mildly. Seems he turned down her request for money when she wanted to get her son into a private rehab place. Then the boy died from an overdose."

"Cripes!" David said. "What was wrong with Jack?" Adam was listening silently.

"And Hilary Greene, who is a very attractive, charming woman, claims to have no animosity toward Jack, although she believes he could be very threatening to some people." I crossed my legs and leaned back. "David, I think it would be a good idea to look through Jack's apartment, especially if he kept old files there. He lived alone and the police will be done with it by now, won't they? Was he working on something on his own? There might be something that the police would overlook."

"That's a good idea, but I don't have a key and I certainly have no authority to give you permission."

"I'm sure we can find a manager for the building," Adam said.

"It's up to you two, then. It wouldn't hurt to check. If Jack did keep anything that belongs to the firm, we'll need it back. Good luck."

"I have to make a couple of phone calls to line some people up for tonight." Adam glanced my way and I did my best not to look guilty. Was it my imagination or had he already talked to the security guards? "Can I meet you back here in a half hour? We can head over to Jack's condo then."

I nodded. "Sure, that'll work." As soon as Adam closed the door behind him, I filled David in on spotting Nora at Deklon Management the night before.

"I can't believe that." David sat staring at me blankly.

I wondered for a moment if David was suffering from shock. Was he able to process what was happening? "I know. It was really a fluke. I just happened to be over on Irving Street and I noticed the sign on the building." I really didn't want to get into a long explanation about my visit to Michael's old neighborhood. "I pulled into the parking lot in back. I was kind of curious about the place."

"What the hell is she doing? This is completely unethical on her part. She has no business even *talking* to the other party in a case unless there's an agreement between the attorneys. And we're going to trial. There's not even a hint of settlement. Christ!"

"What if she's being paid off?"

"Paid off? What do you mean?"

"Well, with Jack gone, who's going to be standing over her shoulder? Let's say she forgets to call an important witness, or fails to refute the testimony of a witness they bring in. It wouldn't be that hard. How would you ever know?"

"What a mess," David groaned. "Look, I didn't want to tell you about this earlier because I didn't want to predispose your mind, but Nora is on notice."

I was stunned. "What? Why *didn't* you tell me?"

"Because my reasons were . . . I don't know, just professional courtesy, I guess. I really never thought Nora had anything to do with this business."

"Getting fired would certainly give her a motive to cause trouble."

"Maybe, but there was no pressure. She'd

195

have several months to find another spot, and we would give her good references. And she had good references from the DA's office too. You know she used to do public defense work. She wasn't terrible, but we just felt she wasn't working up to her full potential."

"To say the least. Besides, I'm pretty certain she has a drug problem."

"Oh." David was silent for a long moment. "I never even thought of that . . . well, no wonder, then."

I explained to David about the medical billings in Nora's personnel file but neglected to mention my explorations of her desk the night before, at least for now. If Adam already knew, I was fairly certain he hadn't said anything to David.

"I remember she took some time off a while back," David said. "I thought it was maybe a weight loss or spa type of thing. I didn't ask, seemed it was personal stuff, so I didn't ask any questions. I'll just have to figure out how much damage she's done and get her off this case, and find a graceful way to get her out of the firm quickly." He hesitated, looking up at me. "Oh, and before I forget, there's another thing that was brought to my attention today."

Uh oh, I thought. Here it comes. David's

been told I was snooping around the office last night. I steeled myself for a lecture.

"Apparently, Jack never changed the beneficiary on his life insurance policy. His ex-wife stands to receive half a million."

"That's a lot of money."

"I know. But I wouldn't be surprised if it comes as a complete shock to Hilary. Unless Jack told her, she probably assumes he changed the beneficiary after their divorce."

"There's something else, David." I wasn't sure what it meant, if anything, but I felt it was important to bring it up. "Looking through the personnel files yesterday, it struck me that Jack, Ira, and Suzanne all came here from the same firm. It's the one thing they have in common. There has to be some logical reason why only those three people received the death threats."

"That we know of, as you yourself pointed out," David responded.

"Was there a particular case the three of them worked on at their previous firm, something that could tie them together?"

"Well . . . uh . . . yeah, there was a rather high-profile case that Jack and Ira handled a few years ago. It was related to the Bank of San Francisco fire. You remember that, don't you? It was all over the news. Maybe Suzanne worked with them on that, I wouldn't know. You'd have to ask her. That's the only one I know of, although there could be others."

"Any cases here that all three were assigned to?"

"No, not at this firm. Suzanne's work would involve her in any large case, especially if it was going to trial, but nothing I can think of that both Jack and Ira worked on."

David sighed. He looked depressed. I left him staring into space and decided to prowl through the litigation section while I waited for Adam to return. My excuse was that I was looking for a three-hole punch, just in case anyone asked. My real reason was to check if Suzanne had come to work today.

Karen was standing by a filing cabinet holding a stack of paper. Dani had spread a newspaper across her desk and was reading, her chin resting on her hand. "Can you believe this?"

"What?" I asked. Karen ignored us.

Dani shook her head. "This stupid astrology column. *Ask Zodia.*"

My ears went up. "Huh? What about it?"

"Will you listen to this one? A woman writes to *Zodia* to tell her she thinks her husband's been lying to her about his real identity and this stupid astrologer tells her to seek counseling! That's the worst advice I ever heard."

I felt my face growing warm. There was no way Dani could possibly know that I was *Zodia*. I remembered that letter from a couple of weeks ago. It was signed *Bewildered*. "What do you think she should have advised the woman?"

"Hire an investigator. Find out for sure and throw the bum out! Sheshh!"

"Hmm," I replied. That was that sort of outspoken advice that had gotten me in tons of trouble with Reverend Roy and his Army of the Prophet last winter. What Dani couldn't know was that the woman's chart had revealed that she was prone to twisting reality and even paranoid fantasies. *Bewildered* really did need psychological help. But I couldn't tell Dani that. I hoped *Ask Zodia* would redeem herself in Dani's opinion someday. No way was I going to reveal myself.

Shrill voices emanated from a closed door next to Jack's office. We all turned in that direction. I asked Dani, "Is that Suzanne's office?"

Dani pulled herself away from the newspaper and nodded.

"We all know what was going on." The voice was high-pitched. I could identify

Nora immediately. An indistinguishable murmur followed.

"He was a sadist!" the female voice screamed. "You were . . ."

". . . my business . . . how dare you . . ."

In response, ". . . you're crazy." I could only make out bits and pieces, and then finally, ". . . none of your goddamn business." This was followed by another shrill outburst. "Get out!"

I glanced at Karen. Her head was down. She was deliberately ignoring the shouting match. Dani had twisted in her chair and was now staring at Suzanne's door. She looked at me and grimaced, as if to say *Watch out.* The quieter voice had to be Suzanne.

Curiosity overruled taste. Dani gawked as I walked to the door and opened it.

"Oh . . . I'm sorry. I didn't mean to interrupt. I was just looking for a. . . . I didn't think anyone was in here." Lame excuse, but what the hell.

Suzanne was a small dark-haired woman in a trim navy blue suit. She stood by the window with a tissue to her nose. Nora Layton was leaning over the desk facing Suzanne, gripping the edge, her knuckles taut. There was something almost feral in her body language. She turned, and when she saw me, stood upright, glared, and marched out.

"I'm really sorry," I apologized. "I didn't think anyone was in here." Given the state Suzanne was in, my interruption was probably a relief.

"That's all right." Suzanne attempted a wan smile.

"I'm Julia. I'm filling in for Muriel while she's on vacation."

"Hi." She took a deep breath. "I'm Suzanne. Suzanne Simms." Sorry . . . I'm just kind of upset. I was out the past couple of days and I can't believe what's happened. Jack and I worked together . . ." She trailed off.

"Oh, I didn't know," I lied through my teeth. "That is tough. I can understand why you're upset." I shut the door behind me and sat down in one of the chairs in front of her desk.

"It wasn't just that. They . . . Jack and Ira . . . they invited me to come here with them and we've worked so closely together."

"You were very close?" I asked softly. Suzanne nodded, tried to speak, and then burst into tears. I pulled another tissue from the box on the desk and handed it to her. I decided to take a chance. "You had a personal relationship with him?"

"Why do you ask that?" Suzanne blurted out. Her face darkened and her jaw tightened.

"I thought maybe that's why you're so upset."

"I know a lot of people thought that, but it's not true," she replied curtly.

"I didn't mean to pry or to upset you. I just thought you might like to talk."

Suzanne grew still. She collapsed in her chair. Quietly, she asked, "How did you know?" I didn't answer. "I guess it doesn't matter anymore. You're right. We kept it a secret here, or at least we tried. Maybe everybody already knows." She hung her head and covered her face with her hands. "It's really pretty awful and embarrassing, what happened, I mean."

"Can you talk about it?" I asked quietly.

"We'd been seeing each other for the past six months. It got pretty hot and heavy and I don't really know why I went for it. I think my perspective was skewed. Working so many hours . . . I'm single and I guess my social life was diminishing as time went on, you know? I was lonely and Jack was very charming and flattering to me." Suzanne took a deep breath and continued. "It was stupid getting involved with someone I work with, I know, but it happened. I fell really hard even though I knew it was never going to go anywhere. Jack wasn't married anymore, but he was no candidate for a serious relationship. He wasn't one to go through life with what he considered 'encumbrances.' " She smiled grimly and rubbed her eyes. "I guess I pushed too hard. I wanted something from him, even though I knew in *his* mind it was just an affair. Things came to a head last weekend, last Saturday night in fact, and we had a huge fight. We'd gone to dinner and back to my apartment after, and, well, things just escalated emotionally, if you know what I mean. I shouted at him and threw a dish. He stormed out, of course. Afterward, I felt pretty stupid."

I stayed silent, unwilling to break the flow of Suzanne's thoughts.

"The next day, I thought maybe there was still a chance," she went on. "Believe me, I can't tell you how awful I felt. I knew Jack would be here working and I thought maybe I could talk to him. I had worried it to death all night and the next day. I drove downtown and came into the office to see him. That's when I found him . . ." Suzanne took a deep breath.

"What time did you get here?" I shivered

involuntarily, sure of what I was about to hear.

"I came into the building about four o'clock, I guess. I . . . I didn't realize at first. The lights were off. I took a step into his office and the lights flickered on, and . . ." Suzanne hesitated, trying to control her emotions. "Then I saw. I saw him. Oh, I think I'm going to be sick."

"Take some deep breaths, it'll be all right."

"I panicked. I hadn't touched anything. My purse was still in my hand. I shut the door and ran to the elevators. I just wanted to get as far away as possible. Is that crazy?"

"Not at all. Quite sensible in fact. Did you by any chance touch his body to see —"

"Oh, no," she gasped. "I didn't even think of that. I was panicking and in shock. I just knew I had to get out of there. And I knew he was dead. It was too late. I should have called the police right away, I know that. But I just wasn't thinking straight. I took the elevator down and got out of the building as fast as I could. I drove all over the city the rest of the day and then finally checked in to a hotel, if you can believe that. Don't ask me why. I just felt I couldn't go home. I'd have to face my roommate and explain to her. So, that's where I've been until today." She rubbed a hand across her forehead. "I haven't been able to get the sight of Jack out of my mind . . . and the blood. I finally realized I'd have to come back. I know the police will find out eventually, if they haven't already, that I was in the building that afternoon. I don't know what to do."

She'd been through a lot, but that wouldn't prevent the police from considering her a suspect. "Did it occur to you that whoever killed him could have still been here?"

"Oh my God," she gasped. "No. It didn't. I really wasn't thinking straight."

"You'll have to tell the police what you've told me. It'll look better if you contact them and tell them everything."

"Even about the affair and the fight we had?"

"It's better if you get everything out. If they dig far enough, they'll find people who saw you together and they'll figure it out for themselves. After all, I did, and I was just listening to gossip."

"I should have called 911 then and there. I should have," she groaned. "But I just *knew* he was gone and there was nothing anyone could do. I guess I was feeling awful about the fight we had, and . . . I know this'll sound crazy . . . but my first instinct was they'd blame me for what happened."

"Do you want to talk to David? He could be a kind of buffer and let the police know you have some information? I'm sure they'll be talking to you soon anyway."

Suzanne nodded mutely. Her eyes were large in her face.

"When did you start working here?" I asked.

"Three years ago. I was at the Browning firm before."

"Did you work on any special case with Jack at the old firm?"

"Well, just one big case with Jack and Ira. That trial was the reason I was hired, and then they asked me to come with them when they moved to this firm. It was the Bank of San Francisco fire."

"I remember that, although I didn't follow the court case."

Suzanne heaved a sigh and tried to collect her thoughts. "The Bank building on Market Street was gutted by an electrical fire and one of the janitors died. He was the only fatality, and the wife brought suit." She rubbed her temples. "Look, I'm sorry, I don't mean to be rude, but I really do have to deal with some of this stuff." She waved her hand vaguely over her desk.

Our intimate chat was over. Maybe it was

just a reaction to having just been so open with me. Regretfully, I nodded and left her there, closing the door behind me. I hadn't had a chance to ask her about the death threat she'd received, but maybe it was better not to bring it up right now. Perhaps that topic would be better coming from David or from the police.

As I stepped out of Suzanne's office, I heard the deep voice of Sergeant Sullivan in the hallway. He appeared in the doorway with the same detective from Monday morning in tow. Adam stood behind them in the hallway.

Sullivan addressed Dani. "We're here to see Suzanne Simms."

Karen spoke first. "What's going on now?" Her voice had risen, and I hoped it wasn't a precursor to hysteria. Both she and Dani were staring at me. Sergeant Sullivan and Officer Ray entered the central room and walked directly to Suzanne's door. I stepped aside as they passed me and entered the office without knocking. I looked at Adam, who was standing in the doorway. His face remained impassive but he gave a slight raise of his eyebrows, as if to let me know he couldn't speak at that moment.

Suzanne's door opened again and the men led her, pale-faced and frightened, out of her office. Sullivan turned to us. "We're bringing Ms. Simms downtown. There's no need to be alarmed. We'll contact Mr. Meyers later." Dani was silent and stunned. Karen, a tissue to her nose and her face red and blotchy, ran to the doorway and watched as the elevator doors closed on Suzanne.

Twenty-One

I left the litigation section and headed for David's office. Adam had reached it before me and was starting to fill David in on the latest development. They looked up as I entered.

"What next, huh?" David leaned back in his chair. He looked exhausted and his face was ashen. I worried about the toll this was taking on him.

"I just wish they hadn't picked her up like this," I replied.

"Well, not putting in an appearance for a couple of days is bound to arouse suspicion," Adam remarked.

David shook his head. "Hopefully they'll just question her and send her home. I'm certain she had nothing to do with this." He looked at me. "Did you have a chance to talk to her?"

"I did. She's an emotional mess. She was seeing Jack, they had a huge fight and she came into the office Sunday to talk to him."

"And?" Adam asked.

"She found him dead. She freaked out and disappeared for a few days."

"Why?" David asked.

I shrugged. "Who knows? I can sort of understand it. It must have been horrible for her. She was just hiding out and didn't want to have to talk to anyone."

"Julia, what do you say we head over to Jack's apartment and see what we can find?" Adam asked.

"We might as well." I grabbed my coat and purse as Adam held the door open for me. I hesitated and turned back to David. "Are you sure you're okay?"

"I don't think 'okay' describes what I'm feeling, Julia." He sighed and looked up at me. "But you two go ahead. Don't worry about me. I'll get through this."

I left David staring out the window. Adam and I took the elevator down to the lobby and switched over to the bank of elevators to the parking levels. Adam pressed the button for B-level. We could just as easily have walked to Jack's apartment, but Adam suggested a car in case we had to lug files or boxes back to the firm.

Jack's apartment was on Filbert, only a few blocks from my grandmother's house in

Castle Alley. His condo occupied the second floor of a four-story modern building wedged between two older structures. I looked up at the glass-fronted façade and sleek windows. Adam stood by my side on the windy sidewalk and reached inside his jacket pocket.

"These are private apartments with a common entrance. I doubt there's a manager to let us in," he said.

"How *do* we get in?"

Adam pulled a flat leather case from his pocket and opened it up. Inside were several thin metal tools. "Stand behind me, as if you're waiting for me to open the door, and let's hope no one comes along and gets suspicious."

"What are you doing?"

"Won't take a minute."

"Is this legal?" I whispered. "What if we get caught?" The weather had turned and a storm front from the Pacific was bringing heavy cloud cover. I shivered and danced back and forth on my toes while Adam fiddled with the lock.

After a minute, it released. Adam smiled rakishly. "We won't. After you, mademoiselle."

We climbed the stairs to the second floor, avoiding the elevator, and once again I watched nervously as Adam worked his magic on the door to Jack's apartment. At least it was warm inside the building and I'd stopped shivering.

No personal touches were in evidence. No family photos. In fact, it looked as if it had been arranged by a professional decorator. The apartment was furnished with heavy masculine pieces, expensive but lacking in warmth. I walked over to a wall of built in bookshelves and thumbed through the CD's. Jack had favored classical and jazz, with the classical leaning toward Rachmaninoff. On the other wall I recognized two large lithographs by a San Francisco artist whose name escaped me. I was sure Gale would know. The lithos illustrated small random shapes scattered over a dark field, very abstract. Very boring.

"These are nice . . ." Adam volunteered.

I shuddered. "They leave me cold."

Large windows illuminated the space with custom shades that were probably controlled by a remote. The entire three-bedroom apartment was immaculate except for a coffee cup in the sink and a robe thrown across the bed. Each room was furnished in much the same style. Extremely upscale Motel 6. Other than the lithos and books and CDs, there was nothing to indicate what Jack Harding was all about.

"The police have taken his laptop and calendar. But if we dig, maybe we'll find something interesting." Adam opened the closet in the hallway. "I'll start here."

I stepped into one of the bedrooms. Jack had set this room up as a home office. There was a large four-drawer filing cabinet containing personal files, household receipts, litigation form files, and working files on cases that were current and some that were obviously older. I found two empty boxes in the closet and filled them with the legal files that needed to be returned to David's firm. Sliding doors opened to another closet, with six more boxes. I started by hauling out one after another and rifling through them. These contained more working files on, all told, four different cases, but two of the boxes held research and relevant copies of court pleadings, as well as deposition transcripts from the Bank of San Francisco fire. What is it about lawyers? They can never seem to dispose of paper.

"Take a look at this," I called out. Adam came around the corner and looked over the folder I'd pulled out of one box. "This was the case that Jack and Ira and Suzanne all worked on at their former firm."

"You're thinking of the threatening letters?"

"Yes. It does link them all together. David isn't overwhelmed by my theory, but their old firm, the Browning firm, represented the main insurer." I stood up and dusted off my skirt. "Suzanne told me there was a fatality in that fire. A janitor was killed."

"I seem to recall reading about that at the time. It was all over the news."

"I wonder who he was. Even more, I wonder about the family he might have left behind."

"I don't recall the details at all."

I thought of David's difficult transits and the involvement of his Moon. Was I right? Was a woman somehow involved? "Adam, what if the janitor had a family? I think Suzanne mentioned it was his wife who brought suit. Since it was these three people from Browning who received threats, could the janitor's widow have decided to take a belated revenge?"

"Let's not get ahead of ourselves. And anyway, why would she blame the attorneys for the insurance company for her husband's death? Jack and Ira didn't represent the owners of the building."

"Who did own that building?"

"No idea, but probably a general partnership, maybe several different companies."

"What if she became obsessed and decided to go after anyone involved in the case? For all we know, there could be more unexplained deaths in the city."

Adam had a dubious look on his face. "Well then, why not kill whoever was to blame for the fire? Why the attorneys for the insurers?"

"Who *was* to blame? I didn't really follow the case. It's a reach, but it might be worth finding out what happened to the people involved and the woman who brought suit. Besides, if the connection between the death threats and Jack's murder is in fact this old case, then that means Suzanne and Ira are in danger too."

"Okay, it's worth a shot. Let's try to locate the widow. You may have a good idea, Julia, but just don't get your hopes up. You can spend a lot of time and spin your wheels on this stuff and ninety-nine percent of the time it turns out to be nothing."

"Maybe the settlement money wasn't enough. Maybe this woman's still around, consumed with revenge."

"You have a very active imagination." Adam chuckled. "Can you find out her name from the documents? I'll run it through our programs and see what I can come up with. Maybe you're right. Maybe the janitor's widow is on a killing spree. Stranger things have happened." He picked up two of the boxes and carried them to the front door. "In the meantime, I'll load all of these in my car and get them up to David's office."

"Adam, one more thing? I don't know if it's really ethical, but can you do some kind of search or credit check on Hilary Greene?"

"Hilary Greene? Oh, you mean Jack's ex-wife?"

"Yes. David told me about her art gallery. If she's in financial trouble, that life insurance policy could be a motive."

"Assuming she knew about it," Adam replied.

"I just want to know if she's been having money problems. And besides all that, I'm really curious what her connection to Henry Gooding is. I ran into him outside her art gallery on Fillmore yesterday." Adam looked at me questioningly. "Apparently he's a wealthy import-export guy who buys a lot of art. It's just that he seems to be popping up everywhere I turn."

"I've heard of the guy. Maybe he's just buying art."

"Possibly. My friend Gale has connections to the art world. She says he's quite the collector, but I think it's just too much of a co-incidence. Oh, and something else, okay? Could you look up someone named Len Ragno? It's a reach, but there's something funny there too. I saw a piece of artwork in Hilary's gallery by an artist of that name and she seemed very tight-lipped about it. Told me it was sold, but somehow, something in her voice didn't ring true."

Adam sighed. "All right." He was jotting down the names in his book. "Anyone else?"

"No. That should do it, I think. You want some help loading these boxes?"

"Not so fast." Adam took my arm and pulled me closer. "You want to tell me about last night?"

TWENTY-TWO

For a split second I thought he was going to kiss me. I hoped he wouldn't notice the flush that spread across my cheeks. "They told you?"

"Yes. I got an earful from the building's guards."

"You didn't tell David?"

Adam shook his head. "No. I'd really rather not. He's got enough on his plate. What the hell were you thinking, Julia?"

I straightened up, doing my best to defend myself. "I wanted to prove to myself it *was* possible to get into the building undetected. And I was right."

"And?"

"And what?" I knew what was coming.

"Julia, please. Don't play games with me. You told the guards that someone else was on that floor."

"Yes, there *was* someone there. And they attacked me in the dark. The lights went out and next thing I knew I was down on the floor. I managed to get into the elevator and get away."

"Cripes." Adam ran a hand through his hair. "That entry is supposed to be locked at eight o'clock at night and all weekend. My guy was making rounds of both floors all night. He never saw or heard a thing."

"There are plenty of hiding places. More than you can imagine."

"Promise me you won't do that again. There's a murderer on the loose and you could be the next target. Any idea who attacked you?"

I shivered. "No. All I heard was rustling and heavy breathing and I bolted for the elevator. I was afraid I'd be chased, but I wasn't."

"It could be any one of those people at the firm. It could be anybody. It doesn't mean whoever it was is guilty of Jack's murder, but they certainly had no business being there. Neither did you." Adam's hand still held my arm. "I don't want anything to happen to you." Was this concern, or was I detecting an attraction? It had been so long since I'd found any man attractive, I couldn't be sure. I didn't want to let my imagination run away with me.

"So . . ." He straightened up. "I'll carry

two down at a time, if you can take this one."

I helped Adam move the boxes from the closet and the office and stack them outside the door of Jack's apartment. We made sure the door was locked behind us and after three trips up and down the stairs had managed to load all of the boxes into the trunk and back seat of Adam's car. Returning to the Montgomery Street building, Adam drove down to B-level and parked near the entrance to the freight elevator. The same freight elevator that I'd been so unceremoniously expelled from the night before.

"You should go ahead up, Julia. I'll take care of these and stack them by your desk." He leaned toward me in the car, brushing away a stray wisp of hair from my forehead and looked into my eyes. "Julia . . ." He hesitated. I wasn't wrong. He was attracted to me and I couldn't ignore what I felt. "When this is over . . ."

"Bad timing, huh?" My brain was short circuiting. How could I be having these feelings when I was still haunted by the image of Michael lying on the street?

"Maybe not bad timing, but it's not quite the right time yet. Soon, though." He smiled.

My face felt hot. I climbed out of the car.

An agreement of sorts had been struck, but I wasn't sure I'd be able to keep up my end of the bargain. Opening that door brought thoughts of Michael, and that old hard stone that was still inside my chest. The prospect of an emotional involvement felt like driving a car a hundred miles an hour into a brick wall without a seat belt. I tried not to think about it. If only the rest of me would follow my head.

When I reached the 41st floor, Ira and Karen were still working in the litigation section. Karen was lining up large brown folders and inserting documents bound with rubber bands into each one. She looked up as I entered the room. "I thought you'd gone for the day."

"No. I had an errand to do for David. What are you up to? That looks like a big project."

"Oh, I'm just trying to organize all these files now that Jack's . . ." Karen hesitated. "I don't know what else to do. I mean, I thought it would be a good idea, since one of the other attorneys will have to take over."

I couldn't think how to respond. Karen obviously needed something to keep her busy. "This morning . . ." I hesitated. "When Nora was shouting in Suzanne's office. Before the police came. What was that all about?"

"I heard that too, and I'm not really sure, myself. Whatever's going on with Suzanne, it's none of Nora's business anyway," Karen grumbled. "She can be such a bitch!"

"Was Nora after Jack? Was it jealousy, maybe?"

Karen looked at me blankly. "I don't think Nora liked Jack very much. I think she was afraid of him."

"Afraid? Why?"

Karen stopped bundling her documents for a moment. "I don't know, really. It's just an impression. It's as though he held something over her head." She grew quiet for a moment, casting her mind back. "At least, that was always the feeling I had."

Now that we were alone, this was an opportune moment to satisfy my curiosity. "I noticed you talking to Billy, the messenger guy, in the hall the other day."

She shot me a dark look. "What are you asking?" Her tone of voice had changed. She was suddenly on her guard.

"Well, it looked like you had your heads together and you were whispering. I was just curious."

"Billy's a friend. We have lunch together sometimes. We live in the same building.

Besides, I don't think it's any of your business," Karen grumbled. "And if you're wondering where we were when Jack was killed, we were both at home. The police have taken our statements."

"I didn't mean that at all, Karen. I was just asking . . ."

"We both live at the Hartford Arms on Sutter. We have rooms there, okay? And at least five other people can vouch for us if that's what you're wondering."

I was familiar with the Hartford. It's a convenient residence hotel, centrally located. People can stay temporarily or long-term for an extremely reasonable rent. In fact, it's probably the best deal in town. A guest gets a room and two meals a day, plus phone, computer hookup, and a rec room.

"So you both live there?"

"Yeees, we *both* live there. Is there anything else you want to know? Otherwise, I'm done here." There was a momentary flash of anger in her eyes that contradicted her usual manner. She turned and walked through the door of Ira's office, shutting it more than firmly behind her. I can take a hint. I left and walked down the hall to David's office. Adam had just stepped into the reception area. I glanced around and noticed that all the boxes we'd retrieved were stacked next to my desk.

"I've got to head back to the office to take care of a couple of other clients but I'll come back in a few hours. Will you still be around?"

"As long as David's here. I'm going to spend some time reading through the transcripts and pleadings in that case we were talking about."

"I wish you luck." His expression seemed to say he doubted I'd learn anything of value.

I stuck my head into David's office. "I'm back."

He looked up and nodded in a distracted manner. I was grateful Adam hadn't told him about the events of last night. I really didn't feel like being lectured. I vowed I'd find the right moment to tell David about it. I shed my coat, dumped my purse on the desk, and lifted the lid of the first box from Jack's apartment. It held four expanding files full of handwritten notes on long yellow legal sheets and two folders of legal research on issues of law. Pretty dry stuff, much of it copies of cases against insurers heard before appellate courts. The second box was crammed with relevant court pleadings, starting with the initial complaint. The third box contained trial transcripts and deposition transcripts. That might be more revealing.

I scanned the pleadings that were available. Other than the initial complaint filed on behalf of the janitor's widow, Rebecca Moulton, the litigation that followed over the next several years didn't appear to reference her or her husband. These copies weren't the complete file, but they were the salient ones that would have been important to Jack.

Rebecca Moulton, the wife of Max Moulton, the janitor killed in the blaze, had been paid a settlement early on. Her agreement was signed a year after the initiation of the lawsuit. The case had continued for several years after that, as each party or insurer was dismissed from the lawsuit. The fire had been particularly tragic because the employees in the building ignored the fire alarm, assuming it was a test. Fire exits had been blocked by trash bags collected by the cleaning crew and this resulted in the inability of Max Moulton, the young janitor, to escape the blaze. Who was his widow? She would still be young. Did they have children? Was she left alone to cope with the death of her husband? Did she have family in San Francisco to help her through? No doubt she'd been grief-stricken, but was she consumed with an illogical rage? Could she have focused her anger at anyone connected with that disaster, no matter how tenuous the connection?

The last box contained more trial transcripts and the depositions of Fire Chief Herbert Belding and Arson Inspector Ted Warren, both of whom had been witnesses at trial. They testified that the fire had started from a short in the work done by the electrical contractor, Terrence Ward. Improper insulation leading to a circuit box had been the culprit. It was clear from reading the transcript that Jack had pounded it into the jury's mind that the negligence of the electrical contractor was to blame. Reading through the exam and the cross-exam, I could almost visualize the exchange in the courtroom. Ward was tongue-tied, he stumbled, he made excuses and backtracked in his story. The man had been demolished and ripped apart under Jack's questioning. The transcript was damning.

I'd settled in on the sofa with the files spread out around me. Engrossed in my reading, I'd lost all track of time. I checked the clock. Almost six. David must still be in, but his office was unnaturally quiet. I stacked up the files I'd read in one pile on the floor and put the others on the desk. I planned to repack the boxes when I was finished. I tapped on David's door and walked in. He was staring at his cell phone and jumped when he saw me.

"Oh, Julia. You're still here? I thought you would have gone by now."

"I've been reading Jack's old files about the bank fire."

"You still think that's related?"

I shrugged. "It certainly could be."

"Find anything interesting?"

"Well, yes and no." Before I had a chance to say anything further, David interrupted.

"Listen, Adam's on his way up. What do you say we call it a day and grab some dinner. Can you join us?"

Dinner sounded great. I was starving. "I'd love to. Where are we going?"

"How about we walk up to North Beach and grab something there? I'll let you pick the restaurant. You know all the best ones."

"Let's go to Franco's. I haven't been there for a while."

Adam tapped on the door and joined us. "Hi," he said with a smile.

"Hi." I felt my cheeks warm. I hoped David hadn't noticed. "I guess we're heading to North Beach for dinner. I'll get my things."

The three of us walked in single file down

Montgomery Street, doing our best to avoid the crowds pouring out of office buildings and heading to bus stops. At the Broadway-Columbus intersection, North Beach was brightly lit and every street log jammed with traffic. A local group of Chinese musicians playing traditional instruments had taken over the wide sidewalk by the traffic lights. We joined the crowd and listened to their exotic music for a few minutes. Adam dropped a five dollar bill into a basket and we continued on our way to Franco's.

The doorway was wide open. Inside, pots of geraniums stood on the windowsill and strands of woven garlic hung from the ceiling. The décor is a little tacky but the incredible food more than makes up for the interior. I was instantly hungry. We were the first diners of the evening and had Franco's complete attention.

"Julia, *comé stai, cara?*" Franco is a dark-haired, stocky man in his fifties who runs his restaurant with the help of his wife, son, and daughter. He likes to serenade his customers while they eat. It's often hard to dine and keep a straight face. What Franco lacks in singing talent, however, he makes up for in sheer force of personality. He also makes the most fantastic tortellini in Alfredo sauce.

"Bene, et tu? Et tua moglie?" I replied.

"Molto bene. Grazie."

Adam held out a chair for me. "Friend of yours?" he asked.

"Oh, I've known Franco for years. I grew up just a few blocks away."

"Ah, so I can't impress you with my knowledge of North Beach restaurants, I guess."

"No need to." We smiled at each other and I could feel my cheeks grow yet warmer. This was not lost on Franco, who discreetly bustled away to the kitchen. He returned with a bottle of Pinot Grigio and three wineglasses. The specialty of the evening was rotelli alla gamberi, a squiggly pasta served with shrimp in a lemon and white wine sauce. I opted for my favorite, after the tortellini Alfredo, that is — broccoli tortellini in a creamy marinara sauce.

David said, "This is fantastic. I'm sorry we have to spoil it with shop talk tonight."

"It's probably a good idea if we do most of our talking away from the firm anyway," Adam replied.

"So, Adam," David began, "what have you been able to learn? Have the police come up with anything?"

Adam reached for the wine bottle and poured some into each of our glasses. "The police have told me that Karen Jansen came into the building on Sunday. She'd agreed to work a few hours that day. She'd called Jack earlier and her phone records back up her call. She came in around three fifteen. She says that when she got to the office, Jack had changed his mind and told her he didn't need her after all."

"What? She told me today she was at her residence all day," I said.

"Well, she lied. She was in the office. She said nothing unusual happened. Jack was grumpy and insisted he didn't need help. She left and walked home. She swears Jack was alive when she left. We know Nora Layton was supposed to come into the office to talk to him about the case they're working on, but she called him and claims he decided there was no need."

Franco returned to our table with a huge tray of steaming dishes. We fell silent as he served each plate. Adam waited a discreet moment before speaking. "The police checked Suzanne's parking record. She arrived at 4:15 and left at 4:35. She says she found Jack, already dead, in his office. But that's twenty minutes. Seems like a long time to just walk in, discover Jack, and leave."

"Not really," I replied. "Maybe she parked

on a lower level and had to wait for the elevator up to A-level and then went to the other bank to take an elevator to the 41st floor. Plus she'd have to sign in at the guards' console."

"Maybe," Adam conceded reluctantly. "There's one more thing. Roger admitted to being in the office Sunday too. He drove in, so it was easy to check. He didn't speak with Jack. He just needed to pick something up from his office and left, he said. But he did see Karen leaving and Jack was still alive."

"Did Suzanne see anybody else while she was there?" I asked.

"No. The police have taken her statement and she says she saw no one. She was pretty upset when they questioned her. The other known entry to the building was a delivery guy from Giuseppe's Pizza. That was on the up-and-up apparently because the security guard even called up to the office on the 16th floor before he let the guy up to deliver the pizzas."

I decided this might be the opportune moment to fess up to David. I took a deep breath. "Listen, last night I got into the building and up to the 41st floor without being seen by the guards. They caught up with me as I was trying to leave, but I did make it up there without their knowing."

"Why did you do that?" David sputtered. "That could have been dangerous."

"Please don't be upset. I had a bee in my bonnet about it and just decided to check."

"David's right, Julia," Adam remarked softly.

David turned to Adam. "You knew about this?"

Before Adam could answer, I said, "I know you're both right, but I couldn't resist. There's a truck tunnel used for deliveries that connects to two other buildings. One on Sutter and one on Market."

"That's right," David remarked. "I'd forgotten about that. You mean the tunnel door to our building wasn't shut?"

"Nope. Interesting, isn't it? Adam told me it's supposed to be closed at eight o'clock during the week and all weekend, but each guy thought the other had taken care of it."

"So, it's possible the same thing happened on Sunday?" Adam asked.

"Could be. If the metal door was up for a Saturday delivery, maybe the guards didn't even think to check it on Sunday."

"They're supposed to make rounds on all four parking levels at some point in their shift," Adam said angrily.

"Hey, the reality is maybe they don't and

say they do," I replied. "Anyway, I just wanted to prove to myself that it was possible, that's all. But there's more."

"More?" David asked.

"Somebody else was there. In the litigation section. I heard something, and then I was hit and knocked down."

"Julia, what did I tell you?" David's face grew red. "You're making yourself a target and you could have been really hurt. I think the police ought to know about this."

"Listen to me, David. What's more important is that one of the guards went down to B level to close off the tunnel while the other one escorted me to my car. So, whoever was in the office that night couldn't possibly have left the building without being seen."

"This is sounding like *Phantom of the Opera*. You mean someone might have been inside all night?"

"Sure, why not? I already told you what I think. There's a good chance our murderer is a female, perhaps even an employee." David remained silent, but he looked uncomfortable.

"And where does this come from?" Adam asked.

I hesitated for a moment. "Adam, I'm not really a legal secretary. I mean, I used to be.

I used to work for David a couple of years ago, but I have my own business now. I'm an astrologer."

"An astrologer?" Adam's incredulity was obvious and both eyebrows went up.

"Yes." I watched his face carefully as he digested the information. "I have my own business. I have a private clientele, I lecture, and I've published a few things." I heard a defensive tone creeping into my voice.

Adam was silent. David smiled. "And I'm one of her clients," he said. "I can vouch for Julia. I wasn't a believer either, but she's turned me into one."

"Well . . ." Adam trailed off. I could see the surprise on his face.

"Trust me, it works," I said. "David and his family have been clients of mine for some time."

Adam shrugged. "Well, it's one way to come up with clues. I can't knock it. I don't have anything better. I'm planning on checking up on the Deklon Management guys. The two charming Farraday brothers. Find out what they've been up to lately."

I realized belatedly that I hadn't asked Adam for his birth information. I was as negligent as Gale. If I asked now, it would be obvious to David why I was asking. I'd have to wait for an opportune moment.

"Oh, Adam, before I forget, the plaintiff in the Bank case . . . her name was Rebecca Moulton."

Adam pulled a small notebook and pen out of his jacket pocket. "How do you spell that? M-O-U-L-T-O-N?"

"Yes."

"Okay." He sighed heavily. "I'll try to find out where she is or whatever happened to her."

When the dinner plates were cleared away, we ordered espresso. I knew I'd need the caffeine to wake up after the heavy meal and be able to concentrate on charts. As we left Franco's, the bells in the twin towers of Saints Peter and Paul across the park were chiming the eight o'clock hour.

"Julia, do you need a ride home?" Adam asked. His smile was warm and suggestive. David glanced over at me. I could feel a blush starting and turned away. Adam's interest was flattering, but I wasn't appreciating the thought bubble I could see over David's head. I'm a very private person. Was I ready to get involved with anyone? No matter what, I didn't want to have to explain myself.

"No need. My car's in the garage."

"I'll walk you to your car in that case. Doesn't hurt to be cautious," Adam replied.

The night was chill and damp. The streets glistened with moisture that reflected the garish neon signs along Columbus. Most of the restaurants had cleared their outdoor seating in deference to the cold while diners stayed warm behind plate-glass windows overlooking the sidewalk. We reached the corner of Kearny and Sutter, where the streets were now silent and deserted. Sandwiched between David and Adam, I could feel the warmth from Adam's body and detect a hint of aftershave. I hadn't had this kind of reaction to a man in a very long time. Maybe I'd just been dateless for far too long. We entered the building from the street level using David's building card, and, in unison, glanced up at the security cameras by the front doors. David pushed the down button to A-level on the elevator console.

"We'll have to sign in *and* out before we can go down to the levels where we've parked our cars," David remarked. Sure enough, as we stepped out of the elevator, the building guard approached us. This was a different man from the ones I'd encountered the night before. I breathed a sigh of relief. Although I'd confessed my explorations to David and Adam, I didn't particularly want to remind them of the incident.

The guard recognized David but asked that he, as well as Adam and I, sign in for the few minutes we were in the building. I was relieved to see that the guards weren't leaving anything to chance, and I was willing to bet that the steel door to the truck tunnel was closed and locked tonight.

David spotted his car immediately as soon as we exited the elevator on B-level. Mine was against the far wall, tucked into a corner. We said good night to David as he pulled out of his space and drove up the ramp. Adam followed me across the parking area to my car. I fumbled in my purse for the keys and unlocked the driver's side door. I turned to say good night, but Adam was standing so close I had to look up at his face. His hand rested on the small of my back. He pulled me close and bent down to kiss me. Intense warmth spread through my body and I silently prayed that my cheeks were not bright red.

"When this is over, Julia" — he hesitated — "I hope you feel the same." I opened my mouth to speak, but no words would come. I thought, *Julia, you idiot, he can read you like a book.* Adam smiled slowly and took a step back. "Do you have a long drive?

"No," I managed to mumble, "just out to the Avenues." I bundled myself as gracefully as possible into the Geo and turned the key. Adam stood by as I backed out and drove off.

I headed straight home and parked in front of my building, again too tired to put the car away. I took a deep breath. The taste of Adam's lips still lingered, but when I closed my eyes, I saw the image of Michael's body lying on the street. I shuddered and did my best to push that thought out of my head. I wanted to remember Michael as he was when he was alive and vital. My ribs were still sore from the attack last night, and tension was making my neck ache. I climbed the front stairs, shed my coat, and threw it over the kitchen chair with my purse. I'd planned to work on the charts a little longer, but knew I wouldn't be able to focus.

I kicked off my shoes and pulled a wine glass off the rack. I dropped two ice cubes into the glass and filled it with Merlot. I know you're supposed to drink red wine at room temperature, but wine aficionado that I am, I don't care. I like it with ice cubes. I fell into the big armchair in my living room, propped my legs on the ottoman, and hit the TV remote. Wizard was curled up in a ball in the other chair and lifted his head to acknowledge my presence. He climbed down and took up a position on my lap. I'd spent two days running around in circles and had accomplished absolutely nothing.

I channel-surfed until I found something that suited my mood. One of my favorites was playing — a grade B sci-fi from the fifties. The hero wore an Army uniform and the heroine's tight sweater displayed jutting breasts. The film was close to the end because the irradiated octopus had wrapped its tentacles around the Golden Gate Bridge and the Army was making its last stand. I downed my wine, wondering where I'd find the energy to walk the hallway to my bed when the phone rang. I reached over and picked it up.

"Julia, it's me." David's voice came over the telephone.

"David?"

"I'm sorry to call. It's worse news. I'm at the building with the police. They've found Ira. He's dead."

Twenty-Three

David had received the call as soon as he'd arrived home. He said the police wanted to see both me and Adam. I promised I'd drive back downtown. Groaning, I splashed some water on my face at the bathroom sink, slipped on a pair of flats, grabbed my coat and purse, and headed back out. When I arrived at Montgomery Street, I used my key card to drive down to C-level where David had told me they'd be waiting. On the west side of the building, near the empty slot of a tandem parking area, were an unmarked car, a black-and-white police vehicle, and a coroner's van. Adam and David stood side by side next to two uniformed men, while two other people in coveralls bundled up a man-sized package and loaded it into the van. Adam walked over to open my door.

"I didn't want them to call you. I don't think you should be here. This is pretty bad."

"I'll be fine." I wasn't so sure of that, but it seemed like the thing to say. "How did this happen?"

"They believe he was run over with his own car. It must have happened when he left the office around six o'clock. They'll tow his car and have Forensics go over it."

"How could that happen? Did someone overpower him and take his car keys?"

"Probably someone he trusted," David said. "The police think he might have suffered a blow to the head before being run over, but they're not sure yet. He must have been unconscious when this happened to him. Poor bastard. At least I hope he was unconscious."

"Are you telling me he was lying down here on C-level when we came back from the restaurant? One floor beneath us?"

David nodded in response. "Someone working late found him. Sometime soon after we left. His car was reversed into the parking spot. It hid his body, so no one passing by would notice it. The man who found him was opening his trunk and happened to look over. Saw him lying behind the back wheels."

The blood must have drained from my face. "Are you okay?" Adam looked concerned.

I swallowed hard and nodded. "This is just so horrible and brutal."

Sergeant Sullivan approached. "I'm sorry we had to ask you to come down tonight, but I think it's better if we talk now rather than at the office tomorrow." Sullivan didn't look any too happy to be hauled out at this hour either. "Ms. Bonatti, is there anything you can tell me about this?"

"Sorry, no. I know Ira was working in the office today. I didn't see him leave. I was away on an errand for a few hours, then I came back."

"And you parked on B-level when you returned?"

"Yes. It was later in the day and there were empty spots there. After that, I was in David's office."

"What time did you leave the building tonight?"

"Well, we — David and Adam and I — walked up to North Beach for dinner. We got back to the building about . . ." I looked to Adam for confirmation.

"Sometime around eight, or quarter past," Adam answered. "We signed in and out and took the elevator down one level to B. We chatted for a bit, said good night, and we all drove off." I blushed, remembering the kiss that Adam and I had shared.

Each of us answered a few more questions about our movements during the day, and then the sergeant told us we were free to go home.

Adam stepped closer. "Julia, I'm following you home."

"There's really no need, Adam. You don't have to do that."

"Uh uh, don't argue. I just want to make sure you get there safely."

"But where do *you* live? I never thought to ask you."

"In the Marina. I've got an apartment there. It's no trouble, Julia. I'll cut through the Presidio and I'll be home in no time."

True to his word, he followed me out of the garage and all the way back to 30th Avenue. I pulled up to the curb in front of my house and climbed out. Adam found a parking space across the street. He walked me up the stairs to my door and waited while I unlocked it.

In the darkened doorway I couldn't see the expression in his eyes, but he touched my cheek, then slowly leaned toward me and kissed me again. My knees turned to jelly and heat ran up my spine as I returned the kiss. We said nothing, both of us intensely aware of where this was going.

Neither of us sure we wanted to go there just yet.

"Good night, Julia." Adam smiled, then turned and walked to the bottom of the stairs. "And call me if you're worried or if you need anything, okay?"

"Adam, wait!"

He turned back. "What is it?"

"What's your birth date?"

Silence for a moment, and then he laughed. "August 5, 1976."

"And the city and time?"

"Uh . . . I think it was around five p.m. In St. Paul."

I smiled. "Good night."

"But you have to tell me what you find, okay?" He waved once, slid into the driver's seat, and started the engine. I stepped through my darkened doorway, still trying to recover from one of the hottest kisses I could ever remember. It really had been too long. I pushed aside my vision of dragging Adam through the doorway and ripping his clothes off before we even got to the top of the stairway. Ice cubes in the bath water. That's what I needed.

As I started to shut the front door, I shivered and turned quickly. I was certain I caught a glimpse of a shadow by the telephone pole on the other side of the street. I hurried inside, shut the door, and turned the lock. Very carefully, I eased back the side of the curtain on the inside of the door and scanned the street. The shadow was gone. Nerves again, I thought. I double checked that the bolt was on and climbed the stairs, shedding my clothes, and crawled under the comforter. Wizard was still the only man in my bed.

TWENTY-FOUR

David's face was sickly gray under his tan. "I'm not handling this very well . . . Someone is trying to ruin this firm."

Adam and I sat with David in his office. Meyers, Dade & Schulz was now closed for the rest of the week, and perhaps longer. I didn't want to say anything to David, but his complexion looked ghastly and I was getting worried about his health. I was determined to stick it out and do whatever I could to help him through this disaster.

I had half woken several times during the night and wasn't feeling exactly tip-top myself. At one point, I'd had another dream about a dragon. This time the giant beast had circled above my building, its wings spread wide, its tail swishing back and forth. I'd stared upward from my window and as the creature passed over me, the sky darkened to black and I woke up. I shook my head to rid myself of the memory. I needed more coffee to face the day. The answering service was taking care of incoming calls and would forward them to the attorneys working at home or to their cellphones. They were able to access the computer network at the firm from other locations, and so the more urgent work could be taken care of. I wasn't sure how long this would be effective, but it would take care of the immediate situation. Unfortunately, court deadlines couldn't be postponed, and so Roger, Karen, and Dani were working on the 41st floor protected by two of Adam's security guards, who were monitoring the hallway and the elevators. David was in a state of shock, as was everyone else, but I thought he seemed to be taking it particularly hard. He had had the gruesome task of identifying Ira the night before.

Adam paced back and forth by the window. "I blame myself. I was more keyed in to possibilities here in the firm, at night or on weekends, but at that hour . . . and on one of the parking levels. I never anticipated this. I should have, but I didn't."

"Nor did I," David replied.

"Have the police told us anything more?" I asked.

Adam said, "Nothing new. According to our man, everyone was gone from both floors at that time except for you and David. The guard remembers Ira passing by the desk to take the stairs down to C-level . . . and that's it. We're checking with companies in the building to see if anyone saw him or saw anyone else around his car. The police checked the tires on his BMW and fragments on the tires, and they know he was definitely run over by his own car."

"God, how awful." I shuddered.

"Somebody must have knocked him out before he got into his car, dragged him behind it, and then drove over him twice. I won't go into the gory details, but he bled to death from internal injuries. The full autopsy report won't be in for a while, but they can most likely tell if a skull injury wasn't related to the internal injuries."

My stomach churned again with the memory of seeing another body bag. I had to change the subject. "Listen, I spent yesterday afternoon reading through Jack's old files from the Bank of San Francisco case. I know Adam thinks I'm grasping at straws, but frankly, that case links both Jack and Ira."

Adam sat down in one of the wing chairs. "I'm sure they worked on other cases together at their old firm."

"Actually, no. I spoke with Suzanne yesterday before the police took her in for questioning. She told me that they hired her just to work on that trial, and when it was over, she moved with them to this firm."

"Following your theory, Julia," Adam said, "Suzanne could have sent a threatening letter to herself to allay suspicion."

I sighed. "That is a possibility, I guess. But the reality is that two of the three people who've received death threats are dead. And the one thing all three have in common is that they came from the same firm and worked on the same case. What do you know about that lawsuit?"

David sat nervously twirling a pencil between his fingers. "Well, I know that every law firm in the city followed it. It was a big one. Jack and Ira represented Rockwood, the main insurer of the building, and the fire itself was eventually blamed on negligent work done by the electrical contractor. I don't know the details, but I think because of all the publicity, the State Contractors Board pulled the man's license to operate. As I recall, the word was he had a drinking problem, and so everyone assumed he'd made some sloppy mistakes."

"Was that true?"

"I wouldn't know. I'm sure he claimed the

fire wasn't due to his negligence."

"What happened after that?" I was hoping David might recall something that wasn't in the official record.

"I don't really know. Rockwood paid on most of the claims and I guess that was the end of it, at least for the Browning firm."

Adam was silent during this exchange, but I could tell the wheels were turning. I studiously avoided looking at him, afraid I would give away what had passed between us the night before. "By the way, is Suzanne here today?" I asked.

"I haven't checked yet, but the police released her late yesterday. She might be," Adam replied.

"Maybe I'll have a chance to talk to her some more."

David flipped open a binder on his desk. "Well, if you two will excuse me . . . as hopeless as everything seems right now, I'm going to attempt to get some work done."

Our conversation was over. Adam and I stood to leave. I opened the door and spotted Dani, sitting on the floor in David's outer office surrounded by the files from Jack's apartment.

"Dani! What are you doing?" I glanced at Adam. He raised his eyebrows but remained silent.

"Hi, Julia." She looked up brightly. "Karen told me these were shipped over from Jack's apartment. I'm waiting for some revisions right now, so I thought I'd organize them and then if they're old, I'll send them off to storage."

I gritted my teeth and forced myself to stay cool. "Dani, look, I appreciate the offer, but David said he wanted to go through them first."

"Oh." Her face fell. "I'm sorry. I didn't know."

"That's all right. Really. I appreciate the offer, but maybe it's better to leave it all until David's done with it."

"Okay. I'm just at a loss as to what to do with myself. I'm waiting for Roger to finish so I can get his filing done. Then I plan to get the hell out of here." She stood and stacked up the loose files on the floor, replacing them in one of the boxes. "See you later." She left the reception area to return to her desk.

I took a deep breath, relieved to see her go. I could understand her looking for something to do, but it seemed odd to me that she'd come in and take it upon herself to go through these boxes. David had unlocked his outer door when he arrived in the morning, and I hadn't seen the need to keep it locked while we were inside his office. I checked that the files had been replaced in the same order, and then Adam and I pushed the boxes against the wall and stacked them out of the way.

Adam turned to me. "I have to get back to the office. I'm meeting a client there in a little while, and I've got to finish work on some post-trial jury interviews. That's a project that's taking a lot of time to coordinate. One of our men will make sure everyone gets to their cars safely or gets a taxi home today. I just don't know what more I can do for the time being." He opened the door and walked down the hall. His jaw was set. He was undoubtedly angry he hadn't been able to foresee the attack on Ira.

I was feeling like a fifth wheel. There wasn't much else I could do at this point either. I headed down the hallway to see if I could help Karen or Dani with anything. Roger was reading over his brief and Karen, her eyes rimmed with red, was playing a card game on the computer. She looked up as I entered.

"Hi Julia, what's up? I have absolutely nothing to do. Can you believe it?" She appeared to have forgotten her anger at my questions the day before.

"Me neither," I said. "I came down to see if you needed anything."

"Nothing's happening right now. We're just taking care of this immediate filing and then we'll head home."

Dani piped up. "Whoever thought there'd be a dearth of attorneys? What's that quote from? Shakespeare? Let's kill all the lawyers or something?"

"Henry the Fifth, isn't it?" I answered.

Karen glared at us. "I don't find that the least bit funny." She bit her lower lip and burst into tears.

Dani swiveled in her chair to face Karen. "You know, I feel pretty bad about this too. I couldn't stand Ira but I wouldn't have wished that on him. Don't think for a second you're the only one with any feelings." She turned back to me. "I might just as well practice. Our gig is tonight and I have to rehearse." She rummaged under her desk and opened her case. She pulled out her electric guitar and worked out an almost silent rhythm with her fingers.

I walked past Karen's desk and peeked into Suzanne's office. It was dark. "Have either of you seen Suzanne today?" Karen ignored me.

"She's not here," Dani volunteered, "but she called. She might stop in later to pick up some things." Dani's head was nodding along with her music.

At that moment, Roger stepped out of his office and gave me a dark look. "Could I have a word with you?"

"Sure," I answered hesitantly. I felt a little like a kid who'd been called into the principal's office. Roger stepped back to allow me access to his office and shut the door behind me. The room was every bit as neat as it had been the night I searched it. I was unsure whether to sit or not.

"Who are you?"

"What? What do you mean?"

"You know exactly what I mean. You no sooner come here than all hell breaks loose. You've been all over this place sticking your nose in where it doesn't belong, asking questions you have no business asking."

"Look —" I started to speak but was interrupted.

"I want to know who the hell you are and what you're doing here. And who you're working for. That's what I'd like to know."

I bit back the urge to tell him to go to hell. His manner was arrogant and demanding and I could feel my temper rising. I took a deep breath. "You already know what I'm doing here. I'm filling in for Muriel. I worked for David, here at the firm, a couple of years ago. Why would you assume it was anything more sinister than that?"

He stared me down and made no response.

I refused to break off eye contact. "If there's nothing else, I'll be on my way. Just call me if you have any more questions, okay?" I added sarcastically.

"You're David's little spy, aren't you? I might have known. Well, in case it's information you're after, why don't you start with him?"

"What's that supposed to mean?" I turned, my hand still on the doorknob.

"Jack was planning to leave the firm."

"So?"

"And take most of the bigger clients with him. That's what David doesn't want you to know. Why don't you ask him if you don't believe me?" Roger's lips turned down in a sneer.

"I still don't see why this concerns me." I was determined not to give away my surprise at his statement.

"Because if you're sniffing around for a motive as to who killed Jack, I don't think you have to leave the office at the other end of the hall, that's why."

My temper flared. "If you're suggesting that David Meyers had anything to do with

Jack's death or Ira's death, you're out of your mind, Roger. Besides, I'm sure the police wouldn't have to dig very deep to find a motive for you." As soon as the words were out of my mouth, I regretted being goaded and losing my cool. I could have bit my tongue. I had no real information other than the fact that Gale had suspected a whiff of scandal around Roger.

But my remark hit home. His face grew pale. "What do you mean?" he said in a sibilant whisper.

"Think about it, why don't you?" I didn't look back at him as I opened the door and slammed it shut behind me. Karen started shuffling papers at her desk, attempting to appear as if she hadn't heard raised voices. Dani stared at me wide-eyed. I ignored her silent query. I took a deep breath to control my temper and stormed down the hall to David's office. I was doing a slow burn by the time I reached my desk. Roger had made me furious. Granted, I trusted David. I considered him a friend, but Roger was his *partner.* How could he even imply something like that?

David stuck his head out of his office. "I can't get anything done today. I just called the Walstone house and left a message with their maid. I'm driving over to Walnut Creek to see her. Feel like keeping me company?"

"Sure, I'm curious to meet her." I took a deep breath to calm myself. I needed to get out of this building before I really lost my temper. "Let me get my coat." David was ready to go and stood waiting for me. "I do need to be back in the city by eight o'clock, though. My grandmother's birthday dinner is tonight."

"Shouldn't be any problem, even with heavy traffic." David hesitated. "Uh, I should warn you. I have no idea what we'll run into when we get there."

"Well, speaking of unpleasantness, I just had an episode with Roger."

"Roger? What happened?"

"He accused me of being, quote, your little spy, which I am, of course, and he more than hinted that you had a good motive for murdering Jack."

"Me?" David looked askance.

"Apparently, according to Roger, Jack was planning to leave the firm and possibly take clients with him?"

"He was?" David looked nonplussed. "Well, believe me, this is the first I've heard." He stared at me. "Julia, you can't possibly think I had a motive to kill Jack? And certainly not for that. Even if Jack was planning to leave and go elsewhere, and maybe some clients would have moved with him, on the whole it wouldn't have hurt us. But Jack never gave any hint he intended to leave. He was full of himself sometimes, and he'd bluster about his own importance." David shrugged. "Whatever the case, I honestly doubt we would have lost any really important clients."

I had the distinct impression David wasn't telling the whole story and there might be more he didn't want to share, but there was nothing to do at the moment but accept his explanation. He'd never given me any reason to distrust him, and I wasn't about to start now.

TWENTY-FIVE

We had a long drive ahead of us to Walnut Creek across the Bay. Talking to Rita Walstone seemed like one more exercise in futility but I knew David felt obligated and being a moral support was the only thing I could do right now. I was still bothered by Roger's nasty implications about David, but I kept any more questions to myself for the moment.

Traffic was relatively light on the lower span of the Bay Bridge heading east. Once we hit land on the far side, we followed the 80 and turned off to Walnut Creek, the traffic lighter as we progressed. The Walstone home occupied a rise on the outskirts of the suburb. It was a two-story pseudo-Colonial white house, arrived at by a semi-circular drive leading up to the front portico. David rang the bell and a small plump woman with dark and graying hair opened the front door.

"Hello, Maria." David nodded. "We're here to see Mrs. Walstone."

The woman's smile was friendly, but she shook her head and looked down as she opened the door to let us in. "Oh, Mr. David, I hope there is something you can do."

"What's wrong, Maria?"

"I take you up."

The foyer she led us through was brightly lit from a chandelier above the main entryway. A tall vase of white gladioli occupied the round table in the center of the room. An atmosphere of well-tended but impersonal elegance was apparent. The housekeeper's plump legs encased in dark stockings made a swishing sound as she climbed the wide staircase. David and I filed up in silence behind her. She arrived at a doorway at the end of the hallway and knocked. Receiving no answer, she opened the door and ushered us in unannounced.

Rita Walstone lay on a chaise lounge wrapped in a dark silk robe. A half-full liquor bottle lay on the floor next to her. She turned her head toward us and tried to rise from the lounge but failed.

Maria bustled in and gathered the bottle up. "Mrs. Walstone, lie down now."

"Well, well, David. How nice to see you." Rita slurred her words toward the end of her speech and fell back against the lounge. "And who have we here?" She peered myopically at me.

"Maybe I should wait downstairs," I whispered.

David shook his head. "It's okay, Julia."

"It's okay," Rita Walstone mimicked, barely able to hold her head up. She had once been a beautiful woman. That much was obvious, but the ravages of drinking had ruined her skin. Still, her dark hair and eyes and strong features must have been striking in her youth.

"Rita, I'm so sorry. I just wanted to stop by and see you. Is there anything you need? Or anything we can do for you?"

"Oh, I think you and your firm have helped me out plenty." She spat the words.

"Is there someone I can call for you?"

"No . . . and don't be sorry. He was a mean bastard anyway and it looks like someone put him out of his misery." At this, she started to laugh and the laugh ended in a hiccup.

I whispered in David's ear, "She'll kill herself if she goes on like this."

"I know," he mumbled. "Rita, look, I think you've had enough to drink. I'm calling your doctor." He turned to me. "Can you see if Maria has the number? We can't leave her like this."

I returned down the stairway and, walking through the tiled foyer, located the door leading down a short hallway to the butler's pantry and into the kitchen.

"Maria, can you find Mrs. Walstone's doctor's number for me, please?"

"Yes, miss. Thank you. I've been so upset, I didn't know what to do."

The housekeeper turned toward a nook at the end of the kitchen, and retrieved a telephone book. "Her doctor's name is Steiner." I leafed through the book and finally located a Richard Steiner, MD. I picked up the phone and explained the problem to his receptionist. She told me to hold, and after a few minutes I was put through to the doctor himself. He agreed to stop by the house the next day and promised to arrange for a practical nurse from an agency right away. I thanked him and hung up.

"Maria, does Mrs. Walstone have any family we could call?"

"Yes, she has a sister. She's coming tomorrow."

"That's good. In the meantime, can you please search the bedroom and the house for any more alcohol and get rid of it? Check all her hiding places, and check the bathrooms and the toilet tanks too, everywhere, just to be on the safe side. The nurse should arrive in an hour or so, okay?

"Yes, thank you, miss. I don't want to be here now, but I was afraid to leave her like this."

I produced one of David's cards from the firm and told Maria to call if she needed any further help. "How long has she been like this?"

"Oh, miss, since a few days ago."

"Since Monday?"

"Yes. Since Mr. Walstone call her from the office and tell her someone die there."

"I see. Has she done this before? Before Monday, I mean."

"Well . . ." Maria hesitated, unsure of her loyalty to her employer. "Sometimes yes. Sometimes she goes on a . . . uh . . ."

"Yes, I get it."

"But, always here, never outside the house, and I make sure I hide the car keys, too. She is a very unhappy lady. To have so much and to be so unhappy." Maria shook her head and returned the telephone book to its resting place. "But she is not always so bad, you know? This is the worst I see her and I was worried."

"I don't blame you. You're right to be worried."

I returned to the upstairs room. David had taken a chair next to Rita and was doing his best to engage her in conversation. "I'm sorry to bother you at a time like this, Rita, but is there any reason you can think of why anyone would want to kill him?"

"I told the police all this . . . last night. No. No reason. He wasn't likeable, but not interesting enough that anyone would want to murder him." She peered through her disheveled hair. "You do mean Ira, don't you?"

"Yes."

"Oh." She laughed. "For a second I thought you meant Jack. Now that would be a long list . . ." Her voice trailed off.

David sighed, struggling to maintain his patience. "Did Ira tell you he had received death threats?"

"Oh, yes." She waved her hand airily, as if dismissing any danger.

"Weren't you surprised?"

"Why? He was a lawyer, wasn't he?" A slight trace of a Southern accent revealed itself in a way that made the word *lawyer* sound like *liar.* I wondered if it was intentional. "Doesn't surprise me at all. Not at all. Guess he should have paid more attention, huh?" Rita leaned back on the lounge and reached for a glass of what looked like straight whiskey. "But he wasn't worried about that," she said. "Had it all figured out."

"Figured out? What do you mean?" I demanded.

"He said he was going . . . tell you." My ears perked up.

David's face was blank. "What was he going to tell me? Did he tell *you* anything? Can you remember?"

"No . . . can't remember . . . if he did." The glass started to slip from Rita's hand. David caught it before it fell to the floor. Rita leaned back against the cushions, her eyes closed. We waited a few moments, but it didn't look as though she'd wake.

I retrieved a large blanket from a shelf in the closet and covered her up, then rolled her onto her side. She didn't stir. "Let's go, David. There's nothing more we can do here." I picked up the glass and dumped the liquid in the bathroom sink. We returned downstairs and said goodbye to Maria. Ten minutes later we'd reached the main road that led to the freeway.

"Maybe we've hit on the motive for Ira's murder," I said. "Maybe he wasn't killed because it was the *plan* to kill him — maybe he was killed because he knew who was sending the threats or who killed Jack."

"Let's not get ahead of ourselves. We still don't even know if the threats are really connected to the murders."

"Oh, come on, David. It's too big a coincidence. Let's face it. A lot of people would have liked to see Jack Harding dead. Ira Walstone included, from rumors I've heard. Do you think it's possible Ira could have killed Jack, and then he in turn was targeted by another person?"

David shook his head but didn't respond, driving silently onto the freeway. We sped across the Bay Bridge, touching ground as we entered the tunnel running under Yerba Buena Island, halfway to the city. Once we were on the upper span again, the city appeared, sparkling in the light. I spotted the Ferry Building, its tiny shape dwarfed against the cluster of taller buildings. In the distance the first hint of afternoon fog clung to the spires of the Golden Gate Bridge on the far side of the city.

TWENTY-SIX

David pulled into the parking garage and drove straight to my car. It was almost three o'clock. By now, everyone in the firm would be gone, and with the office closed, we had no reason to return. We said our goodbyes and I clambered into the Geo, pulled out of the building, and drove home, pushing all the problems of the day out of my mind. I entered an afternoon curtain of fog as I crossed Park Presidio. A few blocks later, I had to turn my windshield wipers on.

The Avenues, as they are now called, were originally considered uninhabitable. Miles of sand dunes over bedrock enveloped in fog. By the late 1930s, as the city's population grew, development began in earnest, and now block after block all the way to the Pacific Ocean is densely inhabited. After the first year in my apartment, I couldn't imagine living anywhere else. It's the best part of the city as far as I'm concerned. I'm two blocks from the cliff that overlooks China Beach and the entrance to the straits. At night, I'm serenaded by the baritone voices of the foghorns.

Years ago, one of the two horns on the Bridge died. The city discovered that replacement parts were nonexistent, so the Coast Guard's solution was to replace both of the old compressed air horns with a one-tone electronic horn. It just wasn't the same. Romantics of San Francisco arose and demanded the return of the two-tone horns which, during the foggy season, typically sound more than five hours a day. Right now, they were in full voice. I started up the stairs and jumped involuntarily when I saw Adam sitting on the cold granite stairs.

"Adam! You scared me."

"Sorry. I didn't mean to. I hope you don't mind that I stopped by. I figured if you didn't show up soon, I'd leave a note in your mailbox."

"I don't mind. Come on up and I can fill you in."

Upstairs, I peeked into my office and saw the light blinking on the machine but decided to listen to my messages later. I threw my coat and purse on the kitchen chair and washed my hands at the sink. Adam followed me into the kitchen. Wizard had been waiting patiently by his bowl, but when Adam entered, Wiz disappeared into the bedroom and didn't come back when I called him. My cat is a jealous cat.

Adam took a chair in the kitchen. "They told me downtown that you'd left with David."

I sighed. "He wanted to drive over to Walnut Creek to see Ira's wife. She was in bad shape."

"Grief-stricken, I'm sure."

"Hardly." I joined him at the table. "She'd been drinking . . . a lot. We contacted her doctor. If anything, she may be more grief-stricken over Jack's death. Her housekeeper told me it started on Monday."

"Well, that's interesting."

"Would you like a coffee?"

"Absolutely. I could really use one right now."

"There's another thing, actually, that I wanted to mention to you." I filled the kettle with water and turned on the gas. "I thought there was something funny passing between Karen and the messenger guy who does the court runs. Billy."

"The biker guy?"

"Yeah. I guess they live in the same residence hotel. Karen claims they're friends. But it just seems like an unlikely friendship.

He's a young guy and she's old enough to be his mother."

Adam shrugged. "Well, I checked both of them out. Karen was already home when Ira was killed. She watched television in the lounge from five o'clock till nine. Lots of people saw her. Billy was out with friends last night when Ira was killed. The police are checking on that, and he claims he stayed in his room all day on Sunday when Jack was killed. Sleeping, he says."

"I guess Karen doesn't have a car but she could still get around," I said. "She's so close to work."

"Did she actually say she doesn't have a car?"

"Well . . . she told me she walks to work." I cast my mind back to the conversation I'd had with the secretary. "Maybe I just assumed that because she doesn't park in the building." The water had boiled and I spooned espresso coffee into a filter and waited for it to slowly fill the mugs.

"I can check on that."

I passed the steaming mug across the table to Adam. "Hang on. I have some half-and-half. Do you take sugar?"

"Just half-and-half is fine." Adam took a sip. "I was hoping you might be free for dinner tonight." There was something in his expression that made my face grow warm.

"Oh, I can't. I have a dinner downtown. It's my grandmother's birthday tonight. Another time maybe." I took a deep breath. "I just keep seeing body bags when I close my eyes, particularly when I think of Ira. Then my stomach starts doing cartwheels. One minute Ira wasn't concerned with anything but reaching his car to head home, and a few minutes later he was dying on a concrete floor in a parking garage."

"It's tough, I know. I guess cops and medical examiners have to somehow develop a facility for disconnecting from the inhumanity of the situation. It isn't easy."

"By the way, I looked for Suzanne today and she wasn't at the firm." I took a sip of coffee. "I'm sure you know by now that Suzanne and Jack were having an affair."

Adam laughed. "I think it was hardly a secret." He reached into his jacket pocket and pulled out an envelope. "Before I forget, the other reason I stopped by. I have some information on your guy Len Ragno or Lenny Ragno."

"Really?"

"He did time at Chino."

"What for?"

"Drugs . . . dealing. What else? Here . . . they faxed me his picture. Have a look."

271

Adam passed over the sheet of paper. It was a grainy black-and-white mug shot, but there was no mistaking the man in the photo. It was Luca Russoli, Gale's protégé.

"Oh no!"

"What? You look like you've seen a ghost."

I filled Adam in on Gale and the Fort Mason art show and the argument I'd witnessed between Luca and Nora Layton as I was leaving. "Luca Russoli is really Len Ragno."

"But why would he want an art showing under a pseudonym?"

"Maybe he's trying to put the past behind him? What'll I tell Gale?"

"The truth, if she's a friend. And Ragno, go straight? I don't *think* so. This guy's been in and out of trouble since he was fifteen."

"Gale's sharp. I don't think I need to worry about her. But no one needs this, to be lied to. I just hope she hasn't gotten involved with him any further."

"There's more." Adam drained the last of his coffee. "You're gonna love this."

I turned back. "What? You're looking very smug."

"I pulled up Ragno's court record." Adam's smile grew wider as he nudged his chair closer to mine.

"Yeeees? You're definitely looking pleased

with yourself. Tell me!"

"Well, the court website lists all court hearings and documents filed. It also lists the parties to a suit or criminal charge, *and the attorneys who appeared.*"

"What are you saying?"

"Guess who Len Ragno's public defender was?" I looked at him blankly. Adam waited patiently for my response, and when there was none, he said, "Nora Layton, no less!"

"Ah, that makes sense. David told me she'd worked as a public defender before joining the firm. Now that's a big connection. They already knew each other. And she would have known who he really was when she saw him at the art exhibit. So maybe that's why they were arguing, or maybe there was or still is a drug connection." I'd really have to tell Gale in person, and I wasn't looking forward to it. "Adam, something that Rita Walstone said today . . . It was hard to understand her, but it sounded like Ira had figured something out, something he was going to tell David."

"Really! Did she say anything more?"

"No. Either she didn't know or she couldn't remember. Whatever it was, Ira never got to speak to David. I'm worried, Adam. I'm worried about Suzanne as well. She could be in danger."

"Worry about yourself first, Julia. You're way too close to this. Besides, my vote's with Ms. Layton."

"Nora? Why?"

"She needed money, and David told me she might have been selling information to Deklon Management."

"Quite likely. She's just about thrown her career away, so what does she have to lose? If Jack was threatening her with exposure about illegal drug use, she could have lost the one thing that was keeping her afloat. The firm had asked her to leave, but she still had the ability to practice law. That could all change with a criminal charge. If so, she certainly had a motive to kill Jack, but so did Ira. Jack contributed to the destruction of Ira's marriage."

"From what David's told me, it doesn't sound as if Ira cared much about keeping his marriage together. And a lot of people had it in for Harding."

"Have you had any luck locating the janitor's wife? We need to find out who she is and where she is."

"Not as yet, but I'll keep trying. Got a couple of other places I can check. If she's still in the city. Don't forget, she got a large settlement. She could have relocated any-where."

"True, but I still hold to my premise that a female is involved."

"Because of David's Moon . . . something? With all due respect, that's astrology, not fact."

I bristled. "I know. Look, I *think* it's a female and possibly an employee, *and* I could be wrong."

"Okay, assuming you're correct, who do we have? We have Nora at the top of our list, Suzanne, even if you think she's in danger, and Karen Jansen and Dani Nichols."

"Let's not forget Rita Walstone and Hilary Greene. Or even Sarah Larkin. Any one of them may not be as harmless as they seem."

"But they don't work at the firm."

"But they all have connections to the firm and to Jack, in one way or another. I can't think of any motive that Dani would have. She doesn't seem interested in anything but her music and the gigs her band is booking."

"What about this Karen Jansen?"

"Dani thinks she's weird. Doesn't believe she was ever married even though Karen's hinted she once was. Plus, she's pretty upset. Both her bosses are dead. There's still some work for her but she could be out of a job."

Adam pushed back his chair. "Listen, I know you need to get going. I should get back to the office and catch up on some work."

Part of me was disappointed he was leaving so soon, another part grateful I wouldn't have to make any decisions about him for the time being. I followed Adam down the stairs, keeping a bit of distance between us. I didn't trust myself after last night's kiss. I opened the front door and Adam turned to me. He reached up and held the back of my neck, his fingers weaving into my hair. Then he leaned down and kissed me again, pulling me closer. I could feel the warmth of his body. "Maybe we really could have dinner some evening?"

"I'd like that," I managed to croak. My face felt hot. A real date?

Adam turned and waved as he reached the street. I closed the door and climbed back up the stairs. There was no doubt in my mind that Adam was more than a little attracted to me, and I in turn, but could I handle it? Wizard was crouched at the top of the stairs, his back to me, signaling his disapproval.

TWENTY-SEVEN

I headed down the hall to my office and hit the button on the answering machine. Three calls. One from a regular client, one from a potential new client referred by Celine, and the last from my grandmother, reminding me about her birthday dinner. Of course I wouldn't forget. I'd return the client calls tomorrow.

I flicked on the computer and plugged in Adam's birth information, generating a new chart. If his time was correct, his Ascendant and Moon were very close to my Sun sign. His Sun conjuncted my Moon. No wonder there was an attraction. I felt like a teenager writing the name of my schoolgirl crush in my notebook. I'd definitely have to study this further, but right now I was running late.

I rummaged in the hallway closet and found a garnet-colored wool sheath with a matching jacket. I washed and dressed quickly and tucked my grandmother's present into my purse, a lovely citrine bracelet I'd found at a small shop in North Beach. I called to Wizard but he ignored me. He was curled up in a ball in the little slipper chair in the bedroom. "Okay, be like that. I'll still feed you." I dished some food out into a fresh bowl, closed the kitty door, and then hurried down the front stairs to my car. Twenty minutes later I pulled into the parking lot of the Mystic Eye and called Cheryl's cell.

She answered right away. "Be out in a sec."

True to her word, Cheryl appeared at the back door and waved. I waited while she locked up and climbed into the passenger seat.

"Oh, you're all dressed up!" she exclaimed. "Is the Asia Inn a dressy place?"

"No," I laughed, "not at all. It's just a funky place in Chinatown over by California Street. It's neat, though. Very old, with private rooms. This outfit is from 'Nonni's Closet.' That's what I call my stash of good clothes. I always try to wear one of the outfits she's given me when we go out."

"Well, I love it. You're sure I'm okay like this?" Cheryl waved a hand over her blouse and skirt.

"Absolutely. You're fine. You'll see. We're

just going to chow down a lot of Chinese food. Kuan's organized the whole thing. It'll be fun."

"I'm looking forward to it. Gale said she didn't mind if I closed up a little early tonight. It's nice to get out. I feel like all I do is work and go home, but now I actually have a home, so I don't mind." She glanced over at me. "What's going on?"

I hesitated. "What do you mean?"

"Something's different. You're smiling."

"What are you talking about? I generally do."

"Mmm, my spidey sense tells me something's going on. Something like a man. Is it that cute cop that helped us this summer? He liked you. I could tell. Are you seeing someone and not telling me or Gale?"

"No," I replied hotly, then sighed. "I'm not 'seeing' anyone, but there is someone I've met. He . . . well we haven't actually gone out or anything, but I'm sure we will."

"I knew it! I knew it!" Cheryl crowed. "That's wonderful. I'd love for you to meet someone!"

"Well, we'll see. We'll see how things go."

"Don't be so damn negative!"

"I'm not being negative. Not at all. It's just . . . complicated." I hit the brakes before pulling out of the alley onto Broadway.

279

"Something's happened." I filled Cheryl in about Maggie's visit and the couple who'd discovered the photo of Michael's accident.

Cheryl was silent for a moment. "I'm so sorry, Julia." She reached across and squeezed my hand. "It's terrible. It's like you're dragging ghosts behind you."

I nodded. "Let's not talk about it anymore tonight. And please don't say anything in front of my grandmother. It's her birthday. I don't want to bring anyone down." I smiled at Cheryl, just to let her know I was okay. "The trick will be finding a parking space on Grant. But we'll give it a try." It took three passes up and down Grant Avenue, across California, and back again before I spotted someone pulling out of a metered spot.

"Watch out, Julia," Cheryl said. "That guy's gonna try to grab it." A large sedan was idling a car length away on the same side of the street.

"Not a chance. It's car wars." I squeaked into the vacant spot before the driver in the other car realized he couldn't reverse in time to block me. His rear lights blinked off, and, angry, he revved his engine and took off down Grant Avenue. I turned to Cheryl and smiled. "Let's get inside. I'm starving."

"Me too."

Kuan and Gloria were at the bar. Gloria was sitting on a stool, sipping wine, and Kuan held a sparkling water in his hand. He came over to greet us. Tonight he wore his formal outfit of all black: black slacks and a black collarless shirt buttoned to the neckline. "Cheryl, very nice to meet you. So glad you could join us."

"Thanks for inviting me. I've never been here before." Cheryl looked around, admiring the retro ambience. The restaurant had first opened in the 1930s and the owner had never wanted to update or remodel the place. The original hexagonal black-and-white tiles covered the entire floor space. The walls were a deep red with dark wood wainscoting. Lanterns hung from the ceiling and heavy drapes hid the private rooms from view.

"I think you'll like the food." Kuan turned to me. "Why don't we get to our table. Gloria's friends should be here any minute."

"Sounds good." I approached the bar and gave my grandmother a hug and a kiss on her cheek. "Happy birthday, Nonni." She was wearing a gold-colored long-sleeved sheath with a soft wool shawl. "You look very elegant."

Her eyes twinkled. "Hi darling, *ti amo.*

Thanks for coming and thanks for bringing Cheryl too. So nice to see your friends."

"Gale was sorry she couldn't be here. She had something else going on tonight."

"Next time." Gloria slid off the barstool and took my arm as we walked toward our room. Kuan held the curtain back for us to enter. "Angela and Dolores will be here any minute. They just called. They're still looking for a parking spot."

We took our seats and I fished the small present out of my purse. "Go ahead and open it."

"Oh, you shouldn't have!" Gloria exclaimed. She smiled broadly. "Can I open it now?"

"Of course."

My grandmother untied the ribbon and tore the paper away like a little kid. She opened the velvet box and gasped. "Oh, it's gorgeous," she said. "What is it? Is it . . . citrine?"

"You guessed it. Do you like it?"

"Oh, yes," she breathed. "I really do. Where did you ever find this?"

"Indira's in North Beach. I thought you'd love it." I reached over. "It goes well with your outfit too. Here, hold up your hand and I'll clasp it for you."

Gloria leaned across the table to show

Cheryl. "What do you think?"

Cheryl touched the bracelet delicately. "It's beautiful. Very different."

Kuan turned as he heard voices and lifted the curtain again. I recognized two women from my grandmother's church. One was Angela, the other Dolores, but for some reason I always mixed up their names. We all said hello and as they took their seats, a dark-haired man in his forties followed the two women in. *Uh oh,* I thought. What's this? I shot my grandmother a look, but she raised her eyebrows as if to innocently indicate she had no idea another person was joining us. *Yeah, right!*

"Julia, so nice to see you again," Dolores said, or was it Angela. "This is my nephew, Gianni. Gianni Scaramelli." Gianni waggled his head a little as he gave me a smarmy smile. At least he had the good grace to hold the chairs out for his aunt and her friend. "Sorry we're a little late. We had such a hard time finding a parking space and then just as Gianni was about to back into one, some obnoxious person in a little car snuck in behind us."

Cheryl's eyebrows went up. She hazarded a questioning look at me.

"That's terrible," I replied. "People can be so rude." Cheryl's face pinched as she

283

tried not to laugh. I introduced Cheryl all around. It was obvious Gianni had been pressed into service to chauffeur his aunt and her friend, but he didn't seem to be in much pain as he leaned forward to get a better view of Cheryl's cleavage.

I decided to play along and be polite. I was about to ask Gianni what kind of work he did, but Angela jumped into the breach. "Gianni's a certified public accountant, you know." The remark was directed at me. "He has an office in North Beach, just up the street. So, if you ever need help with your taxes . . ." She turned to her nephew. "Gianni, give the ladies your card. You brought your business cards tonight, didn't you?"

He reached into his breast pocket and retrieved two cards, handing one to me and the other to Cheryl. He still hadn't spoken. Cheryl studied the card for a moment. "Oh, I knew you looked familiar. I've seen the sign above your office." She turned to me. "You must have seen him around too, Julia."

Kuan gave a signal and a waiter bustled in carrying a huge round tray. I leaned close to Cheryl and whispered, "Sex offenders website, wasn't it?" Cheryl kicked me under the table.

The waiter scurried around our table, delivering the first course, a melt-in-your-mouth beef dish. This was followed by shrimp with glasses of Chinese ginger liqueur. Cheryl had already polished off one glass and was working on her second. Next came platters of rice, pots of tea, and more covered dishes of pork, beef, and vegetables. The food was non-stop. Cheryl was happily chatting to Dolores across the table, and Gianni, seated next to Cheryl, was hoping to catch Cheryl's attention.

When the fourth course was cleared away, Angela, who could barely contain herself, said, "So, Julia. Do you have a boyfriend now?"

I almost gagged on my bite of shrimp. Before I could reply, Cheryl laughed loudly. "She does now." I shot her a withering glare.

Gloria said, "Really, dear? Who are you seeing?"

I managed to down my mouthful of food and shook my head. "No one. Cheryl's mistaken." I kicked her again. I felt my grandmother's gaze as she squeezed my hand under the table. I was going to be questioned about this.

Without warning, the lights dimmed and two waiters entered, carrying a birthday cake sizzling with little sparklers. Gloria gasped. "Oh, no, you didn't!"

Kuan chuckled as the waiters placed a single candle in the middle of the cake and began to sing "Happy Birthday" off key. We all joined in. Then we heard drums and a trumpet and cymbals as the lights dimmed even more.

"What's that?" Cheryl asked. The curtain parted and a huge dragon's head appeared between the drapes. I gasped involuntarily.

Cheryl leaned over. "Are you okay?"

I nodded and took a deep breath. "Sorry, just frightened me for a second." My dreams of the menacing monster and its swishing tail came flooding back. The dragon's head was followed by a train of scaly cloth supported by men whose black-clad legs and feet were visible under the body of the dragon. Three musicians followed the dragon as it danced around our table, the dragon's head moving up and down and sideways, serenaded by clashing cymbals, drums, and trumpet bursts. The noise was deafening in our small room. Gloria held her hands to her ears, but she was laughing. The dim lighting, the sparklers, and the clanging and banging of the instruments sent shivers up my spine. The dragon represents celebration, but still, there was something sinister in the eyes and fangs of the huge papier-mâché head. The men made three passes around our table and finally exited, the dragon's head last as the men danced backward.

"Oh, how wonderful," Dolores exclaimed. "I've never seen a private dragon dance before."

Kuan was having fun, I could tell. As the lights came up, he stood. "The dragon is welcomed everywhere because he brings good fortune." He bowed his head in Gloria's direction. "Dragons possess great power and wisdom and the longer the dragon, the more luck. For our space, we could only hire a small dragon with five joints." Kuan glanced around the table. "But it's important to use an odd number of joints."

"I thought the dragon dance was only for Chinese New Year," Angela said.

"Well, the practice first started in the Han Dynasty for ceremonies to worship ancestors, but eventually it came into use for all sorts of celebrations. If this was a religious ceremony, the dragon's head and tail would have to be burned and the body stored until next year."

"I think it's wonderful," Gloria said. "Thank you, Kuan. That was so thoughtful of you."

"May it bring great good fortune," Kuan replied.

After dessert and more tea, and once the plates were cleared away, Angela and Dolores were the first to leave. I breathed a sigh of relief when the odious Gianni left with them. I asked Gloria and Kuan if I could drive the two of them back to Castle Alley, but they declined, saying they'd rather walk. "Are you sure?" I pressed.

"Yes, dear, we'll be fine. It's a nice night for a walk."

I hugged my grandmother and gave Kuan a kiss on the cheek. "Thank you, Kuan. I'll see you both soon."

Cheryl and I climbed into my car and, waving to Kuan and my grandmother, headed down Grant Avenue toward the Mystic Eye. I pulled into the small parking lot at the rear.

"I'm so sorry, Julia." Cheryl looked contrite. "I don't know what made me say that, about a new man in your life."

"Ha! I knew I should have stopped you after two glasses of that liqueur. Don't worry about it. Are you okay to drive home?"

"Sure, I'll be fine. The hot tea helped." Cheryl opened the passenger door.

"Hey, before you go, there's a place I'd

like to stop into. Do you feel like walking across the way to Stoned?"

"Stoned? The club?"

"One of the women at David's office plays in a band. Tonight's their night. She invited me, so I thought I'd pop in for a drink."

"Uh uh, not me. I'm pooped. It's almost eleven. Aren't you tired?"

"Kind of, but Googie Adano, the owner, is a friend. I thought I'd say hi. Kill two birds with one stone."

"Thanks, but no. I'm heading home and collapsing until I have to come back here tomorrow." Cheryl climbed out and then leaned down. "Leave your car here. It'll be safe."

"Good idea. See you Saturday."

"Oh, don't remind me. I have to get all the snacks organized for the open house." Cheryl blew me a kiss. "Have fun."

I climbed out and locked my car, waving to Cheryl as she got in her car and drove away. I hurried down the short alleyway and crossed Columbus, weaving through the crowds of late night strollers. I wished I'd worn something more casual, because now I was totally overdressed for a club night, but they'd have to take me as I was. I wanted a chance to observe Dani and her band and nose around.

I walked the last two blocks to the entrance and pushed a ten-dollar bill through the tiny window. Googie's partner, JJ, was collecting the cover. He's a very large, very tattooed biker who helps Googie manage the business. His tough macho exterior is good window-dressing, and he can double as a bouncer when needed. He's scary looking enough to keep customers in line but he's as gentle as a large pussycat. JJ smiled in recognition and stamped the back of my hand with a purple stamp.

"Julia, nice to see you . . ."

"JJ." I nodded and smiled.

"Whatcha doing here, girl? Surely you're not here for the culchuh?" JJ growled.

"I'm with the band."

"You shoulda said somethin'." He pushed the ten-dollar bill back to me. "Go right in, honey. Googie's around . . . you'll see him."

The blast was deafening. Dani's band, Hoarse, was on, and Dani was on stage with her bass playing a solid rhythm. The lead singer, a male, stood rigid at the mike and screamed out lyrics I couldn't for the life of me understand. I made a circuit of the interior, carefully avoiding the center where patrons screamed, cavorted, slid, and collided to the music. Actually, I thought Dani was pretty good . . . as a bass player, that is.

The rest of the band she could do without. I spotted Googie on the far right wall behind the bar, wearing a florid Hawaiian shirt decorated with rhinestones.

Googie is devastatingly witty and works very hard at running his business, his dream come true. He absolutely loves what he does and spends every day and night at his club. What amazes me is that after all this time at the noise-a-thon, he still has eardrums left. I ducked under the bar and waved to him.

"Julia, sweetie." Googie sped from the other end of the bar to embrace me and kiss me on both cheeks. He pulled back and looked at my outfit. "Oh, I'm so sorry, madam, the Junior League Tea was cancelled."

I laughed. "Just came from my grandmother's birthday dinner."

"How's she doing?"

"She's great. Kuan organized a big do at the Asia Inn."

"Well, then you've stopped by to tell me you're leaving me your hair in your will?"

I rubbed the top of Googie's thinning hairline. "No, sweetie, no. Just to see you and hear the music."

"Likely story. Come up to my office where we can talk." Googie walked to the end of the bar, grabbed a handle in the wall, and pulled. A black rectangle opened. He gave a wave to the bartender on duty, who nodded in return, and then took my hand and led me up a narrow stairway dimly lit with tiny white lights at the baseboard level. Once the door to the bar was shut, much of the noise disappeared, though the entire structure still reverberated. We climbed the stairway and Googie unlocked another heavy door that opened into a corridor leading to his office at one end and his and JJ's living quarters at the other. Their apartment looked out over Broadway, a street once lit by the infamous neon sign of the topless dancer with flashing nipples suspended from the building at the corner.

"Now what are you really up to? You know, I have to come back soon for a reading, I'm actually thinking of sinking some more money into this hellhole, but I want to consult with you first."

"Of course. Actually, that's what started this . . . a reading for a friend. You know I'm acquainted with one of your musicians?"

"Oh, who, darlin'?" Googie offered me a cigar. I shook my head no and Googie lit one.

"She's playing bass right now with Hoarse."

"Oh, right, she seems real sweet. Not like that testosterone-ridden nerd who sings with them, but she's all right as these kids go. What's up?"

"What dates have they played this past week?"

"Well, we have them booked for tonight and the next three Thursdays. If they bring in a decent crowd, we could move 'em up to Friday nights. But they've been doing the Sunday evening jams."

"Were they here last Sunday?

"Oh yeah. They were. You could always double check with JJ. He has a better memory for that stuff." Googie waved his hand vaguely in the air.

"What time do they start up and how many sets do they do?"

"Four sets. On Thursdays they set up around seven thirty and start playing at eight thirty, and then go to last call at one forty. Unless of course they're sharing the bill with someone else, which they're not right now because it wouldn't be worth it for me. Sundays, they play six to ten. They're the main band. They play the whole first set, then the jammers have their turn."

That schedule didn't give Dani an alibi for either murder. "That's an awfully long night, isn't it?"

"Oh, no, sweetface, they have to work for their money. You know what an oppressive capitalist pig I am." Googie smiled. "Listen, I'm thinking of a whole new look: white on white, with silver appointments, swing bands, and elegant jazz trios. Drinks, caviar, the whole thing . . . evening dress only. What do you think?

"Wow! That's a change."

"This whole urban punk thing has been done to death . . . it's as common as dirt and hardly alternative anything. I'm thinking Café Googie . . . or maybe Café Giorgio. Sounds classier, doesn't it?" Googie trailed off and smiled. "Besides, I'd love to see JJ in a tux. Can you hang around till we close up?"

"No, I can't. Thanks anyway. I just stopped in to say hi and pick your brain. It's a long story, which I won't bore you with now. I'll say hello to Dani and maybe buy her a drink. Don't mention I've been asking questions, okay?"

"You got it."

"Oh, one more thing if you don't mind, Googs."

"Anything for you, honey. After all, you're a Sagittarius. I trust you."

"Ever hear any rumors about a man named Roger Wilkinson?"

Googie squinted his eyes. "Name rings a bell, but I can't place it. Is he one of my people?"

"Pretty sure. Here. Here's a photo of him." I pulled out the article Roger had written on health care abuses, which I'd fortunately remembered to stuff in my purse. It boasted a professional shot of Roger in a suit.

"Oooh, yes. I know who he is. Although I only knew the first name."

"Well, tell . . ." I prompted.

"I don't remember the details offhand. It was a few years back but there was quite a scandal. JJ might remember. I'll let you know what I can find out."

"I'd appreciate that. And again, don't tell anyone I was asking, okay?"

"Don't worry." Googie made a silent gesture zipping his lips shut. "If I can find out more, I'll let you know."

I found Dani on the other side of the room. The jukebox was playing Patsy Cline, which was a welcome relief, and Dani was chatting with a young guy with a beer in his hand.

I approached slowly. "Hi, Dani."

She smiled vacantly at me, then vagueness turned to amazement as she recognized me. "Julia! Ohmigod, I didn't recognize you.

You're all dressed up," she laughed.

"I just came from a dinner party, but I was nearby so I thought I'd stop in."

"Hey, I'd like you to meet my boyfriend." She turned to the young man. "Antho, this is Julia. She's working at the firm this week." Antho turned a somewhat pockmarked round face toward me and smiled a toothy grin. His eyebrows and lips were pierced in various spots. I thought his name reminiscent of the disease that affects a lot of sheep, but I smiled anyway and shook his hand.

"Antho's our singer and lead guitar," Dani announced proudly.

"Can I get you a beer or a drink, Dani?"

"Nah, I've got one, thanks, and I've got to go back up in a minute. Did you catch our last set?"

"I did. It was great," I lied. "I just came by to hear you and say hi."

"Can you stick around for the next set?"

My head spun at the thought of another minute in front of the stacks of amps. "Oh, I'd love to, but I'm on my way to meet a friend. Some other time maybe."

Dani spun around and glanced at a signal from another guitar player on stage. "Uh oh, gotta go. Listen, thanks for coming by, Julia. I'll give you some of our flyers tomorrow when I see you." She kissed Antho quickly on the cheek and took off for the stage.

All in all, the hour spent at Googie's didn't net very much. Whatever alibi Dani might have for either of the murders didn't involve a gig at Stoned. Googie's memory was maddeningly vague, but I knew what a gossip he was and that if he remembered anything more about Roger, he'd let me know. I waved good night to Dani, now on stage, and made my way through the growing crowd to the front door of the club. I said good night to JJ, slipped out the door, and retraced my steps to the parking lot of the Eye to head home.

I pulled up to my garage door and searched for the opener. It wasn't in my purse, the last place I'd seen it. I checked the glove compartment. Empty. Where had it gotten to? I gave up the search, backed out to the curb, and climbed out. I'd have to search for it tomorrow. I climbed the stairs, unlocked the door, and called to Wizard. He didn't come to greet me. I heard his bell jingle somewhere in the apartment. It wasn't like him not to rush to the top of the stairs to greet me. I turned on the lamp on the hallway table and spotted his paws underneath.

"Wiz, what are you doing? Come on out

for a hug." I petted his paws and made kissing sounds. Wiz returned the affection with a gurgle and rushed out to my arms. "What are you doing hiding there?" I cuddled him as I walked into the living room. I flicked on the wall switch and stood in stunned horror. My apartment had been trashed.

TWENTY-EIGHT

The room was in shambles. A ceramic vase lay shattered in a hundred pieces on the floor. Books had been tossed off the shelves and two of the sofa cushions had been ripped open. I couldn't breathe and could barely move. Wizard mewed and snuggled closer in my arms. I went back to the hallway, terrified something might have happened to my bronze Buddha. It was still in its place, probably because it weighs a ton and is impossible to lift. I sighed; it hadn't guarded my nest very well tonight. In the kitchen, dishes from the cabinet were smashed. Food from the refrigerator, what there was of it, had been thrown against the walls to drip on to the floor. Bureau drawers had been dumped out in my bedroom, jewelry flung all over the room. The pillows on my bed and the comforter were slashed. The clothes hanging in the small closet, mostly just a couple of suits and some jeans and sweaters I'd been wearing that week, had been ripped off the hangers and cut to ribbons.

I felt like I'd been punched in the stomach. My hands started to shake. I knew now why Wizard had been hiding under the table, terrified. Then the thought occurred to me that someone could still be in the apartment. Perhaps I'd just interrupted the intruder. I lowered Wizard gently to the floor and shushed him, then made a dash for the small coat closet in the hallway where I keep a toolbox. Opening the door as quietly as possible, I released the catches on the metal box and grabbed a long thick screwdriver. It was the only thing I could think of in a hurry. If I had to defend myself, there was a good chance I could do a job on someone with it. I slipped off my shoes so I could walk silently, and, against my instincts, returned to the bedroom. I peeked under the bed. My hands were still shaking. Wizard had followed me and now was hiding under the tall bureau, his tail sticking out. I was tempted to join him. I picked up the phone and dialed Gale's number, praying she'd answer. She picked up on the third ring.

"Gale. It's me. Can you come right over?"

"Julia? Sure, honey. What's wrong?"

"Tell you when you get here." I hung up. Tiptoeing softly, I walked to the end of the hallway and the office. Nothing in there had been touched. Thankfully, my computer was in one piece. The charts were still stuck on the bulletin board, so whoever it was had either taken no interest in this room or had been interrupted. I checked the desk drawer where I store my laptop. It was intact. I breathed a sigh of relief. The filing cabinet where I keep my hard copies of client charts was undisturbed. Everything seemed in order.

There weren't too many hiding places in my apartment, and the ones that did exist I knew very well. I looked in the large walk-in closet in the hallway where most of my clothes were stored. As usual when I pulled on the knob, the door stuck. I leaned all my weight on the handle and it released. If that clothing had been destroyed, it would have been a real blow, but it was fine. I checked in the bathroom, in the shower stall, and peeked under the bed again for good measure. I walked very softly down the hall to the living room and made a circuit of the space, then checked the coat closet by the top of the stairs again and the small laundry room next to the kitchen.

Returning to the bedroom, I pulled out a

small case I keep under the bed. It holds a flashlight, a small radio, and a pair of tennis shoes in case of earthquake. I grabbed the flashlight and clicked it on. There was only one possible hiding place left in the apartment, and that was the storage area under the front stairway. I tiptoed down the stairs. The triangular-shaped door beneath the stairs is painted the same color as the wall of the hallway and the handle is camouflaged by color as well. Anyone not familiar with the apartment might not even notice it. I steeled myself in case my intruder was hiding there and would lunge out at me. Screwdriver in one hand and flashlight in the other, I pulled open the door and stepped back quickly. Nothing happened. I'd been holding my breath. I shone the flashlight around the almost-empty space. Nothing but two boxes of old tax papers and files and a large plastic storage container for extra blankets. I shut the door and turned the hasp to lock it.

The doorbell rang. I jumped involuntarily. It took me a moment to catch my breath. "Who is it?" I called out.

"It's me," Gale said from the other side of the door.

I opened it and let her in. "How did you get here so fast?"

"I was just down the street on Clement having a drink. Are you okay?" Gale took my hand. "What's going on?" She glanced at the screwdriver I was clutching tightly. "Holy crap, put that down. You look like you've seen a ghost. Let's go up to the kitchen."

"Somebody broke in. Come have a look. You won't believe it." Gale followed me up the stairs. "I think I may have surprised them."

Gale walked into the living room. "What a mess!" She turned away and followed me into the kitchen. "How did they get out?"

"The real question is, how did they get in?" I flicked on the light in the laundry room where the back door led to the outside stairway at the side of the building. Broken glass littered the floor. I pushed the curtain back. One small pane close to the door handle had been knocked out. I hadn't noticed it in my search of the apartment.

"Isn't that a double lock deadbolt on this outside door?"

"No," I said in consternation. "I never got around to it."

"Well, at least we know how he got in."

"Or she." My heart was slowly returning to its normal rhythm. "Gale, there's no way into the rear of the house or the back yard except through that small door at street level next to the garage, and that's always locked and bolted." My house, like a lot of houses in the Avenues, stands shoulder to shoulder with its neighbors. A narrow side pathway to the rear is protected by a locked door in the outside wall of the house.

"Well, let's go down and make sure. Give me that screwdriver and you hold the flashlight." We crept down the back stairs and walked along the side of the house toward the door to the street, skirting the garbage bins. The door was locked and bolted as it usually was. Another doorway under the house led into the garage. That was shut as well as the outer garage door.

"Does the big garage door lock automatically when it goes down?" Gale asked.

"Yes. Oh," I groaned.

"What?"

"My garage door opener. I couldn't find it when I came home. It's been in my purse 'cause I've been parking on the street. That's how they got in. They came in through the garage and up the side stairs to my laundry room."

"Let's check your purse." Gale and I trudged upstairs and I dumped the contents of my purse out on the kitchen table. I rummaged through everything. The opener wasn't there. "It's gone."

"Someone stole it?" Gale sat and leaned her elbows on the table, surveying the contents.

"Must have. I'm very careful. I always zip the top so nothing falls out."

"Somebody at the firm? Somebody as in possibly the *murderer*?" We stared at each other silently. "So it's safe to assume whoever did this still has the opener. You'll have to get a new one and change the code."

"I'll need to tell my downstairs neighbors about this. They're not going to like it. I'm hardly their favorite person after all the commotion last winter when those crazy people were picketing our building."

"Too bad, they'll have to suck it up. I'm sure they'd rather be safe."

"I can bolt the door at the back of the garage for now. Then it won't be possible for anyone to get into the back of the house. Wait here, I'll be right back."

I went down the stairs again and made sure the door into the garage was locked from the inside. Upstairs, I pushed the small bolt across the laundry room door, for all the good that would do.

Gale shrugged out of her coat and hung it over a kitchen chair. "I need a drink."

I pointed her to the cabinet where I keep

liquor. She surveyed the few things I had and finally poured two generous shots of tequila. She handed one to me and belted hers down while I sipped.

"I think you should call the police. I don't think you should spend the night here."

"I really don't want to leave. I'm just thankful Wizard wasn't hurt and the office is intact."

"You know, this almost feels more like a personal attack, doesn't it? Your clothes torn up and dishes smashed? Aren't you going to call the police?"

"I don't want to. I'm exhausted and all they can do is take fingerprints, if they'll even do that. They'll keep me up half the night. Some stuff's been destroyed but I don't think anything was stolen. I don't really have anything worth stealing anyway . . . maybe my laptop and the Buddha, but that's it." I took a large sip of tequila. "But Gale, if this happened, I must be getting close to something. Besides, if David or Adam hear about this, they'll shut me out and I don't want that. I don't want them to know."

"Who's Adam?"

"Oh . . . that's right, I haven't had a chance to tell you." I tried to keep a straight face but I could feel myself starting to blush.

"Yes . . ." Gail had a great big smile on her face.

By now, I really was blushing. "Later. I'll fill you in later."

"Not too much later, I hope." Gale sniffed. "You know, honey, just because I don't say anything doesn't mean I don't think about how you're doing."

"I know that. You don't have to say it."

"Maybe it's time, you know. It'll be almost three years this November. And other than a few dates that didn't go anywhere, there's really been no one. It's not right." She reached over and took my hand. "You can't protect yourself forever, you know."

I gritted my teeth. "Who says I can't?"

Gale laughed and threw up her hands. "Listen, let's get busy. I'll wash up in here." She pulled a bucket out from under the sink and filled it with warm water and soap and began to wash the spilled food from the kitchen walls. I swept up the broken dishes and dumped them in the garbage with the ruined clothing. Then I filled a plastic bag with the pillows and comforter. I didn't have the strength to tackle the rest of the debris and decided to finish the mop-up in the morning.

"I'm not going to let you stay here alone. I'm spending the night. Can you loan me a bathrobe or something?" Gale was rooting around in the refrigerator. I wasn't sure she'd find very much. "God, Julia. Don't you have any *food* in this house? I'm starving. No wonder you're so thin. I swear!"

"Oh, I totally forgot. You had a date with Luca tonight?"

"I did. He's been getting on my nerves. I sent him home. Food?"

"Oh. Well, I did have some soup, but I think it's mostly gone now. Wait." I opened the freezer and pulled out a plastic container. "I'll heat this in the microwave. It's Gloria's lasagna."

"Perfect. Thank you. And I'm going to the supermarket tomorrow to stock up your fridge."

"Please don't bother. Most of the time I forget to eat anyway." I pulled a hunk of hard Romano cheese from the refrigerator. When the lasagna was heated, I grated some to add to Gale's dish. "Thanks for staying. I really appreciate it. I'll take care of all the rest of this mess in the morning. Let's turn on all the lights and I'll jam a chair against the back door. And I can lock the door between the laundry room and the kitchen. Do you mind sharing the bed with me? Or you take the bed and I'll sleep on the sofa."

"Nah, I don't want you to do that. Plenty

of room for both of us on the bed."

I found a nightie and robe for Gale and dug extra blankets and pillows out of the storage closet. I put a log in the fireplace and lit it with the gas jets. We finally settled down and finished our evening with another shot of tequila. Well, maybe three. Wizard decided to come out from his hiding place and join us. Once he realized he was safe, he curled up in a ball in front of the hearth. I decided this might be the best time to broach the subject of Luca and come clean with Gale.

All in all, she took it pretty well. "To be honest, I knew something wasn't right," she said when I finished. "I mean, this guy's supposed to be from Italy. He speaks Italian, but he didn't know the name of the Prime Minister. A big red flag went up for me."

"I'm so sorry."

Gale grimaced and waved a hand in the air. "Don't be. You know, I was totally attracted to him, but after the show, he kept turning up on my doorstep like a lost puppy, and I found that very unappealing. I mean, I like what I do and you *know* I like men, but playing mommy and nursemaid, no. You can have it. I don't have the patience for it." I wasn't sure if Gale was just putting a good face on it. But it was true that she didn't like needy men, so maybe it was for the best. Gale snuggled into her robe. "Are you going back to David's office tomorrow?"

"I guess. I should turn up. I haven't actually done much of anything there, but I've certainly done a lot of running around." I reached over and gave her a big hug. "Gale, bless your heart. I can't thank you enough."

She waved a hand in the air. "It's nothing, sweetie. You'd do the same for me. Kisses. Now let's get some sleep." The log had burned to embers. I shoveled a little ash on top to damp it down and followed Gale down the hall.

TWENTY-NINE

I woke at seven o'clock, even before my alarm went off. The dragon had reappeared. This time I'd dreamed of crows, hundreds of them — a murder of crows — circling the sky over my apartment. The crows had cawed and scattered as a dragon appeared on the horizon. My chest had constricted in fear. I'd tried to run but my feet wouldn't move. I took a deep breath and shook my head to clear the cobwebs. What was going on in my head? I was haunted by a creature that doesn't even exist.

Gale was curled in a fetal position, snoring ever so slightly on the other side of the bed. Wizard was cuddled into a ball behind her knees. Faithless creature. My neck was stiff and my head was pounding, probably from the shots of tequila we'd downed the night before. If my intruder had returned, I wouldn't have heard a thing. I tiptoed out to the kitchen, swallowed two aspirin, downed a glass of water, and filled the kettle. Wiz came running when he heard me crack open a can. I dumped the contents into his bowl and scooped coffee into the filter. Once it was ready, I filled two mugs and put them on a tray with the sugar bowl and a small pitcher of cream and carried the tray into the bedroom. Gale stirred and sat up.

"Is that coffee I smell? You're a goddess. Throw it in my face."

I sat in the little chair next to the bed and sipped my coffee, waiting for the caffeine to kick in.

"You're going to need some help today," Gale observed. "I'll call Edwin, my handyman, and see if he can come over first thing. You can't leave here until he takes care of the windowpane and the locks. If your garage door opener doesn't reappear, I think you'll have to go to Sears or someplace to get a new one and a new code. I've got an appointment this morning, and then I've got to go over to the Eye. My accountant wants me to dig out some old records, so I'll be tied up for a while. But I can come back later and help if you want me to?"

"Thanks, I should be fine. No need to come back. Once the locks and the windowpane are taken care of, I'll call David and let him know . . . actually, no, I won't let him know what happened. I'll make some excuse about being late."

"Julia, that law office should just be closed."

"It pretty much is, but I think David can't totally desert it. He's so lost right now and just can't stay away, and I feel like I made a promise to help him out this week. I don't want to leave him hanging."

I found Gale a toothbrush. She washed her face and put on the clothes she'd worn the night before. I heard her on the phone in the kitchen explaining to her handyman what was needed. In the meantime, I jumped in the shower, dried off, and put on a pair of slacks and a sweater I retrieved from the hallway closet. I brushed my teeth, pinned up my hair, put on some makeup, and was ready to face the day. Gale finished another cup of coffee and gave me a hug on her way out the door.

"Edwin will be here in half an hour and take care of everything. Call me later, okay? Let me know how you're doing?"

"I will."

As it turned out, Edwin lived only five blocks from my house, and he arrived fifteen minutes after Gale had gone. When the doorbell rang I trotted down the stairs and, pushing the curtain to the side, peeked out. A tall, dour-looking, white-haired man wearing jeans with a tool belt around his waist stood outside my door.

"Good morning to you, my dear. Are you Julia?" He spoke with a thick Scottish accent.

"Yes, I am. It's nice to finally meet you, Edwin. Thanks so much for coming on such short notice."

"Not a problem. Just show me what's needed." Edwin followed me up the stairs and I pointed out the window in the laundry room door. "Well, we'll need to put in a small wee pane for this window and clean out the old glass. I have the deadbolts to install. You'll need two, dear?"

"That should do it. One on the laundry room door to the outside and one at the front door."

"Won't take me but an hour or so. I'll see what I can do about getting you a new garage opener and let you know. In the meantime, I'd suggest you keep that back door to the garage locked."

"Thank you, Edwin. Would you like some coffee?"

"Many thanks, but no. I'll just get right to work."

While Edwin was salvaging my apartment,

I returned calls from clients and chatted for a short while. Finally, I left a message for the new client Celine had referred. I tried Maggie's cell, just to check in with her, but she wasn't answering. I left a message instead. An hour had slipped by and true to his word, Edwin was completely finished.

It was now nine o'clock and a good time to reach David to let him know I was on my way. There was no answer on his private line. I called the main switchboard, hoping someone would pick up, but it clicked over to the answering service. I asked for David and was told that he had not arrived at the office or checked in for his messages. I wondered if he'd changed his mind about going in.

I tried Adam's cell phone next. I didn't intend to mention the break in. If Gale hadn't answered the phone last night, my second call would have been to Cheryl. Not that I wouldn't have called Adam if I'd really needed him, but I was convinced that he and David would just stonewall my efforts. Adam answered on the first ring. "Hey. What's up?"

"I've been trying to reach David at the office, but no luck. He hasn't come in. At least that's what the answering service told me."

"That's strange. He told me he was going

315

to be there this morning. He wanted to take care of a few things. Let me try to get hold of someone there. I'll call you back."

"Thanks." I hung up. More than likely David had changed his mind. In the meantime, I needed to get busy and start taking care of *my* life for a change. I pulled a stack of bills from the top drawer of my desk. Rifling through, I lined them up in the order of their due dates. I wrote out checks for each, marked the bills paid, and sealed and stamped the envelopes. I stuffed them into my purse to drop in the mailbox. I studiously avoided looking at the charts on the bulletin board. I didn't even want to think about any of those people. The phone rang. I grabbed in on the first ring. It was Adam.

"Julia. Listen. David's all right, but he's been admitted to the hospital."

"What? Where is he? What's wrong?"

"He's at St. Joseph's. I just talked to their housekeeper. Apparently he had some arrhythmia early this morning and Caroline didn't want him to go into the office. She was worried, so she called 911."

"Oh, how awful. I've been afraid this whole thing might affect his health."

"Just so you won't worry too much, he's doing fine. He wants to go home, but his doctor insisted he stay for a couple of days to run some tests. Caroline's with him."

"I'll go over there to see him. Can I call you later?"

"Sure. I have a meeting at a client's, but I'll be back at my office around noon."

"Talk to you then."

St. Joe's was on Castro near Market. I could be there in twenty minutes. I grabbed my jacket and purse, put my new keys on the key ring, and stuck the extra keys Edwin had left for me in a desk drawer. When I approached the hospital, I turned up the side street and, taking a ticket out of the meter at the entrance to visitors' parking, found a spot midway down the first aisle.

At the entryway, a nurse stood guard over an elderly man in a wheelchair, waiting to load her patient into the family car. A young girl, perhaps ten years old, holding a bouquet of flowers, stood next to the elderly man. I pushed through the glass doors and approached the front desk. The reception counter was topped with an autumn arrangement of gourds, dried leaves, and red and gold chrysanthemums. Cutouts of jack-o'-lanterns done by young patients in the children's ward decorated the wall behind the counter.

A friendly woman with white hair, wearing a pink smock, told me David was in

Room 324. I took the elevator up and wandered down the hallway. The room numbers ended at 318 and the corridor dead-ended at the Radiology Department. Irked, I retraced my steps, passed the nurses' station once more, and turned to the left. Halfway down the corridor I found David's private room. The television was muted and Caroline sat in a chair next to the bed reading a magazine. An IV set up on the back of David's hand connected to a bag of clear fluid suspended on a metal stand.

I tapped gently on the door. Caroline looked up and smiled. "Julia. I just tried to call you. David didn't want you to go into the office at all." Caroline is tall, slim, and blonde, with a long face and aquiline nose. She was wearing a gray skirt and sweater and certainly didn't look as if she'd just rushed her husband to the hospital. If she'd greeted me at the doorway of her Russian Hill home she couldn't have been better put together.

"How is he?"

"He's fine," she said with a smile.

David's voice boomed. "Please don't talk about me in the third person. I'm not dead."

"Shhhh, dear. You'll have the nurse in here lecturing you again." Caroline sighed and, shaking her head, sat back in her chair.

"I hope you didn't come empty-handed." David peered at me over his glasses. "Did you bring me some jelly donuts?"

"Oh, I'm sorry. I didn't even think to bring anything. Are you allowed donuts?"

"No, he's certainly not," Caroline interjected.

"I just want to get out of here. Have no use for doctors," David grumbled.

"He's staying for a day or two, Julia. And I'm here to make sure he stays. It wasn't a heart attack. But they do want to run a few tests."

I pulled a second chair over, next to Caroline's. "I've been worried about you the last few days, David."

"Well," he grumbled, "I'm fine. Really. I'll be out of here in no time. No time at all. How did you find out?"

"I called the firm to let you know I'd be in around ten, and the answering service told me you weren't there. Then Adam called your house and found out what had happened."

David stared in disgust at the breakfast tray in front of him. "Look at this slop." He picked up a spoon from the bowl and let a sticky porridge drip in globules back into the bowl. "I can't live on this. Can you imagine what they charge for this?"

Caroline patiently ignored his complaints. "So, Julia, what are you planning to do with the rest of your day? You can see how mine is shaping up."

"Well, I want to stop by Adam's office and then I might go by the *Chronicle*. I have a good friend who works there. I'd like to find out what stories the newspaper ran about the Bank fire."

David shook his head. "Suit yourself. Frankly, I'm not sure you're not just spinning your wheels, but good luck. Let me know if you find out anything interesting." He pushed the tray away. "Oh, before I forget, I got a call from one of our probate attorneys who, as it turns out, is the executor of Jack's will. His sister definitely inherits everything, except of course for the life insurance policy. Hilary is still the beneficiary."

"Have you talked to Jack's sister about it?"

"I left that up to the estate planning attorney. Apparently Sarah hasn't softened. She's refused to have anything to do with the funeral arrangements, so we'll probably have to foot the bill for that. Hilary may want to organize a memorial for Jack, but I haven't heard anything definite yet."

"What about Ira's arrangements?"

"I don't know what Rita's planning. I'm going to try calling her later."

"Well, both Jack's sister and his ex-wife will benefit from Jack's death. And Rita Walstone from her husband's."

"I find it hard to believe that any of those women could commit a murder."

"Someone did." I stood and gave David a kiss on his cheek and hugged Caroline. "If I find out anything interesting at the *Chronicle,* I'll let you know. And I'll pop in to see you tomorrow."

"We'll see you then, Julia." Caroline smiled in return. She'd need the patience of a saint to keep David contained for the next day or so. I didn't envy her the task. I heard David's voice call out as I headed down the corridor, "Don't forget the donuts."

I left the hospital parking lot and drove on Market straight downtown. The offices of Sinclair Investigations were at Ellis and O'Farrell and parking there was horrendously expensive. The only other option was public parking under Union Square. I turned off Market and circled the Square in bumper-to-bumper traffic, but when I finally approached the entrance to the underground parking, a standing sign told me the lot was full. I went around the square once more and drove the few blocks to Montgomery Street. I pulled into David's building and used my parking card. Parking here meant walking a few blocks, but at least it was free.

I emerged from the building and headed down Market. As I approached Grant Avenue my stomach reacted to smells from a pizza parlor one door up. I couldn't resist and stepped inside. Other than a quick piece of toast this morning while my new locks were being installed, I hadn't eaten a thing.

The interior of the shop was taken up by a large workspace behind glass where the dough was spun wider and wider until it reached the size of a full pizza pan. Ingredients for toppings were arranged in metal containers set into the counter space. A heavy-set man with graying hair and an apron covered in flour had just placed the thin dough onto a pan and was sprinkling cheese over the top. He ignored my arrival, adding oregano and olive oil over the entire slab. When he finished, he pushed the completed tray through a hatch at the back of his work area, where another man picked it up and shoved it into one of the large pizza ovens in the rear.

"What'll it be, lady?" He finally looked up at me.

"I'll have a piece, just cheese and tomato."

"Comin' right up." He walked around to the back room and returned with a paper plate of piping hot pizza. As the aroma assailed my nostrils, I seriously thought about ordering an entire pizza for myself, but discipline reigned.

"Anything to drink?"

"Just a glass of water." I handed him a five dollar bill, and got three dollars in return. Best deal in town. I stuffed a dollar into the tip jar and carried my plate over to a small table by the front window. I was the only walk-in customer. Most of the shop's business was undoubtedly phone orders and take-out. I devoured my slice, took a gulp of water, and wiped my mouth to make sure no dribbles of oil were running down my chin.

The big man hollered, "Yo! Ready." A different man came from the back room and headed out the front door carrying two large boxes. Something about the tilt of the man's head seemed familiar, but I couldn't place it. He stepped out to the street, heading east on Market. As he passed, he looked up at the window where I sat and for a brief moment hesitated, then continued on his way.

It hit me in a flash where I had seen him before. It was Antho, Dani's boyfriend.

THIRTY

I was eating at Giuseppe's Pizza and Antho was delivering pizza to make ends meet. I had probably passed this place hundreds of times but had never noticed the name on the door. Given its proximity to the financial district, it wasn't surprising that offices in the area would use Giuseppe's as their favorite place for take-out and deliveries. Dani had never mentioned that her boyfriend worked for the very business that had delivered to the 16th floor of the Montgomery building on the day of Jack's murder. Had Antho been the delivery guy on that fateful day? And had Dani bothered to tell the police her boyfriend had access to the building? She would have known if he had been working that Sunday. I stood up and tossed my paper plate and napkin into the trash bin by the counter. The heavy-set man was preparing yet another pizza. This one with pineapple and hunks of ham, a desecration of the real thing in my humble opinion.

"Excuse me."

The pizza maker didn't look up when he answered. "Yeah?"

"The guy who just left . . . he looks familiar to me. I think I know him. Is his name Antho?"

His hands stopped moving and he looked up. "Are you a friend of his?"

"We have a friend in common. Listen, by any chance, what days does he deliver for you?"

"What's this about?"

"I was just wondering if he did your deliveries last Sunday?" I imagined takeout orders wouldn't be too heavy on a day when most offices were closed, so Antho might have been the only guy working on a Sunday.

"Are you a cop?" The pizza maker's tone became belligerent. "If you are, then I'll spare you the trouble, because the cops have already been here asking questions, and I don't have time for this crap."

"No, no, really, I'm not a cop," I assured him. I wracked my brain for a good lie that might elicit some information from this bulldog. "Look, this is kind of embarrassing. I'm a friend of his girlfriend. They had a fight 'cause he didn't show up for a date last Sunday afternoon and she's been thinking he's seeing somebody else. He told her he wasn't, he was working."

"Oh, for chrissakes, whaddo I look like, his mother?" The man shook his head.

"I told you it was embarrassing."

He stared at me, a disgusted look on his face. "Yeah, that's his regular day. He's the only guy I can get to do deliveries on Sunday. He works one to five. The kid plays music so he won't come in till the afternoon. You happy now?"

"Thanks. That's all I wanted to know."

"Good. Now can I get back to filling my orders? I got work to do." He shook his head. "What next?"

"Thanks," I said as I pulled the door open and beat a quick retreat. He was still muttering to himself as the door closed behind me.

Was this too much of a coincidence or what? The one person not connected to the firm who entered the building on Sunday, the day of Jack's murder, was the boyfriend of a woman who worked at the firm. Delivering pizza would give him lots of mobility anywhere in an office building. He wore a shirt and a cap with a logo and walked around with pizza boxes in a big vinyl warmer bag. He might get mugged for the pizzas, but otherwise, no one would even glance at him twice.

I cut up to O'Farrell and found Adam's building, a four-story gray edifice next to the parking garage next to Macy's. The lobby area was marble with brass fixtures and so was the elevator. Sinclair Investigations took up a section of the top floor. A receptionist greeted me and I asked for Adam Schaeffer. She made a quick call and then pointed to a side corridor. "You'll find him down there."

Adam was standing in the hallway, waiting, and indicated his small office. "Welcome to my domain." I stepped inside. A large window overlooked the three-way intersection of Market, Stockton, and Ellis.

"I was hoping you'd call, but this is better. What can I do for you?" He smiled.

"I was wondering if you'd found any information on Hilary Greene?"

"I'm sorry. I didn't forget, and I'm not ignoring you. I've just been so busy with a couple of new clients. But we can have a look now. We can probably find a birth date, maybe even a social security number. And we can definitely do a property search."

"Great. I'll watch over your shoulder."

Adam sat behind his desk and turned to

the keyboard. "Did you have a chance to talk to David?"

"Yes, I stopped by the hospital. He's complaining a lot, so I'm sure he'll be fine."

"Good." Adam plugged in the address of the art gallery on Fillmore and, sure enough, it told us the date it had been sold, the price for the small one-story building, and the buyer's name: Hilary R. Greene. Bought one year after her divorce from Jack.

"Is Greene her maiden name? I thought she told me she'd been married once before Jack. Can we look up marriage records or name change records with this program?"

"We can access city and county information. That should give us any marriage records or name changes."

Adam entered a search for "Greene," and, scrolling by year, started searching for Greene with an "e." There had to be hundreds with no "e," but only about two hundred with an "e." Patiently, he moved the down arrow as I looked over his shoulder.

"Do you know the name of her first husband?"

"Not a clue."

We finally found it, second from last in the list of Greenes. A license had been issued in San Francisco County on May 4,

1999, to Edward Greene and Hilary Ragno.

"Well, well, well," Adam said. We stared silently at the screen for a few moments. "So Hilary is related to our Len/Luca, huh?"

"Looks that way," I responded. "And Henry Gooding is connected to Ragno."

"How do you know that?" Adam asked.

"Because it was Gooding who suggested him to my friend Gale for the art show."

I made the decision to tell Adam about the break-in at my apartment. I was still afraid he might try to keep things from me, but I felt I needed to confide in someone. I was still very shaky about the whole thing. And given David's condition, I hadn't wanted to say anything to him at the hospital.

"Julia, why didn't you call me?" Adam was thunderstruck.

"I don't know . . . I'm sorry. I know you would have helped. I called my friend Gale, who stayed the night with me."

"More importantly, why didn't you call the police? Whoever did it might have left fingerprints."

I couldn't find the words to convey the feeling of invasion, and my desire to clean up the mess as quickly as possible.

"I do think you should talk to Sergeant Sullivan about this."

"I don't want to tell him my theories. He'll think I'm completely nuts. He'll dismiss anything I have to say. I just know it. Unless I can find something more solid . . . and I'm frustrated."

"Whatever you want in the way of help, you've got it. I don't think you should be sticking your nose into this anymore, though. Someone's obviously singled you out. You don't have a security alarm in your home?" Adam asked.

"No. I went through some trouble last year, but after that, I never felt the need."

"Maybe that's something I can set up for you and have it installed. I can stop by later to check things out."

"Well . . . okay. Thanks." I was certainly attracted to the man, but I was starting to feel a little fenced in. Security systems, no less! "You probably still haven't had a chance to locate Rebecca Moulton, have you?" I asked.

"I did check a couple of databases on that one, but nothing yet. I'll keep trying. I'll call you if I find anything, okay?"

"And another thing. Do you remember the pizza delivery last Sunday to the building?"

"Ye-e-e-s," Adam said slowly.

"Well, Dani Nichols's boyfriend, Antho, *is*

the delivery guy on Sundays for Giuseppe's Pizza. It was him. He was actually the guy who delivered the pizza."

"Well, that's not so suspicious. Dani works in the building. They both live locally and he has an afternoon job when he's not playing music. I wouldn't hoist a red flag over that. Besides, the police checked on that delivery, and it was a real order that came from an accounting firm. So I can't see that he could've engineered an excuse to actually be in the building at that time."

"I guess you're right." I felt deflated.

"Look, it's nerve-wracking not to have any answers, and after a while, it preys on your mind, and you start to suspect everyone and everything. I don't mean to squelch your ideas, but . . . just let the police do their job. The things that need to come to light, will."

"I guess you're right. I'm seeing things in the shadows." Not to mention bad dreams. I glanced at the clock on Adam's desk. It was almost two o'clock and I wanted to get to the *Chronicle* to talk to my old friend Don Forrester. I wasn't sure what hours Don might be working and I didn't want to miss him. I picked up my purse and stood.

"Hey, what's the rush? Was it something I said?"

"Sorry, no. I have another stop to make. I can fill you in later."

Adam stood and followed me out to the elevator bank. He pressed the down button and took my hand. I could see the receptionist watching us. "I wish we were alone right now."

I smiled. "Me too, but we should be discreet. I have the feeling you're already the subject of gossip." Adam was a good-looking man, and perhaps several women in his office had eyes for him. I stepped into the elevator. "Oh, before I forget" — I held my hand out to stop the door from closing — "what are you doing Saturday night?"

Adam smiled. "Hmm. Are you asking me out on a date?"

"Well . . . sort of. There's a Halloween open house at the Mystic Eye from four to nine, if you'd like to stop by. That's where I'll be."

"I'd love to . . . if I can get someone to cover at the firm. If there's any way I can make it, I'll come. Sorry I can't promise, though." He raised his hand in a goodbye as the doors closed.

I exited on Market Street, a little disappointed that he'd been so vague about the open house, but I shrugged it off. A trolley was approaching. I hurried across the street and made it to the doors just in time. I climbed in, paid the fare, and got off a few blocks later.

The newspaper building is dominated by a clock tower at the corner and extends a block in both directions. The interior of the lobby has been renovated in a bland, utilitarian sort of way, but at least now the elevators work a whole lot better. Don's office, or should I say cubbyhole, occupies a corner of the Research Department on the second floor. I stepped off the elevator and approached the front desk. I asked for my friend and gave my name to the receptionist, a young woman in her twenties with large hoop earrings, choppy black hair, and dark purple nails. While I waited, she picked up her phone, spoke briefly, and instructed me to go down the hall and turn right. I already knew where Don's office was located, but I had to observe the formalities. I reached his door, which was covered with a collage of horror pic glossy photos and a grinning paper skeleton. I knocked and stepped inside, declaring, "If you think this is going to keep people like me out of your hair, you're sadly mistaken."

Don looked up from his video game, a half-eaten tuna fish sandwich in his hand. He and I have been friends since college.

When I was living in my apartment in the Sunset District, Don had dated my roommate, Denise, who'd dumped him to join a cult. He'd been morose for months, but eventually ended up marrying his high school sweetheart and now they had an adorable little four-year old boy.

"Julia . . . hey . . . whatcha up to?"

I glanced around. Don's walls were covered with vintage horror flick posters featuring Dracula and the Wolfman. His desk lamp was a plastic skull topped by a purple shade. "Sorry to beard you in your den, so to speak, but I'm here for a favor, if you can do it. And by the way, you've really spruced the place up."

"You like it? Kathy says I'm the biggest kid in the family." He took another bite of the tuna sandwich. "Plus, I've reorganized this entire research section and all our computer files. If they fire me, they're screwed." He turned his bag of potato chips toward me. "Help yourself."

"Thanks." I took two. "Listen, I'm trying to get copies of anything the *Chronicle* ran about the Bank of San Francisco fire. To be more specific, anything regarding a death in that fire."

"I remember that. It was . . . what? Five years ago? But between the fire and the lawsuits and any historical follow-ups, that covers a lot of ground."

"I know. I don't need that. Just anything in regard to the death of the janitor in the building. His name was Max Moulton."

"And can I ask the reason for this query, ma'am?"

"It's about the murders at the Meyers, Dade & Schulz law firm."

Don raised his eyebrows. "And you're involved how?"

"I . . . uh . . . I'm working for my old boss there, temporarily . . ."

"You do manage to find trouble, don't you?" Don narrowed his eyes. "You think those murders are connected to the fire?"

I nodded. "It's possible. No one else agrees with me, though."

"This'll cost you. I want a free solar return on my birthday."

"You got it." Don was very fond of the solar return as a predictive tool. Astrologers, meanwhile, are somewhat divided on the subject. Solar returns are based on the theory that at the exact moment the transiting Sun returns to its natal position — in other words, on the individual's birthday — the resulting chart foreshadows the year to come. Myself, I've never been convinced this method works very well, but some clients, like Don, have actually gotten interesting results.

Don had turned to a monitor on the other side of the littered desk, double-clicked an icon, and typed in "Bank of San Francisco." The screen filled with lists of references.

"Let's see, the front-page story was printed on November 1st. The fire started the night before. Halloween, strangely enough. Wait a minute, what's today?"

"October 30th."

"There's a reference to injuries and one death." He read aloud, " *'Authorities believe the body discovered is that of a janitor trapped on an upper floor.'* No information about the cause of the blaze here." Don moved his mouse down the list on the screen. "Let's try another search. Let's use the word 'death.' " I leaned forward so I could see the screen. "Here we go. There's an article on November 3rd about the accidental death of Max Moulton. Is that your guy?"

"Yes."

"Then there's a January 7th article the following year, about the lawsuit brought by his family, his wife I guess. There's some related articles that reference the fire in relation to safety and inspections in high-rise buildings. Do you want any of those?"

"No. Just anything to do with accidental

death, wrongful death in regard to that fire. Particularly if there are pictures."

Don continued to scroll down the list on the screen. "Here's something. This is November 1st, two years after the fire. *The Bank of San Francisco claims its second victim.'*"

My ears perked up. "What's that?"

Don read the précis in a monotone. *" 'Death by suicide of electrical contractor, Terrence Ward. The ill-starred Bank of San Francisco claims its second victim . . . Terrence Ward was found dead today of an apparent self-inflicted gunshot wound. The electrical contractor was suspected of negligence in the deadly fire but was never charged.'"*

"Any reference to family he might have left behind?"

"No, but we can check the obits for the week following this. Hang on." Don moved to another site. "Here it is. *'Beloved husband of Elva Ward. Parents deceased, no children. Funeral services to be held in Minneapolis.'"*

"Can you get me copies of the November articles and the later obituary, and any pictures the paper might have run?"

"Sure, take a few minutes. I'll print them out. Wanna wait here?"

"Yes." I sat behind Don's desk, sniffed the

tuna sandwich, and helped myself to a few more chips. If I balanced just right, I could rest my feet on the windowsill and see people hurrying below me on Mission. Jack could have been killed for any number of reasons. There were certainly plenty of people who disliked him if not actually hated him. Ira was murdered either because he knew something about Jack's murder or because his and Jack's deaths were connected to the threats they'd received. If that connection was related to the Bank fire, Suzanne might really be next. I grabbed Don's phone and dialed Adam's office. He picked up on the first ring.

"I'm sorry to keep bugging you."

"You're not bugging me." I could almost see his smile through the phone. "What's going on? Where are you?"

"I'm at the *Chronicle* doing some research. Can I give you another name to check out?"

"Sure."

"It's Elva Ward." I spelled the name. "She was the wife of the electrical contractor, Terrence Ward, who was blamed for the fire. And he committed suicide." Adam was quiet for a long moment. "Are you still there?"

"Yeah. Look, I know you're kind of stuck

on your theory, but isn't that reaching a bit?"

"Maybe. Quite possibly. But I'm curious about whatever happened to her too. After all, she would be the second widow to come out of this."

"Maybe this guy offed himself for his own reasons. Nothing to do with the fire."

"Maybe."

"Okay, no problem. I'll look her up and see what I can find out."

At that moment, Don returned with several sheets of paper clipped together. "Gotta go. I'll call you later." I hung up.

"Here's you go, Julia." Don passed the sheets of paper to me.

The *Chronicle* story that had appeared right after the fire detailed the events leading up to the death of Max Moulton. It ran with pictures of the fire itself, and a smiling shot of Max in better days. He was young, thirty years old according to this article, with a wide generous mouth and fair hair worn a little long over the ears. The second article referenced the suicide death of Terrence Ward. It appeared on page fifteen as a filler, and wasn't run with any pictures of the dead man or his family. I was disappointed. "Any chance you could keep searching and see if any papers anywhere might have included pictures of him or his relatives?"

"Sure. But you'll really owe me. Two solar returns."

"You do drive a hard bargain." I smiled. "We'll set a date before your next birthday." I tucked the pages into my purse and thanked him. Don powered up his video game, pushed his glasses back onto his nose, and prepared to wreak death and destruction on cyber persons.

I left his office and followed the corridor back to the elevator bank. When I stepped outside at the corner of 9th and Mission, a brisk wind was blowing, although the day was still bright and sparkling. I hurried toward Market and waited at the traffic light to cross over to the trolley car island. Traffic was heavier now. I hoped I wouldn't have to wait too long to get back to Montgomery Street and my car.

The sidewalk at the intersection was jammed with people, all of us waiting for the light to change. Cars sped by, attempting to beat the traffic light before it turned yellow and then red. I felt someone pressing against me. Irritated, I turned to see who was pushing into me, but before I could turn my head, I was shoved forward. I stumbled and reached for a pole to catch my balance. My hand slipped and my heel caught on the curb. Cars were wheeling past as I fell forward. A horn blared and I heard the shriek of tires as I hit the concrete.

THIRTY-ONE

Instinctively, I'd clasped my hands around my head and curled into a ball. I sensed rather than saw the heavy black tires that narrowly missed me. A woman on the sidewalk screamed. Metal crunched against metal as another car hit the car that had just avoided me. I waited for an impact but none came. A horn blared and arms reached down to pick me up.

"Hey lady, what the hell's going on . . . are you drunk or something?"

"Or something," I muttered as the crowd surrounded me and two people helped me to my feet.

"Are you all right?" a man with a florid complexion asked. A woman I assumed was his wife was grasping my arm. I looked around and realized traffic had come to a standstill. Strangely enough, my purse still hung on my shoulder. I checked the street to make sure the contents hadn't spilled out.

"I'm fine. Really." I quickly scanned the crowd. I *had* felt that hand on my back. I hadn't imagined it. "I'll be okay."

"We can get you a cab," another onlooker volunteered.

"Thank you. Really. I just slipped. Stupid of me." I nervously scanned the crowd. Had I imagined seeing a man in a heavy leather jacket as I fell? Doing my best to control my wobbly knees, I took a deep breath and walked across Market to the trolley island as the light changed. My hip was sore and a scrape on my leg was oozing blood. As I reached the waiting area, the trolley slowed to a stop. The same man who'd helped me to my feet stood close by, watching me as we climbed into the trolley. I hung on to the pole near the front as we progressed in fits and starts toward the Ferry Building and the end of Market. At the corner of Montgomery, I limped off the car and crossed to the sidewalk. Fortunately I didn't have far to walk, only half a block to the entrance to the office building. I took the elevator down to the parking level and climbed into my car, breathing a sigh of relief. I'd had a close call. I wanted nothing more at that moment than to get home in one piece.

I drove out of downtown, stopping and

starting in traffic. When I reached my apartment, I managed to climb the front stairs and fit the new key in the lock. I made sure to lock the door behind me and put the bolt on as an extra measure. I walked slowly up my inside stairway and hung my jacket over the railing. I collapsed on the top stair and gingerly pulled off each shoe. Wizard's bell jingled in the hallway as he trotted to meet me. He tentatively touched my foot with his paw. "Oh, Wizard." I picked him up and held him close. He began to massage my stomach with his paws. I rubbed his head and took a few deep breaths, grateful to be home and alive. I was a real mess.

I gathered up my shoes and purse and coat and limped to the bedroom, carrying all twenty pounds of Wizard as well. Wiz hopped out of my arms and took up a position on the bed. In the bathroom, I washed off my cuts and scrapes and applied ointment and Band-Aids to strategic spots. I pulled on a pair of loose jeans and slipped on a T-shirt, then took two aspirin and went back to the kitchen to make myself a cup of tea. My hip was sore where I'd fallen and I was sure it would be black and blue the next day. I slammed the kettle on the stove in frustration. My house broken into, my clothes slashed, and now this. A nightmare.

Carrying the hot tea, I limped down the hall to my office and pulled all the natal charts I'd done off the bulletin board. I lined them up along the long table under the window. So far, I had solar charts for Jack and Ira, both now deceased; Roger and Nora; plus Suzanne Simms, Dani Nichols, and Karen Jansen. I still had no birth dates for Jack's sister Sarah, his ex-wife Hilary Greene, or Ira's wife Rita Walstone.

Wizard placed a tentative paw on the threshold of the office, but then, sensing my mood, withdrew. I pushed the rolling chair across the room and sat down, careful not to lean on my hip. I could see the city skyline in the distance and the narrow spire of the Transamerica pyramid. I imagined David's office building a few blocks to the right, impossible to pick out from this far away. The events of the past week and the influx of new information had kept me from concentrating on these charts in a determined way. I needed to study them again with a fresh eye. I read and re-read and re-arranged the charts and my notes. I pulled out a large notepad and methodically went through each one, jotting down major points and natal aspects. Then I made a second column for current heavy transits.

Almost everyone at the firm with the

exception of Dani was touched by the Pluto transit through Capricorn. Nora had very difficult Neptune and Saturn aspects in her birth chart and Pluto was squaring her Moon. Pluto was opposing Karen's Moon and Saturn was hitting Nora's Neptune by transit. My head hurt. It was one thing to work on one chart, or two or three, but there were eight charts, including David's, in front of me and I couldn't come to any definite conclusions.

Was I wrong in thinking that the murderer was a woman? Or wrong in thinking it was one of David's employees? But at the time I'd felt fairly certain of that. Could the woman be Rebecca Moulton, or connected with her? Where was Rebecca, anyway, and was she out for revenge? Who was Elva Ward and what had happened to her after her husband's suicide? I didn't feel I could rule anyone out, not even Hilary Greene, Sarah Larkin, or Rita Walstone.

I was feeling anxious and irritable and I wasn't quite sure why. I didn't like the idea that no one had heard from Suzanne since she'd been released by the police. When I had access to the personnel charts, I'd made a note of everyone's home numbers. I pulled the sheet out and tried Suzanne's number first. There was no answer and no voicemail. Then I called Dani's home number, hoping she'd be there. She was. She answered on the first ring.

"Hi Dani, it's Julia. I'm home right now. I was just hoping that maybe you'd heard from Suzanne. I never had a chance to talk to her."

"Not today. I did see her yesterday. She came into the office late in the afternoon. She was still working when I left."

"Oh." I couldn't decide what to do. "Well, that's good to know."

"You know something I don't know?"

"That's the trouble. I don't. I'm just kind of worried about her but I never got a chance to talk to her."

"Ah, she's probably just upset over . . . you know . . . over Jack and everything. Call me later if you're still worried. I'm home tonight. Just practicing some new stuff."

"Thanks, maybe I will."

I tried Suzanne's number again and still got no answer. Frustrated, I went back to work on the charts. My head was starting to throb and my hip and leg were sore and hurting. My neck was stiff and I hoped it wouldn't go into complete spasm. I wasn't thinking clearly and I felt it was critical to do so. Wouldn't the killer and his victim share certain mutual points in their respective charts? That's it, I thought. My computer contained a program that would line up all planetary and angular points in linear fashion from 0 degrees of Aries through 29 degrees of Pisces. I printed each sheet for the individual charts as soon as the computer program had sorted them. There were even more correspondences between the charts than I had at first noticed. I thought maybe I should just go back to David's chart and focus on that. After all, that was the one that had started the ball rolling, and I could pick up on anyone who had planets that actually touched his natal points.

The phone rang and I jumped.

"Julia." It was Adam. "I'm just checking up on you to make sure you're okay."

"Of course . . . I'm fine," I lied, slightly annoyed but flattered he was thinking of me. "Just working on some charts." I decided not to mention my near miss with the traffic on Market Street. I just wasn't used to people actually worrying about me. Of course, at the rate I was going, I'd be worried about me.

"What deep dark arcane secrets have you discovered?"

"None at all. I'm trying to put my mind in neutral and go over all the information again. I can't help the feeling that the answer's right under my nose."

"Guess what?"

"What?"

"I found her."

"Who?"

"Who? Rebecca Moulton."

"You're kidding. Where is she?"

"Right here in the city. She lives near you in the Richmond District."

"I'd love to talk to her."

"I'll go with you if you can wait. I've got to take care of a few things first."

Adam's deep voice sent a thrill through me. I hated to admit it, lone wolf that I am, but I wanted to see him, away from the firm and away from this case. "What's her address?" I managed to ask in a neutral voice.

"She's at 323 25th Avenue. She owns the property. She must have bought it with the settlement money. It's a duplex, like your place. She lives downstairs and probably rents the upstairs to a tenant," Adam replied.

Rebecca Moulton was only five blocks away. "When are you free to see her?" I asked.

"Oh . . . either later tonight or tomorrow morning."

In spite of my bruises and stiffening

muscles, I was antsy to move sooner. "Listen, I'm stuck with the stuff I've been working on. I might go see her now."

"You think that's a good idea? I'm a little nervous about your going alone." Adam sounded worried.

"I'll be fine. Really."

"Well, why don't you give me a buzz when you're back?" There was a timbre to his voice that made my legs weak. I wanted to have these feelings again, but the thought that there might actually be a breakthrough in Michael's accident preyed on my mind. It felt like ice water in my heart. "Promise?" he asked.

"I promise." Smiling, I hung up. I could feel warmth creeping up my neck to my cheeks.

After stacking all the charts on my desk and turning out the light in the office, I decided to change into something more presentable. I stripped my jeans off slowly and straightened up just as slowly. My lower back felt unstable and stiff at the same time. I sat on the side of the bed and checked the bandages on my legs and arms. I pulled on a loose skirt and sweater and, not sure if I could stand stockings against my skin, picked out a pair of soft flats. I caught a glimpse of myself in the mirror. A large purplish bruise was forming on my left shoulder. At least the sweater would cover that. I lifted my arms to pull the sweater over my head and a sharp pain in my shoulder blade jolted me. I took a deep breath and tried again, this time successfully. I slipped a jacket on, grabbed my purse, and headed down the stairs. It was dinnertime. Hopefully Rebecca Moulton would be at home.

Thirty-Two

Typical of the houses on the Avenues, the Moulton house was a two-story, late 1930s wood-frame and stucco duplex, painted yellow, with a garage at street level underneath the house itself. The trim was white, with white shutters at all the front windows. Window boxes on the two stories overflowed with bright flowers and trails of English ivy. A large terra-cotta pot with trailing geraniums stood next to the polished oak front door, which sported a man-sized paper skeleton. Three small pumpkins sat at the side of the top steps. The brass of the door handle was original and highly polished.

I rang the bell and after a few moments, a woman in her mid-thirties opened the door. She wore jeans and a striped sweater. Her long brown hair was pulled back in a ponytail. Her complexion was clear with only a slight touch of makeup.

"Rebecca Moulton?"

"Yes. Well, it's Rebecca Wilson now."

"My name is Julia Bonatti. I'm working for David Meyers at Meyers, Dade & Schultz."

A look of confusion crossed her eyes. "Should I recognize that name?"

"Probably not, but two of the attorneys at that firm worked on the lawsuit you brought against the Bank of San Francisco and its insurers."

"Oh." She didn't exactly look thrilled to hear my explanation. "Well, you better come in then." She stepped back and held the door open. A tall coatrack stood by the front door. On it hung two small jackets, with a basketball and a skateboard underneath on the lowest shelf.

"Have a seat in there." She indicated a room through an archway to the right. "I'll be right with you. Just have to turn down the stove," she called over her shoulder as she hurried down the hallway.

Soft lamplight illuminated the living room. Plush area rugs covered polished hardwood floors. The furniture was large and overstuffed in a light-colored tweed pattern. The table at the end of the sofa held family photos in small frames. I sat in the armchair closest to the fireplace, where a log burned, and waited for Rebecca to return. She came back in, wiping her hands on a dishcloth.

"I'm terribly sorry to bother you like this, especially without calling, but there have been problems at our law firm. Some of the attorneys . . . well, if you've been watching the news recently, two of the attorneys at the firm have been murdered."

"Murdered?" The shock was evident in her voice. "What's the name of the firm again?" Her brow furrowed.

"Meyers, Dade & Schultz."

She shook her head. "I'm sorry, I don't recognize that name. What does this have to do with me? The Bank of San Francisco case was settled years ago."

"This may have nothing to do with the fire there, but the police and the private investigators working for the firm don't want to leave any stone unturned." I neglected to mention that no one was even slightly interested in my theories.

"I'm still not sure I follow."

"They think it's possible there might be a connection between that court action and the two attorneys who died."

"You mean they represented the bank?"

"No, they were the attorneys for the insurance company."

"Look." Her face had become very pale.

355

"That was a tough time for me. I left it to the lawyers. I don't even remember all the companies involved. I hope you're not implying that I have any connection with this?"

"Oh, of course not," I lied. "But we thought it might be a good idea to talk to you to see if you know of anyone or have heard from anyone who might have a reason to wish them harm."

"It's still not easy for me to talk about all that. One day my husband was here and the next he was gone. He just didn't come home from work one night and I was left with two small kids to raise, but I have no gripe against the insurance companies involved. It's because of them that I at least got my settlement."

"You seem to be doing well."

"I'm doing all right. I bought this house and invested the rest for my boys. I remarried last year and my husband has a small business. We're not wealthy, but we're managing." She shook her head. "But there's no amount of money that will ever compensate me for the loss of Max. And the boys will never know their father. There's not a day I don't look at them and think of him, dying, trapped in that burning building. The irony is that he was only working there at night because he was finishing school. His dream was to be an engineer. I don't blame the insurance companies. I blame that drunk . . . that electrical contractor who did a rotten job on the wiring and killed my husband."

"Was he ever found guilty of negligence?"

"No. Can you believe that? The district attorney originally pressed charges but they dismissed it. The only thing that happened was he lost his license." Her hands had started to shake. She pulled a cigarette out of a box on the coffee table and lit it. "Sorry. I guess no matter how many years go by, it doesn't go away."

"His name was Ward, wasn't it? The contractor that was supposed to be at fault?"

She grimaced. "Yes, I remember *his* name. It's hard for me to go back over all that stuff again. But, yeah, Terry Ward, I think. May he rot in hell."

"Do you know what happened to him?"

"I think I heard he died. I guess his wife's a widow now too." She smiled ruefully.

"Do you know if he had any other family?"

"No idea."

"Do you remember who told you Ward had died?"

Rebecca shrugged. "I guess it must have

been my lawyer."

"I thought someone mentioned he committed suicide."

"That may be right. I just don't remember. I was in very bad shape for a long time. If he did, it had to have been out of guilt."

"I'm glad to hear you've remarried. That must be good for your children."

Her eyes softened. "Yes, it is. My older son, Todd, is twelve now and my younger one, Jeff, is seven. They needed a dad and my husband is really good with them. I'm sorry. You just wanted to ask a few questions and I went on and on."

"That's quite all right," I assured her.

"I didn't mean to lay all that on you." She shuddered. "Murder. Well, I'm glad I know nothing about it." I heard quick running footsteps in the hallway. A young boy appeared in the archway, half-dressed in a pirate's costume, an empty plastic pumpkin in one hand. It had to be Jeff, the seven-year-old.

"Mommy, when are we going trick-or-treating?"

Rebecca turned her head. "It's tomorrow, honey." She turned to me and smiled. "He just couldn't wait to try on his costume."

"Mommy, can I have a cracker?"

She sighed. "Just one. I'll get it for you.

Don't climb up on the counter."

"Todd said I could."

"And I said no."

Jeff looked crestfallen. He hung his head and turned toward the kitchen, rhythmically banging his pumpkin against the wall.

I caught a whiff of dinner from the kitchen, some sort of pot roast I guessed. Rebecca smiled. "I love them so much. And whenever I look at them, I remember that their father never got to spend this precious time with them. My life's okay. Maybe great compared to most, but yes, I admit to bitterness, and I still grieve. I still have some days when I wake up and it all comes flooding back. Maybe that'll go away in time, I hope."

I could certainly relate to that statement. I thanked Rebecca as she let me out the front door. The wind had picked up, blowing fiercely off the ocean. I pulled my coat closer and hurried to the car, turned the key in the ignition, and flicked on the heater.

As much as I didn't want to admit it, I was no further along. If Rebecca Moulton, or Rebecca Wilson, as she was now, was bitter, it wasn't toward the insurance company that had settled with her without a murmur. Jack and Ira had represented Rockwood Insurance only, which then went on to countersue others, but not the widow of the man who'd died in the blaze.

I decided to take a chance and see if Hilary Greene's gallery was still open. I couldn't help but wonder if she'd been told she was the beneficiary of her ex-husband's life insurance policy. It wasn't exactly the kind of question one could easily slip into casual conversation. I drove up to Geary and headed toward the Pacific Heights end of Fillmore. Parking was just as bad as it had been before, but I lucked out and found a spot a block away from The Greene Room between a fire hydrant and a driveway. The lights in the window were dimmed, but a brighter light shone from the office in the rear. I tried the door and it opened. The bell tinkled as I entered and Hilary Greene peeked out from the back room.

"Hi, Hilary. Remember me?"

"Oh, yes . . . Julia, isn't it? Come on in." She looked surprised to see me again. The stone sculpture still occupied the center of the room. I moved closer and noticed that the artist's name had been removed from the card.

"I came back to take another look at this," I said, pointing to the sculpture.

"Oh?" A flicker of alarm crossed her face.

"Maybe you could give me a little information about the artist? Or should I say, what he's calling himself these days?"

I was surprised at the rush of anger I felt. The events of the last few days had worn my patience thin, and I was motivated by a feeling of protectiveness toward Gale. She'd been set up by Henry Gooding and Luca. Whatever the reasons, I didn't like it. Hilary remained quiet.

"And maybe while we're at it, you can tell me what Henry Gooding has to do with Len Ragno," I added.

Hilary took a deep breath and her shoulders dropped. "Okay . . . I guess you already know everything by now."

"Not really." My anger remained. "I'm hoping you can fill me in."

"Len's my brother. Years ago, he got into trouble with drugs. He went off the deep end and got desperate for money. He was arrested and charged and he did his time. But he was *always* a talented artist. He's clean now and he's straight."

"So why use a different name?"

"Why not? It's not against the law. Why shouldn't he call himself Luca Russoli? It suits him. And besides, who's going to want to buy high-priced art from an ex-con? I want him to stay straight and I want him to be a success. He deserves it. So what if I help promote him under a pseudonym?" She was silent a moment. "How did you find out?"

"It just so happens I saw his work at an art show the day before I walked in here. I couldn't help but notice the similarities."

"My own damn fault. I should have taken the card off that piece."

"And what does all this have to do with Henry Gooding? I know he approached Gale Hymson about an exhibit of your brother's work."

Hilary smiled then. "Henry and I are planning to be married. We've been seeing each other for some time. He found out about Len and he's been helping to promote his work. He was the one who first thought it would be a good idea to create a new identity for him." She rubbed the base of the sculpture with her hand, as if to erase her mistake. "We're not hurting anyone. I'm just trying to help my brother. I don't blame you for being upset, but, believe me, we weren't out to make fools of anyone."

As much as I didn't like it, her explanation made sense. In fact, it was the only explanation that did make sense. "I know your brother was represented by Nora Layton at his trial. She was his public defender. Do they have any other connection?"

Hilary hesitated and glanced over her shoulder. "Why don't you ask him yourself?"

THIRTY-THREE

Hilary led me to the back room where she'd served me coffee a few days before. Len was leaning against the far wall, his arms crossed on his chest.

I stared at him, unsure what to say.

"Julia," he said with no trace of an accent, "I just want you to know my sister's telling the truth. I never meant to hurt anyone. Especially Gale." He had obviously over-heard our entire conversation in the gallery. "Nora's been after me since I got out, but I don't want anything to do with her. I have no idea how she found out about my show. There were no pictures on the invitations, but she somehow knew. Maybe it was just a bad coincidence."

"I saw you two arguing outside the build-ing that night. What was that about?"

Len sighed. "She wanted me to say I'd been with her at her condo the day before. The police were questioning her about a murder. She said she was home that whole day and didn't have an alibi."

"What did you tell her?"

"I told her to go to hell. She was furious. Then she threatened to blow my cover and tell Gale and everyone who I really was." Len shook his head. "She's trouble. There's no way I want to open that can of worms. I told her she was on her own. She could do whatever the hell she wanted."

"Look, I'm not trying to cause any trouble for you."

"It doesn't matter." He smiled ruefully. "Gale gave me the boot anyway. So you can tell her whatever you want." His voice betrayed his resignation.

I wasn't going to volunteer that I'd already shown Gale his mug shot. I turned to Hilary. "I'm sorry to barge in. It's been a rough day."

Hilary walked me to the door. "Forget it. I'm sorry if your friend's upset."

"She's okay. I doubt she'll say anything, but I needed to find out what was going on."

"Just don't mess it up for him, okay? Just give him a chance." Hilary's look was pleading as I stepped outside. The lock clicked on the door behind me. As I walked slowly back to my car, the lights in the window went out.

I started the engine and pulled a U-turn, following Sacramento, a street that runs straight through Laurel Heights. I remembered jotting down Suzanne's address when I'd called her earlier and rummaged around in my purse for my notebook. I thought about calling Dani again but finally decided to go straight to Suzanne's apartment and find out for myself if she was home. At the next red light, I found the note I'd written. Suzanne lived at 430B Laurel Street. I pulled up in front of a three-story Victorian painted in different shades of blue and gray with white trim and lots of gingerbread. Several lights were on in the front windows of the building. Parking was touch-and-go on this street too but I finally found a spot around the corner between two driveways.

I headed back to Suzanne's house and pushed open the unlocked front door. I stood in a tiny vestibule with individual old-fashioned buzzers for each apartment. I buzzed number two, Suzanne's apartment. If she wasn't there, then I hoped her roommate was home. After a moment, the intercom clicked and a woman's voice answered.

"Suzanne?"

"She's not here right now." The voice was slightly lilting.

"Oh. I'm sorry to bother you then. This is Julia Bonatti from the Meyers firm. Could I talk to you a moment?"

"Sure. I'll buzz you up. Just push the door." I heard some clicks in the vicinity of the door lock and pushed the inner door open. A hallway table with a lamp and a large mirror was the only furniture in the entryway. The walls were papered in a small print designed to recall days of yesteryear. I climbed the stairway to the right which, in true Victorian fashion, was disconcertingly narrow and steep. My muscles were stiff and rebelling and my legs were sore. At the top of the stairs, I spotted an open door decorated with a small wreath of dried flowers and bay leaves. A petite blonde woman in jeans and a sweatshirt stood in the hallway. "Hi, I'm Joanna. Come on in. Your timing's good. I just got back a few minutes ago."

"Hi, Joanna." I smiled back. "Look, I don't mean to be an alarmist, but when did you last speak with or see Suzanne?"

"Well, it would have had to have been Wednesday morning. She was getting ready for work and we had coffee together. I told her I didn't think she should go in."

"Did she tell you what happened? That she'd discovered her coworker's body Sunday afternoon?"

"Yeah." Joanna nodded her head sadly. "Look, I'm her roommate and her friend, but I really couldn't say anything about this Jack guy. I knew he was a jerk and so did she. I warned her."

"What do you mean?"

"Oh, I just mean I put my two cents in and told her to be careful."

"What made you dislike him so much?"

Joanna shrugged her shoulders. "He wasn't much to look at, but he was charming and smooth. He didn't do anything for me, but who knows? Some women would find him appealing. I guess what I'm trying to say is, he didn't exactly strike me as the kind of guy who would ever help you with the groceries or feed your cat if you went out of town."

"Gotcha." I knew exactly what she meant and it pretty much echoed everybody else's opinion of Jack. I wasn't sure if that was enough reason to murder the guy, but somebody obviously had a reason.

"Did she ever talk about the relationship?"

"Not a lot. And I never really wanted to straight-out ask for any more details. As time went on she seemed less and less happy about the whole thing. I was concerned about her 'cause I know she's all alone in the city. Her family's back east somewhere. And she doesn't have any really close friends here, other than me, that I know of. She spent most of her time working."

"You know the police brought her down to the Hall of Justice for questioning on Wednesday, right?"

"Yes. She left a message for me."

"Did she come home after that?"

"I don't know. I just got back. I have to travel a lot for work."

"She was at work yesterday afternoon. Dani saw her. But now the office is closed and I haven't been able to reach her."

"Oh." Joanna's face paled.

"Could I use your phone?"

"Sure."

I dialed the number for Sergeant Sullivan from the card he'd originally given me. I tried the cell number first. He picked up on the second ring.

"Sullivan."

"Sergeant, this is Julia Bonatti from the Meyers firm."

There was a moment's hesitation. "Oh, yes?"

"I know you spoke with Suzanne Simms a couple of days ago, but I'm at her apartment with her roommate and no one's seen her since yesterday afternoon. I've been trying to reach her, but I've had no luck."

"Really? That's interesting."

"I think it's pretty alarming, don't you?"

"Considering we advised her to stay close in case we needed to talk to her again, that's right. Would her roommate like to come downtown and file a missing persons report? There's no waiting period to file and we'll see what we can do."

"I'll talk to her about it." We hung up. Sullivan didn't sound like he was going to be much help at all. Joanna listened apprehensively as I repeated my conversation with the sergeant.

"I guess I should do that. File a report."

"What kind of car does Suzanne drive?"

"It's a Nissan, dark blue."

I gave Joanna my cell number in case Suzanne checked in with her. I was getting more concerned by the minute and didn't like this one bit. I walked back to my car and managed to squeeze into the driver's seat in spite of my stiffening back. It was almost nine o'clock and I still hadn't accomplished anything at all. When I reached home, I trudged slowly up the stairs to my front door. Wizard came to greet me once again.

"Poor Wiz, all alone every day. What kind of life is this, huh?" In response, Wizard trilled deep in his throat and gently bit my hand. He followed me out to the kitchen. I made yum-yum noises and opened a can of tuna grill, one of his favorites, and filled his bowl. I downed two more aspirin and filled the tub with hot water, adding bubble bath and Epsom salts. I stripped off my clothes and stepped slowly into the tub. It was scalding hot, but it would help my muscles relax. After half an hour, I felt infinitely better but had to climb out before I fell asleep.

I dried off and pulled on a robe. In the kitchen I made a cup of tea and carried it into the office, where the light on the answering machine was blinking. The first call was from Adam to tell me he'd be in his office till ten tonight and I should call if I needed anything. The second call was Gale, reminding me about the Halloween event at the Mystic Eye tomorrow night, and the third was from Googie.

"Julia, have some interesting stuff for you. Give me a ring."

I dialed Googie's number while I sipped my tea. "Googie, it's me. What's up?"

"Well, you know your little friend with that article in the *Bay Area Gazette*?"

"Roger. Yes."

"Apparently he attended a rather weird gathering."

"Weird? How?"

"It was a very expensive, very private club, if you know what I mean, for people with, shall we say, eccentric tastes."

"Googie, be more specific please."

"You know, rubber suits, chains, hanging from rafters, and all that peculiar stuff. Me, I don't understand it at all. Somebody went too far and a young man died. There was a lot of gossip, stories circulating, and this guy was definitely a member of that group if you know what I mean. Everyone more or less knew the people involved."

"There must have been a police report. Do you know who was named?"

"No. No one wanted that kind of police attention, so anyone who was part of that crowd was shunned by anyone who had any sense. Your guy was terrified this would make the news or make the rounds. Didn't want anything to jeopardize his squeaky clean rep. He may have had nothing to do with what happened but he certainly didn't want to be named in any reckless endangerment charges or manslaughter."

"I can see why. I'm sure the Bar Association wouldn't approve."

"You got it, girl. Well, apparently he has a little political pull, called a friend of his, an assistant DA, and suddenly, lo and behold, there's no record of his name."

"Googie, how did you find all this out?"

"Oh, I have friends. Everyone was gone by the time the police got there so a lot of people were rousted and word travels fast. That's how I heard about it. He may not have been charged with anything, but people have long memories about this kind of thing."

"That's great, Googie. Thanks."

"Toodle-oo, sweetie." Googie hung up.

So that was it. That had to be what Jack Harding was holding over Roger's head. Roger couldn't afford to have it known that he was involved, even circumstantially, in a manslaughter investigation. Jack was exactly the kind of person who would use that information against him, and Jack must have threatened Nora Layton with exposure of her drug problem. I recalled Hilary's words. Someone thought that killing Jack was the only way they could survive. Jack thought nothing of sleeping with Ira's wife and didn't care if Ira knew it. The Walstone marriage had probably been over years ago because of Rita's drinking, but Jack had felt it necessary to muddy the waters further.

The only woman in his life who'd survived and prospered was his ex-wife Hilary Greene. It was hard to imagine, but it seemed Hilary was made of some very tough stuff indeed. If she really was marrying Henry Gooding, though, what possible motive would she have had to kill Jack? Just to collect on a life insurance policy? And that's assuming she even knew he hadn't changed the beneficiary. After all, to whom would he leave it? His alma mater? A favorite charity? Although Jack didn't strike me as a person who would even consider a charity, much less have a favorite one. There was no one else, only a sister who hated him so much she refused to bury him.

I finished my tea and went back to the charts on the desk. I pulled out the computer printout with the list of multiple placements of everyone's chart organized according to zodiacal degree. I looked at the correspondences between these charts again. Nothing made sense. I couldn't find the clue I needed that I was sure was there. I wrapped my robe tighter and limped back to the bedroom. It was too late for a nap and too early for bed, but my hip and leg were throbbing and my aching muscles had the last word. Ignoring the mess, I flopped across the bed sideways and pulled the blankets over me. A little sleep would help. Wizard climbed up on the bed purring, and before I knew it, my eyes closed and I slipped away.

THIRTY-FOUR

I was floating somewhere near the rafters of the empty gallery at Fort Mason, looking down at the same room that had housed the art exhibit. It was devoid of decoration now, and several large sculptures were covered in white draping. I strained to see with dreaming eyes but couldn't discern what lay under the coverings. In that knowledge peculiar to dream states, I knew that under one of the drapes was something other than a sculpture of stone. I floated down, my feet touching the floor, and became aware that I wasn't alone. A dark shadow passed in my peripheral vision. I turned and saw nothing, but when I turned back to the rows of sculptures, one of the white coverings had disappeared.

The stone was morphing, taking the form of a tall faceless figure in a black tuxedo. I needed to know who he was. My heart was beating faster but as I moved toward him the face remained blank, as if the sculptor had neglected to chisel features. The figure raised a champagne glass and, smiling, beckoned me to come closer. He pointed at another large covered shape in the center of the studio. I couldn't understand why I hadn't noticed it sooner. The dark figure reached up and grasped a small steel ball hanging from the rafters. He pulled downward and the drapery covering the sculpture became taut, finally lifting upward to reveal a dragon carved in a deep green-colored stone, the light playing on its surface as if it was made of malachite. The dragon raised its fearful head and stared at me, its tail beginning to swish back and forth. I watched, transfixed. I was afraid but couldn't move to escape the fearsome creature coming to life. Wisps of smoke curled from its nostrils and two long flames shot out as the beast reared its head with a great roar. Its tail swept the room, knocking sculptures from pedestals, shattering all in its path. Shards of stone and wood flew everywhere. With a powerful thrust of its haunches, it leapt off the pedestal toward me. Blackness obscured my vision. I awoke on the bed, sweating and shaking, filled with a deep sense of dread.

Wizard was making questioning noises in

his throat and looking at me strangely. I reached over to pat his head but he scooted away. I sat up and rubbed my eyes. Early morning light was filtering through the curtains. I'd slept all night. I stretched and cracked my neck, trying to recover fragments of my dream. It made no sense, but dragons were stalking me, forcing themselves into my consciousness.

Stumbling to the bathroom, I splashed water on my face and drank a few sips from my cupped hand. I felt hot and dehydrated. Then I padded out to the kitchen, fed Wizard, and put the kettle on for coffee. Once the caffeine kicked in, I hopped in the shower and dressed. I straightened up the bedroom as much as possible and glanced at the clock. Nine o'clock. Perfect time to visit David as I'd promised. If I left now, I'd probably reach him just as the breakfast dishes were being cleared away. I wondered if he was enjoying the porridge a little more.

I made a pass through the apartment compiling a mental list of what needed to be done. The sofa cushions could be repaired, nothing valuable was broken or stolen, but I'd need to buy another set of sheets, pillows, and a comforter. I rarely entertained — well, maybe one client at a time — but it would be nice to have more than two dishes. Whoever had trashed my apartment had broken almost every single dish, cup, and saucer. They hadn't had the time or inclination to destroy the wine glasses in the rack above the sink. I thanked the stars my office had been left untouched; my computer and my laptop were safe and my client files hadn't been disturbed. That would have been horrible and expensive. I dreaded to think anyone could have harmed Wizard. I could only guess the intruder hadn't had enough time. Or was there some logic to the fact that what was damaged was personal and intimate? The door from the laundry room had to have been the avenue of escape. Perhaps he or she was bolting down the street just as I was surveying the damage. The clothes that had been destroyed were old. They were my faves, things I wore every day, but I could live without them. Thanks to my grandmother, they could be replaced. I still couldn't shake the feeling of being invaded. I made sure the deadbolts on the back door were in place and the window over the kitchen sink was locked. I still had to deal with my downstairs neighbors and a new garage opener but in the meantime the locks would protect me.

I hurried down the front stairs and climbed into my car. Pulling a U-turn, I drove up the hill to Geary and over to St. Joseph's. On the way I stopped at a bakery and bought three jelly donuts. I hoped Caroline would forgive me. When I arrived at David's room, Caroline was reading. I took a peek at her book cover. It featured a large bloodstained knife. "Good book?" I asked.

She looked up. "Hi, Julia!" Then she smiled. "Yes. I'm thinking of committing a crime right about now myself. What's in the bag?"

"I'll give you three guesses. I hope you don't mind. There's one for each of us." I looked around. "Where is he?"

She shook her head. "In there." She indicated the bathroom. "He's getting dressed and wants to go home."

"Well, that's good."

She made a face of disapproval. "Not if the doctor advised him to stay one more day, it isn't."

"I hope you'll forgive the jelly donuts. I took pity on him."

She smiled. "Pass that bag over, I'm starving." I sat next to her and opened the bag, handing her a napkin. She reached in daintily and retrieved one of the donuts encrusted with sugar. She took a bite. "Oh, yummy. I can't remember the last time I ate one of these. I make sure to never keep these in the house. David would inhale them all in one sitting." I joined her with a donut of my own just as David exited the bathroom fully dressed.

"Oh my word," he said. "You remembered. Thank you. I hope you two aren't going to eat them all." He sat on the edge of the bed and pulled the rolling tray closer.

"You get one," Caroline said. "Just one. Julia was kind enough to bring one for each of us."

"Couldn't come at a better time. All I had this morning was that dreary slop in a bowl. I can't wait to get home."

"How are you feeling?" I asked.

"Terrific. I've never felt better. This was all a tempest in a teapot. I'm just sorry Caroline got so scared." He took a large bite of the donut. "So, Julia, any news? Any new developments? I don't know what that sergeant is up to. I called him yesterday and he hemmed and hawed and said he'd keep me in the loop. In other words, nothing!"

"Not much," I lied. "I did discover a few things, though."

"Tell me."

"Well, quite by accident, I learned that Dani's boyfriend, who I met the other night, works delivering pizzas part time, and he was the person who delivered to the building the day of Jack's murder."

"Really? That's interesting. Dani didn't say anything."

"He might never have mentioned it to her. Maybe she didn't know at the time. And you know my theory about the Bank of San Francisco fire . . ."

"Oh, what's that about?" Caroline asked, wiping her fingertips on a napkin.

I turned to her. "Of the three people who received death threats — Jack, Ira, and Suzanne — the one thing all three have in common is that they worked on the trial that resulted from the fire. They represented the insurance company that paid a settlement to the widow of the man who died in the fire."

"I remember all that. It was so horrible and so unnecessary."

"But here's the thing." I turned to David. "There was another death connected with that event."

David's eyebrows rose. "I don't remember that."

"You wouldn't. It happened a couple of years later. The electrical contractor took the brunt of the blame. He wasn't charged, but he lost his license and later committed suicide."

"How awful," Caroline said.

David shrugged. "I agree, but I don't really see what that has to do with our firm."

"I read through the trial transcripts, at least the ones before the settlement was hammered out, and Jack Harding destroyed that guy in deposition and on the stand in court. He was really brutal."

"I believe it. That was his MO. He was a pit bull in court. Juries never liked him but he was a good trial attorney nonetheless." David sat lost in thought for a moment. "You really think that case could be connected? Couldn't the contractor have committed suicide for other reasons?"

"I keep going back in my mind to something Hilary said to me. She said that somebody must have felt that killing Jack was the only way they could survive."

THIRTY-FIVE

I dialed Suzanne's apartment as soon as I returned home. Joanna answered immediately. She'd made the official missing persons report and managed to talk to Sergeant Sullivan, who took an interest now that one of his suspects was AWOL. Suzanne had last been seen around four o'clock on Thursday afternoon, over a day and a half ago. I couldn't help but wonder if she was just once again avoiding everyone and hiding out at some hotel in the city. I wished now I'd asked her where she had stayed before. If she'd gone to ground again, she might have chosen the same place. Hotels in San Francisco are prohibitively expensive, but there were plenty of less expensive spots to stay along Lombard Street. So many, in fact, it would be impossible to call each one. I really hoped that was where she was but I couldn't quell the uneasy feeling that she was next on the killer's list.

The phone rang. It was Gale. "What time are you coming down?"

"I have some errands to take care of, but I'll be there as soon as I've finished. You're starting at four o'clock?"

"Yup. And we have tons of snacks and drinks to lay out. If you're free, it would be a big help. And I know you'll look so cute in the cat costume I got. Can you wear black, though? Wear your black jeans and a black leotard if you have one. Oh, and a pair of black flats."

I sighed. "Okay."

"It'll make sense when you get here. So many people are coming. All our readers and our regular customers. People you haven't seen for a while. Zora's doing readings and Jonathan is doing Tarot and Nikolai wants to do a special presentation. Should be lots of fun. See you soon. Ciao."

By the time I arrived at the Eye, Cheryl had already done most of the work. Gale had hired a crew to decorate the main room with orange and black crepe paper streamers and spotlights on top of the tall bookcases. Cheryl's window decorating project was stunning. She was putting the finishing touches on a long table groaning with bowls of fruit, platters of cookies and chips, and several different kinds of crackers and cheeses. There were non-alcoholic drinks and a punch bowl full of some sort of pumpkin-colored beverage. Creepy horror music played in the background and dry ice in several containers added to the atmosphere. Cheryl was sporting a witch's costume and Gale was decked out in something exotic that suggested an escapee from a Turkish harem, face veil and all. Zora had set up in a private room and Jonathan in another. Ten minute readings were ten dollars, with the reader keeping the take.

Nikolai, dressed in street clothes, was there when I arrived. "Where are your robes?" I asked him.

"Ah, Julia, twice in one week!" He bent down and kissed the back of my hand. "I vill vear my black robes tonight. You'll see."

Gale grasped my hand. "Come to the back and get dressed. You'll love this little outfit." I followed her into the office and shut the door behind us as she handed me several items. "Here it is. These furry elastic things, you slip over your ankles and your shoes, and here's a tail to attach and fuzzy fingerless gloves with cat ears and a mask."

"Well, thanks for this. You know me, I'd just have come in everyday clothes if you hadn't done this."

"We'll have tons of people, I think. Free snacks, readings, and a floor show. Would you mind taking a turn at the counter? We should have lots of sales too."

"Not at all. I'm here to help out any way I can."

"Good girl. And I'm sure all our neighbors will be coming by too. I've had a newspaper ad running in the local North Beach paper, plus publicity on all sorts of social media sites thanks to Cheryl. I can't let the Mystic Eye miss an opportunity like Halloween. If this goes well, maybe we can make it a regular thing."

Zora was circling the table with a paper plate, sampling all the goodies, ensuring she had energy for the evening. As four o'clock neared, we spotted the first group of costumed guests waiting outside on the sidewalk. Four young girls and two guys. We opened the doors and welcomed them in. One of the girls added her name to the blackboard for a Tarot reading while her friends headed for the food table.

Nikolai, now in his robes, took up a position by the door to welcome visitors. Within a half hour, the room was crowded. About a third of the guests were in costume, the rest in civvies. My eye caught a man in a dragon costume — a large papier-mâché head with eyeholes and a cape with a long train made from shiny golden scales. Another dragon! They were everywhere. From the conversations I overheard, the younger people all seemed to be heading to parties later in the evening, and a few asked if we could store their purchases until the next day.

I joined Cheryl behind the counter. "Let me give you a hand."

"Thanks. I could use some help." Cheryl rang up the next customer and bagged his purchases. She turned to me and whispered, "Gale told me about the break in at your apartment. Why didn't you call me?"

"I would have if Gale hadn't answered right away. Turned out she was close by. I'm really okay, just a bit shaken and left with a mess to clean up."

"You know, I have your back too. If you ever have any trouble again, you make sure you call me."

"I will. I promise."

"You better." She glared at me for a moment, then squeezed my hand.

We manned the counter for the next half hour, racking up sales. Zora and Jonathan had a line of customers waiting for readings, and the ambient noise and chatter in the large room grew until Cheryl and I could barely hear ourselves speak. She turned to me. "Phew! We've never been so busy. It was a great idea to do this. I was afraid we'd go through all this work for nothing."

I spotted my grandmother in the crowd. She waved and worked her way toward the counter. "Hello, Cheryl! How are you?"

"I'm great. So nice to see you again, Gloria. I'm glad you could stop by."

"Well, I thought I'd walk over and wish you all the best. This is a lovely idea of Gale's. You know," she said, leaning across the counter toward Cheryl to speak quietly, "a lot of my friends from the church think the Mystic Eye is a den of iniquity."

"Well, I hope you've straightened them out," Cheryl replied.

"I have, I certainly have. And I tell them how popular my lovely granddaughter is too." She smiled at me. "And about all the wonderful books, not to mention books on religion, too, and the jewelry and perfumed oils. Father Hewitt at Saints Peter and Paul doesn't approve of anything that smacks of paganism, but he's . . . well, he's rather intellectually limited, in my opinion."

Cheryl smiled broadly. "That's good of you. This is a wonderful shop and it saved my life when I moved back to the city."

Gloria patted Cheryl's hand in encouragement and turned to me. "I can't stay, dear, but I just wanted to pop by and say hello. I have to hurry back. It'll be dark soon and Kuan's manning our doors in case any trick-or-treaters show up early." She turned back to Cheryl. "Sadly, we don't get as many children as we used to, not like when Julia was growing up. So many families have moved away." She shook her head. "Too crowded and expensive for them, I guess."

I moved around the counter and gave my grandmother a hug. "Want me to walk you back?"

Gloria laughed. "No, I think you better stay right here in your cat outfit."

I smiled. "Say hi to Kuan for me."

"I will, dear." She turned away and began to maneuver through the crowd to the front door.

Gloria had no sooner headed for home than Cheryl and I were deluged with even more customers buying books and candles and jewelry. We rang up their purchases and bagged them as fast as we could.

When we finally had a lull, I said, "Why don't you take a break, Cheryl? Grab a little food before we get another rush?"

"Thanks, I think I will. Does your grand-mother know about the break-in?"

"No, certainly not."

"Good thing I didn't open mouth, insert foot."

"That was smart. I'd never hear the end of it and you'd worry her to death."

"I figured. Be right back." Cheryl ducked under the wooden hatch and weaved through groups of people toward the food table.

Gale suddenly appeared next to me. "Isn't this wonderful?" she breathed. "I think a lot of people are discovering the Eye for the first time. I wish I'd lined up more readers though. I think Zora and Jonathan are going to be pretty drained by the time this evening is over. I really never expected this large a crowd. I thought we'd have a sedate little gathering with a few new people stopping in."

"Hey, free food, free drinks even if they are non-alcoholic, discounted readings, and Nikolai — how could they resist? What exactly is he going to do?"

"I'm really not sure," Gale replied hesitantly. "He said it would be a surprise. I'm just glad he was willing to be here tonight. He's probably the biggest celebrity in the occult world in San Francisco." She raised her eyebrows and made a concerned face. "I just hope he doesn't do anything too outré. With him, you never know."

When Cheryl returned, I slipped out from behind the counter and grabbed a mini sandwich and a few potato chips. The food table looked like an invasion from the Russian army had taken place. I cleaned up as much as I could, then lugged a box from the storeroom and refilled the bowls of chips and platters of sandwich swirls. The drinks had held up well in the large cooler under the table even though the ice had melted.

At seven thirty, Gale stepped to the middle of the room and hit the large gong that was a permanent fixture in the store. The sound reverberated through the busy chatter. I was reminded of her performance at the Fort Mason art show. "Hi everyone," she said. "Thanks so much for joining in with us on this magical evening. As you all know, we have a special appearance by Nikolai." A cheer erupted around the room and a few people whistled. "Yes," Gale said, smiling, "I know how you feel. Nikolai is one in a million and we're so happy he could join us tonight."

Someone in the crowd shouted, "We want to see demons!" More people cheered and clapped. Jonathan and Zora had left their respective reading rooms to join the crowd. Jonathan carried a straight-backed chair to the center of the room and stepped away.

Cheryl whispered to me, "I don't know about demons. At least I hope that's not what he's doing, but he really wouldn't tell anyone."

Gale glanced over her shoulder as Nikolai in his long black robes, his gray beard shining in the low-level lighting, headed for the center of the room. "And here he is, in the flesh. Welcome Nikolai, everyone!" The room erupted again in cheers and applause.

Nikolai acknowledged the greeting and raised his hands for silence. He bowed his head as if saying a silent prayer and then looked up. Gale dimmed the lights even more and a somber mood settled over the room.

"Tanks, everyone," Nikolai began. "Tonight I vould like to do sometink different. Because this is a very special night, a night when the veil between the vorlds can be lifted for a short while, I would like to haf a volunteer. Someone who isn't afraid to remember their past."

The room became still. Many people glanced around. Many wondered if they should volunteer but no one stepped forward. Nikolai scanned the crowd, his eyes finally resting on a young woman almost hidden behind taller people. He stepped toward her and the crowd parted. The woman looked up at the large man in the black robes, her eyes wide. "You, my little one. I choose you." Nikolai took her by the hand and led her to the chair. She sat and fussed with the sleeves of her sweater. She was nervous. Nikolai kneeled on one knee close to the shy woman and whispered in her ear. She nodded in response. He stood and turned to the room. "Ve must haf absolute silence now." Standing behind his subject, he rested his hands on her shoulders and began to speak.

"Close your eyes. You are totally relaxed. Picture a varm beach and soft sand under your body. The varmth is moving up your legs, now to your spine and to your shoulders and neck. You are in total control but your eyes are closing . . ." The woman seemed to be fighting the urge to close her eyes, but she finally did. Perhaps Nikolai had chosen a good subject for hypnosis. "Ve are going back . . . back . . . back to vhen this problem first began. You vill remember, remember the tings dat caused you to hide yourself, to fear."

Nikolai waited. The room held a collective breath. "You are dere. Tell me vhat you see." The woman began to speak in a strong, deep voice, a voice that couldn't possibly come from her petite body. I was transfixed.

"There's blood. I am killing him." Someone gasped. "Oh, the blood!"

"Who are you killing?" Nikolai asked in a
calm voice.

"He . . . he . . . he hurt my daughter. He's
come back. He thinks he can do what he
wants . . . I'll show him. I'll make him pay.
I'll hurt him like he hurt her. I just wish I
was stronger. I could make him suffer more.
A knife is too good for him."

"Are you alone?"

"Yes. My husband is dead. There's no one
to protect us."

"Who is this man?"

"A soldier."

"What color is his uniform?"

"Red. All red. He has a black hat."

"What are you doing now?"

"I am stabbing him," she snarled.
"Blood . . . everywhere . . . red . . . blood."
The woman uttered a shriek, her arm rising
and falling in a feverish mime of stabbing
motions. Her voice rose. She spoke rapidly,
desperately, in a panicked tone in words that
were not English. French perhaps? A chill
ran up my spine.

"Can you tell me the year?"

The woman shook her head.

"Who is king?"

". . . *Louis. Louis le bien aimé.*"

Nikolai spoke soothingly. "You are safe. You are very safe."

The woman became more agitated. "I must hide him. I must bury him while the ground is still soft. Before the frost comes. Before anyone discovers what I have done."

Nikolai calmed her. "I vant you to disengage for a moment. You are safe here. How do you feel?"

"Good." She breathed deeply. "A quick death is too good for him, but I am satisfied. I am happy he is dead. Happy I have done this thing."

"You took revenge but you defended a loved one. You had to do dis ting. Dere is no further need for guilt. No longer in dis life. You vill not be afraid to stand up for yourself, to speak up for yourself. You have suffered enough. You vill come back now. You vill only remember dose tings that cause you no pain. You vill remember dey can no longer hurt you. Dat vas all in the past. You must let go." Nikolai took a deep breath. "On the count of ten, you are coming back. One . . . two . . ." Silence enveloped the entire room. "Ten. Open your eyes."

The gathering waited in deathly silence. Finally the young woman opened her eyes. Her face was wreathed in smiles and tears streamed down her face. Nikolai knelt next to her once more and, their heads together, they whispered to each other. She nodded and grasped his hand and rose from the chair. Another woman stepped forward and took her friend's hands. She smiled at Nikolai and thanked him. She put an arm around her friend and led her out of the shop. People parted to make way for them. The entire room breathed a sigh of relief. Two people were crying. I felt tears well up in my eyes as well.

Gale, standing next to me, signaled to Cheryl to put some music on, but the party atmosphere was gone as if a tidal wave had swept through the room. Nikolai turned and approached us.

"Well, you certainly put a great big damper on our party, didn't you?" Gale said accusingly with a smile on her face.

"Vell, that vas not my intent. Revenge is a terrible ting. Understandable, but guilt is ultimate result. But the poor little ting. She vas tied to the past and crippled with guilt. She could not move on. I saw her in the crowd and I knew she vas the one who needed me."

Gale patted him on the arm. "Thank you. That was an amazing experience. We all felt it. I believe you did help that woman." She turned to me. "It's almost eight thirty. Maybe we should start clearing up so we can close right at nine."

"I think lots of people are leaving." I looked around. A line of customers was standing at the counter with items in their hands. "I'll ring them up." I slipped behind the counter and nodded to the first customer, a man with several books in his arms. It took another half hour before Cheryl and I had handled all the purchases.

I heard a loud crash and looked across the room. One of the smaller tables had tipped over, spilling books across the floor. It was the man in the dragon costume. Somehow his tail had become entangled in the table leg. As he'd moved away, the table went with him and plates of leftover food fell to the floor. Like my dream in which the dragon's swishing tail caused havoc. The man apologized profusely to Gale and then shed his robe. He began picking up the debris from the floor. Gale waved away his apologies and joined him to clear up.

The dragon's tail. I drifted away, staring into space. Cheryl glanced over at me. "Julia, are you all right? Hey!" She shook my arm.

I turned to her. "The dragon's tail." She looked at me questioningly. "I think . . . it's what Nikolai said about his subject: *She could not move on.*"

"What?"

"The *Cauda Draconis.*" I hurried to a bookcase in the far corner where the astrology books were displayed. I grabbed an ephemeris and counted the degrees. "It must be," I mumbled. She was born with the South Node of the Moon conjunct her Sun. She was fifty-five years old. I counted the degrees. Solar arc Pluto had advanced to her natal Sun and her South Node. She was the widow I had been searching for. How had I missed this? The South Node, the *Cauda Draconis,* the tail of the dragon, the point of karmic undoing. And now Pluto was activating this unfortunate aspect. She could not move on. She could not escape the past. She had nursed her pain for a long time and now was lashing out. Karen Jansen was a very dangerous woman.

"I have to go, Cheryl."

"What? Now?"

"There's something I have to make sure of."

"Where are you going?"

"Right down the street. To David's offices. I have a very bad feeling about something." Cheryl followed me to the back. I pulled off my cat accessories and did my best to scrub

399

off the whiskers Gale had drawn on my cheeks.

Cheryl watched silently. "I don't think you should go alone."

"Adam has security at the firm. I won't be alone. Don't worry, I'll come back for my car later. It's quicker if I walk." Cheryl sighed in response. "I could be wrong, but I don't think I am." I slipped on my jacket and tucked my cell phone into a pocket of my jeans, putting my parking card and the key to the firm in the other pocket. "Lock this back door after me."

Before Cheryl could speak again, I hurried down the alley and across Broadway. It was just a few blocks to the Montgomery Street building. A nighttime mist had turned the streets into glistening black ribbons. I ran, crossing Pine and Sacramento and arrived, out of breath, at the glass front doors. Suzanne was in danger. I was sure of it. And if my hunch was correct, she was inside. She'd never left the firm on Thursday evening. I said a silent prayer that she was alive and that I could find her.

The lobby was brightly lit and empty. The revolving door in the center of the entrance was securely locked, but my key card would work on one of the two doors at either end. I swiped my card, heard the click, and pushed the door open. A row of sagging pumpkins sat along the concierge's counter: the contest entries from the week, now soft, their features sagging into bizarre expressions like melted wax.

When the elevator came, I stepped in, waved my key card at the little red light, and hit the button for the 41st floor. The doors closed and the elevator descended! Desperate, I pressed the button for 41 and kept it depressed, as if willing the elevator to move upward. Instead, it kept descending slowly.

THIRTY-SIX

I took a deep breath and pulled myself together. I knew what would be waiting for me when the doors opened. Two different guards, not the men I had met earlier in the week, were facing me. One man was younger, well over six feet and two hundred pounds, who looked like he might be of Pacific Islander descent. He stepped inside, blocking the doors from closing. The other man, older and red-faced with a prominent belly, looked me up and down. Belatedly I realized that my whiskers were still smeared on my face and I'd forgotten to remove my tail, which peeked out from my jacket.

"Step out of the elevator, please, ma'am," he said.

"I have to go up to the 41st floor. I work here. I work for David Meyers at the Meyers firm," I said as I stepped out.

"I didn't hear about any costume party in the building tonight, did you?" he asked his colleague, smirking. The younger man, unsmiling, ignored the sarcasm.

"Look, you don't understand . . ."

"No, lady, you don't understand. The firm is closed. No one is there tonight, and if you really work here, as you say you do, then you'll know there's been a murder on that floor and another one in the parking area. Only private security is allowed up there."

"A woman has gone missing and I think she's being held up there."

The older guard did a double take, then shook his head. "I don't think so. I think that's the craziest damn thing I ever heard."

"Please. Call Sergeant Sullivan at the Hall of Justice. Talk to him. I think I'm right, and if I am, she's in danger."

I could see the wheels turning behind his Neanderthal brow. It was slowly occurring to him that he might be the one to take any blame.

"I can give you his number."

"Oh, we have it. We're supposed to let him know about any suspicious activity."

"Then call him. Please. And let me go up there. If there's nothing to find and I'm wrong, then I'll go away and leave you alone."

We were at a standoff. I needed him to release the elevator and he needed to protect his job. He flashed a questioning look at the other guard, who hadn't changed his position, and turned back to me. "I'll give you ten minutes to look around. That's all. And then I'm calling the security guy. I want to see you back down here and out of the building. Don't even think about coming back again later because unless I program it, that elevator isn't going anywhere. Sergio." He turned to the younger guard. "Take her up. Don't let her out of your sight and then bring her back down." He shot a glare at me. "Ten minutes."

"Okay." Sergio nodded. I stepped back into the elevator and he followed me. The older guard returned to his console and the doors finally closed. The elevator moved upward, directly to the 41st floor.

When we reached it, Sergio slipped a key into a lock below the keypad. "I'm holding this car here so we can go down without waiting." We stepped into the corridor and Sergio followed me to the door to the attorneys' offices. "Look," he said, "I'll be watching you, but this place makes me nervous after what's been happening in the building."

I used the key David had given me and pushed the door open. Frankly, the very fact of the guard's presence made me feel a whole lot more secure. I reached around to flick on the overhead light but nothing happened. The room remained in darkness. Sergio pulled a flashlight out of his back pocket. "Lights not working? I don't like this," he mumbled. "I'll hold the flashlight for you while you look."

I felt cold and clammy even under my clothing. I moved slowly past the desks and closed office doors, Sergio's flashlight following my progress. I ducked under the yellow tape and opened the door to Jack's office, and again tried the lights. Nothing. The main switch to the whole area had apparently been turned off. I waited a moment for my eyes to adjust to the darkness, then felt my way over to the desk to try the lamp. No luck. Why would all the electricity to this section be off when the motion lights had just worked in the corridor? I moved as silently as possible around the room and felt my way to the coat closet that I remembered was there. Sergio was still tracking me with his beam of light. I opened the closet door. My foot hit something soft and bulky. At the same moment, I heard a crash. Sergio's flashlight made a crazy pattern on the walls as it flew through the air and landed on the floor.

"Sergio," I called out. No answer. I fell to

my knees and reached out. My fingers touched a wool garment and a sweatered arm. Without a flashlight I was blind, but I was sure it was Suzanne. I felt warmth and touched the side of her neck. There was a pulse. I shook her arm but got no response. She was unconscious but not dead. I leaned closer and whispered in her ear, "Suzanne . . . can you hear me?"

I sensed a shift in the atmosphere and heard ragged breathing. In the dark, I crawled backward away from the closet and felt my way to the side of the desk, hunkering down. If I was blind, so was Karen. The sound of her breath came closer. A low sound, almost a growl, and thumping footsteps on the carpeting. She was at the closet door. Another sound. I imagined her foot making contact with Suzanne's prone body. She waited for a response from the prostrate figure. When none came, she moved away.

Where was Sergio? Was he unconscious? Surely if we didn't return soon, the guard downstairs would start to worry. Would he call one of Adam's security guards or the police? Or would he be afraid of losing his job and decide to come up himself? That would be deadly.

My senses were on full alert. The room felt empty. Was she gone? If only I could see something, anything, even a glimmer of light. I crawled slowly away from the desk to move to the closet, hoping to wake an unconscious Suzanne. Then I heard sounds, grunting sounds, from the central room. She was struggling with something heavy. Sergio? Was she strong enough to move an unconscious man? Under cover of this noise, I crept forward. Staying low, I moved to just outside Jack's door. I stepped silently in the dark, reaching the space between the two secretarial desks. The sounds were now coming from the corridor outside. Was she dragging Sergio's body to the elevator? I was desperately casting about for some object I could use to defend myself. I remembered the stun gun I'd seen in Dani's desk. I knelt. Sliding open the bottom drawer as quietly as possible, I felt around for the small black object. I could only pray it was fully loaded with batteries. My fingers finally felt something hard and plastic. It was in my grip, but now I had to quietly close the drawer that blocked me and leave my temporary shelter before it was too late.

I pushed the drawer closed, holding it with my fingers before it made a final metallic click that could give me away. My heart was pounding. Taking a deep breath, I moved forward, hoping to stay invisible and escape the central room. If I could reach the elevator, I could get downstairs and find help. Where was the security detail? Had Adam found someone to cover the shift tonight? If not, maybe Adam himself was here.

Sergio had locked the elevator in place when we first arrived. From my angle I could see the area in front of the elevators. I could tell the doors were still open because light from the interior spilled into the hallway in a bright rectangle. I moved closer to the door to the corridor. Sergio's prone body was half in and half out of the elevator. Where had she gone? And why had she left him like that? I couldn't tell if he was dead or only unconscious. If I could reach him, and if I was strong enough, it might be possible to drag him into the elevator with me and get us both to safety. I'd have to find his key to release the elevator. If I could hook my hands under his arms and pull him backward all the way into the elevator we could both escape.

I slid the stun gun into a pocket of my jacket and hunkered down, rushing toward the elevator door. As I stepped over Sergio's jutting legs, I felt a rush of air and a hand grabbed my arm. I was pulled backward and flung across the corridor, away from the waiting elevator doors. I hit the wall, winded, and slid down. She loomed over me and reached out to grab me again. I rolled away and stood up as fast as I could. I ducked under her outstretched arm and ran down the hall toward David's office. If I could get inside, I could lock myself in and call for help. The key was in my pocket. I pulled it out and struggled to fit it into the lock in the semi-darkness.

She moved swiftly. My fingers fumbled and the key slipped out of my hand. As I reached down to find it, I heard a rush of air and sensed something coming at me. I ducked and jumped to the other side of the corridor. A heavy crack rang out as an axe cut into the hard wood of David's door. The axe from the emergency cabinet. She grunted as she struggled to pull the weapon out of the wood. This was my chance. I turned and ran back toward the elevator, but she was too fast. She cried out as she tackled me in the dark. I landed face-down on the carpeting. Her grip was strong. Her fingers curled into my hair. She lifted my head and banged my face into the carpet. I felt blood flowing from my nose. As my head was pulled back once more, I twisted and with all my strength hit the side of her rib cage with my elbow. I heard a gasp, and her grip on my head loosened. I rolled over and managed to pull one knee up against the weight of her body. I clawed for her eyes but missed as she pulled her head back and grabbed for my throat. I kicked upward and she released her grip. I kicked again and pushed her off. I scrambled up, holding onto the wall for support.

"You don't have to do this, Karen," I gasped. "I know everything. I understand now."

"Do you?" her voice snarled in the darkened corridor. "You, all of you, you filthy lawyers, bloodsuckers, you killed him. You killed me, you took my life, and every single one of you is going to pay for that."

"Maybe he *was* unfairly accused, but that doesn't give you the right to take a life." My fingers felt for the hard plastic casing of the stun gun in my pocket.

The ambient light from the elevator highlighted her frame. "You couldn't possibly understand. Watching him day after day, shunned by everyone, losing his license, slandered in court by those bastards. He did *nothing* wrong. There was *nothing* wrong with his work. He was a convenient scapegoat. Pin the blame on him while everyone else walked away with a bundle of cash." She sneered. "*He* couldn't defend himself. He couldn't hire lawyers to clear his name.

But that didn't concern any of them."

My mind was racing. Where was Adam's security? At least thirty minutes had elapsed. I slid the stun gun out of my pocket very slowly, hoping she wouldn't spot the movement in the darkened hallway. "Nobody killed your husband, Karen." I spoke quietly, almost a whisper. "Nobody took his life. He killed himself."

She lunged at me. Howling. I wheeled away from her and as she reached out, I stepped closer and shoved the stun gun against her neck. I pressed the trigger. My hand vibrated as the electrical charge coursed through her body. She trembled and uttered a gagging sound, finally crashing to the floor.

I leaned against the wall and slid down. My legs were shaking. I could barely breathe. The overhead lights flickered on, temporarily blinding me. Someone stood at the end of the corridor. Adam. It was Adam. I sobbed in relief.

THIRTY-SEVEN

Adam rushed to my side. "Julia. My God. Are you all right?"

I nodded. I couldn't speak.

He reached down and helped me stand, then picked up the stun gun and slipped it into his pocket. "Are you hurt?" he asked tenderly.

"I'm more shaken than hurt."

Adam kneeled next to Karen and felt for her pulse. He straightened out her body, securing her hands and ankles with plastic ties. "She'll be okay in a few minutes. Good thing I got here when I did."

"You have to help Suzanne. She's in the closet in Jack's office. And one of the guards is unconscious by the elevator."

"I saw. Just wait here for a moment." Adam hurried down the hall to the litigation section. He returned a moment later. "I tried to wake her but I think she's been drugged. She's breathing okay, though. The paramedics can have a look at her when they get here."

I felt like bursting into tears in relief. "Where was your security guard tonight?"

"He called to tell me he was down with the flu and I arranged for someone else, who obviously didn't show up. I just stopped by to check up on him and the guard downstairs told me a woman had been let up to the 41st floor."

"Sergio, the guard. How is he?"

"He's out cold. Concussion, I think. Looks like she clobbered him with a fire extinguisher. I just called an ambulance for him. They'll be here soon." He reached for my shoulders. "Here, let's get you into David's office. You can rest on the sofa until the police arrive."

"Okay." My legs didn't want to cooperate. I wasn't sure whether from fright or injury. And I'd have more bruises soon. "The key . . ." I pointed to the floor. "I tried to get inside and lock myself in, but she was too fast."

"I'll get it." Adam scanned the floor, picked up the small key ring, and unlocked the door. He led me into the outer office and helped me out of my jacket. I collapsed on the sofa. Adam pulled a handkerchief out of his pocket and wiped my face where my nose had bled. "Stay here and relax. You've had a struggle and a shock."

He left, shutting the door behind him. A moment later I heard the elevator ding. Perhaps Sergio had regained consciousness and Adam was helping him into the elevator. Or maybe the police had arrived. I closed my eyes and leaned back on the cushions. I was crashing after the adrenaline high. I stirred myself a few minutes later. I needed to call the Eye and let Gale and Cheryl know I wouldn't make it back tonight. I could pick up my car in the morning. I was sure Adam would drive me home. I stood, my legs still a little shaky, and walked to the phone on the desk. Then I remembered that my cell phone was in my pocket. I dialed the Eye and Cheryl answered immediately.

"What's going on, Julia?"

"Everything's fine. I found Suzanne, the woman who's been missing. And Adam's here with me. We've called the police. They should be here soon."

"Well, that's good news. I'm glad you're not alone. We didn't want to leave in case you called. You're sure you're all right?"

"Yes. Couldn't be better." *Except for a bloody nose and a few bruises.* "I'll come by tomorrow and get my car. Is it okay if I leave

414

it there tonight?"

"Of course. Don't worry about it. I'll call you tomorrow."

"Thanks, Cheryl." We hung up. I breathed a sigh of relief that the worst was over. I wanted to find Adam and see what he was dealing with. I tried to turn the door handle but it wouldn't budge. Had it locked automatically? Where was the key? I knocked on the door and called out to Adam. No answer. "Adam?" I called again, feeling a rush of fright.

"I'm here. Come on out," he responded.

"I can't. I think the door's locked from the outside."

"Oh, sorry. Hang on." The door opened. I stepped out to the corridor and pulled the door closed behind me. The hallway lights were now on, but Karen was no longer on the floor. Had she managed to remove the plastic ties?

"Where is she?"

"I took her down in the elevator. The security guards are with her. She's not going anywhere."

A strange odor assailed my nose. "What's that smell?"

"I don't smell anything," Adam replied.

"It's smells like . . ." The phone in my pocket trilled. I had a text. I reached into my pocket and pulled it out. It was a text, two texts from Don. I clicked on the first one.

"Who is it?" Adam asked.

"Oh, it's from Don, my friend at the *Chronicle.* I forgot I asked him to look up some stuff for me." The first text said, *Look what I found. Elva and her son in a Minnesota newspaper.* I opened the second text and saw a clear photo of Elva Ward, aka Karen Jansen, and . . . I froze. The man next to her — the face caught by the camera — was Adam Schaeffer. A jolt of fear shot through me.

Adam was watching me carefully. I did my best to cover my shock. "It's nothing. Don . . . uh . . . Don found a photo of Terrence Ward in a local newspaper." I was certain the blood had drained from my face. I attempted a smile.

"Why don't you show me?" Adam advanced and held out his hand. The voice that had seemed so comforting a moment ago now held a hint of threatening power underneath. My mind reeled. How could I have been so blind?

"It's nothing . . . really." I tried to slip the phone back into my pocket but Adam was too fast. He snatched it from my hand and opened the text. His face hardened. I stayed

416

perfectly still, my knees beginning to quiver in fear. He looked up at me with dead eyes.

"I'm so sorry, Julia. This wasn't the way it was supposed to go."

I took a step back, away from him, pressed against the door to David's office. I felt the key in the lock against my spine. "How was it supposed to go?"

"I thought . . . well, it's too late now, isn't it?"

My heart sank. "There's no ambulance coming, is there?"

Adam shook his head. "No police either. You've left me with a real mess to clean up. What am I going to do with the guard and with you?" He shook his head. "It's too bad . . ."

A red plastic container sat against the wall of the corridor. Gasoline. That's what I'd smelled. They planned to set a fire. I had to escape. I slid a hand behind my back and felt for the key. "So you and Karen . . ." I had to keep him talking. I slid the key quietly out of the lock. "Where is she?" The door to the emergency stairway was on the other side of the elevator bank. This key would work to get out of the stairwell. If only I could run, but he blocked my path.

"She's taken Suzanne downstairs to the van. We should have taken care of that

417

earlier, but we couldn't. We couldn't get her out without being seen. Now we're going to take both of you out of here. Sergio's still unconscious. He saw nothing."

"You'll never get away with this. I told the guard downstairs to call Sergeant Sullivan. The police are already on their way."

Adam smiled sadly. "I doubt that. I just called to let him know Sergio was fine and the situation is under control."

"Why, Adam? Karen I can almost understand, but you . . ."

"He wasn't my biological father, but he was my father in every other sense of the word. He didn't deserve what was done to him by Harding and the others. We've bided our time and worked hard to get this far and we *will* get away with it. Every single person who had a hand in destroying him will die."

I thought of Don at the *Chronicle.* Eventually he'd learn something had happened to me and put two and two together. But by then it would be too late.

"Go get your jacket." He reached around me and opened the door to David's office. I walked to the sofa and picked up my jacket, praying Adam hadn't noticed the key was no longer in the lock. "You were never here. Make sure you leave nothing behind," he added. He watched while I turned away and slipped my arms into my jacket. I pushed the key under the sleeve of my leotard.

"No purse?"

I shook my head.

"You first. Don't try any tricks. We're taking the service elevator down to B-level." He pushed me ahead of him and closed David's office door behind him. He glanced down at the lock, realizing the key was missing. He looked at me. "Hold out your hands."

I complied and opened them so he could see I was hiding nothing. He reached into my coat pockets and patted them. Then he felt his own, wondering if he'd forgotten where he'd put the key. "Never mind, let's go. In a few minutes it won't matter." He grabbed the container of gasoline and shoved me down the corridor toward the elevator bank. We turned the corner. Sergio, still unconscious, lay on the floor, half in and half out of one of the elevators. The door to the service elevator at the end of the bank of elevators stood open. Adam shoved me toward it. "Get in."

I stepped over Sergio's legs. I hesitated and turned back. "Look! His eyes are open." Adam turned to follow my gaze. I bolted away, throwing open the door to the emergency stairwell. I was halfway down to the 40th floor before I heard footsteps above me.

"Get back here!" he shouted. He pounded down the stairs but I was already at the door to the floor below, fitting the key into the lock. I pulled it open and raced away through the darkened office, the lights flickering on behind me as I ran.

I had to stop moving. I wasn't sure where the sensors for the lights were placed, but as long as I was moving they'd give my position away. I turned a corner and stopped. From the light filtering down behind me I saw a long stretch of corridor, individual offices to my right, secretarial bays to the left. I had to find a hiding place. I slipped into the first bay to my left. It contained two large desks with counters facing outward and a long counter against the wall, with more desk chairs, printers, and telephones. I scooted under one of the desks and pulled the rolling chair in behind me, doing my best to slow my breathing and make no sound.

For what seemed an eternity I heard nothing. Then I caught a slight squeak of leather and quiet footsteps on the carpeting. They stopped. He was next to me on the other side of the counter. I covered my nose and mouth in case he had super hearing and could judge my position. The footsteps continued, muffled by the carpeting. I waited. David had said other departments at the firm occupied this entire floor. The corridor must continue all around the perimeter of the building. I mentally kicked myself for not exploring the 40th floor when I'd had the chance. By now, Adam would be familiar with every nook and cranny, but surely there must be exits to the central part of the building and the elevator bank. If I could slip out quietly, how long would it take an elevator to come to this floor?

I waited. This cat and mouse game was making my whole body tremble and I didn't like being in the mouse position at all. My legs were cramping. I had to stretch and move before everything went numb. I decided to take a chance and peek out, to see if there was a path to safety. Then I heard him.

"Come out, come out, wherever you are," he sang. I froze. He was closer than I'd imagined. Then he sighed. "It's no use, Julia. I'll find you."

I listened. My heart was beating so loudly, I was sure Adam could hear it. How could I have been so trusting? How could I have been so attracted to him? He was a monster.

And if Adam was telling the truth, then the guard downstairs would do nothing. Maybe eventually he'd get worried, but that would be too late for me. Karen would be waiting in Adam's van with a trussed-up Suzanne. And the guard might not make rounds on the parking levels until Sergio returned. Karen wouldn't dare drive away, not without Adam at the wheel. My brain was doing cartwheels trying to figure out all the possibilities.

The odor of gasoline was everywhere. He was splashing it on the carpeting and against the walls as he walked. The hallway was completely silent; not even the rush of air indicated movement. The lights had been extinguished — Adam must have turned back. I crept out quietly and peeked around the corner of the secretarial bay.

The hallway was dark and unoccupied. I stood and, pressing against the wall to outwit the motion sensors, moved sideways along the corridor, finally reaching the halfway point. Double glass doors to my left led to the elevators and duplicate glass doors opened to the other side of the floor. I steeled myself to make a rush for the elevator button. I'd be exposed for a few minutes waiting for the elevator, but it was my only chance. I took a deep breath, ready to make a dash for safety, and then saw movement, a reflection through the glass.

Adam. He was on the other side of the floor. I pulled back against the wall. He stopped and turned, looking behind him. I held completely still in the dark, pressed against the wall where I had a clear view through the glass partitions. He hesitated again and glanced toward the elevator bank. He squinted his eyes. I could see him clearly. I didn't dare move a muscle. He stared right at me. He had seen me. He sprinted through the glass doorway, passing the elevator bank.

I ran. If he was coming in this direction, I had to go back. I raced down the corridor in the direction from which I'd come. I ducked into an office where a heavy legal tome sat on the corner of the desk. I shoved it and several papers onto the floor and flew through the next doorway. I hoped my ruse would work. I had to buy time.

I crept behind the door of the second office. Something hard pressed against my back. It was as high as my hip and prevented me from moving further behind the door. I reached behind me. A kind of heavy cloth, an edge and an opening. My fingers touched cold metal. Golf clubs.

Adam was in the corridor. Walking slowly.

I pictured him in the doorway of the first office. I turned slightly and carefully lifted up one of the clubs, praying I wouldn't make a sound. A door squeaked on its hinges. Silence. I imagined Adam pushing the executive chair away from the desk and looking under it, hoping I was there. The club was firmly in my hands now. I raised it straight up. Pressing against the wall, I waited. I heard a small thud. Adam had returned the book to the desk. Then I heard his breathing on the other side of my door. He entered and stood quietly for a moment. I needed him to walk toward the desk. I waited. He took two more steps, ready to move around the desk and check underneath.

I shoved the door away. Adam turned. I swung the club with all my strength, hitting him squarely on the side of the head. He swayed and blood flowed from his cheek and nose. Clutching the golf club, I ran. I flew down the hall, through the glass doors, and pressed every button on the elevator bank. My heart was pounding. I glanced back. He was on the other side of the glass doors. His head and jacket were covered in blood. He reached for the door handle, his hand leaving a smear of blood on the glass. *Please, please,* I prayed. How long would it take the elevator to reach the 40th floor?

Adam lost his balance for a moment, but then a determined look crossed his face as he attempted to stay conscious. He reached out to pull the glass door open. The elevator dinged and opened. I fell inside and grasped the golf club, jabbing at the buttons while the doors closed excruciatingly slowly. With only an inch of aperture, bloody fingers reached inside and curled around the rubber edge of the elevator door. The door wouldn't close. In desperation I pounded his hand with the golf club. He howled in pain. Fighting nausea, I pushed the slippery fingers away, allowing the doors to close completely. I was free.

THIRTY-EIGHT

I'd like to think I was cool, calm, and collected when I reached A-level and the security desk, where the guard was biting into a large submarine sandwich. I still don't have a very clear memory, but I think I was screaming. The guard dropped his sandwich on the console and a few slices of salami and tomato slid away.

"Don't let them out," I shouted. "Lock the gate!"

"What the . . ." The guard stared at me.

"They're in a van." I remembered that the metal grate to the parking garage would open automatically. Surely there must be a way for the guard to prevent that. "They've kidnapped a woman. You have to stop them. Call the police."

"I just did, lady. I've also called Sergio, but he's not answering."

"Call them again. Tell them it's an emergency."

The guard nodded and picked up the phone as we heard an engine coming up the ramp. That's when the building's fire alarms began to sound. "What the hell's going on?" the guard hollered.

The van reached the metal grate and waited, engine running, as the grate moved slowly upward. Karen was at the wheel, Adam in the passenger seat. A splash of blood covered the inside of the window next to him. The guard ran to the console and flicked a switch. The gate had risen but the lower bar of it stood only four feet from the concrete, not enough to allow the van to exit. I peered through the glass wall. I had a full view of the parking areas and the ramp to the street. The rear lights of the van flashed, and tires squealed as the vehicle reversed. The engine revved again. The van flew forward and crashed into the gate, bending it and flying past it up the ramp to Montgomery Street. I heard brakes squeal, and shouts and then a crash. I ran out through the door, heading for the exit ramp, and looked up toward the street. The van had smashed into a patrol car. Four officers, guns drawn, stood in a semicircle, shouting instructions.

THIRTY-NINE

"She was born Elva Karen Schaeffer in 1966 in St. Paul, Minnesota. Her son Adam was born out of wedlock when she was just fifteen. He was four years old when she married Terrence Ward, so for all intents and purposes, he considered that man his true father." David and I were seated in hard wooden chairs across the desk from Sergeant Sullivan on the second floor of the Hall of Justice. A few days had elapsed since the capture of Karen and Adam and the attempted murder of Suzanne Simms, not to mention of yours truly. The fire department had arrived in time and quickly doused the blaze on the 40th floor. But it would be a good while till the damage was repaired and Meyers, Dade & Schulz returned to normal. Sergio was doing well apart from a fractured jaw and concussion. He was set to be released from the hospital soon, although he'd be taking nutrients through a straw for several weeks. Suzanne had revived and was in good shape. Adam and his mother had been arrested on the spot.

"How did she become Karen Jansen?" I asked.

"She changed it legally three years ago, after her husband's suicide," Sullivan replied. "Jansen was her mother's maiden name, and she used her own middle name for her new first name. The two of them have been planning this for a long time. Schaefer always went by his birth name, his mother's maiden name. He'd already established himself as a private investigator even before the Bank of San Francisco fire, so that part of their plan was already in place. He wangled a spot with Sinclair Investigations, which is an old, established firm. When Karen discovered the Meyers firm used Sinclair to run their background checks on employees, it was a gift."

"But how could they be sure Adam would be the one to be assigned to the Evolving Soul Meyers firm after the first murder?"

"They chose their timing carefully. It's not that large an organization. The CEO of the agency, Bill Sinclair, is on an extended vacation in the far east. Two people were down with the flu, one investigator was in the hospital having surgery, and the remaining two operatives were up to their eyeballs in assignments. That's when Karen made her move and killed Jack. Schaefer wanted to be on the scene at all times. He wanted to know everything that was going on at the firm, but frankly, they could still have carried out their plan even if he hadn't been." Sullivan turned to me. "If you hadn't gone back to the firm that night . . ." He trailed off. "I hate to admit this, but they damn near got away with it. Killing Ms. Simms was their final goal. We had no forensic evidence at all. Everyone's prints are all over the place. No way to tell who touched or did what. Literally anyone could have gotten to Jack Harding and Ira Walstone in that building."

"What happens now?" David asked. He was subdued but still looked ten times better than when I'd visited him at the hospital.

"I'm certain they'll be held without bail. Who knows if the judge will decide on the death penalty."

I gasped involuntarily. "I hadn't even thought of that."

Sullivan shrugged. "I wouldn't be surprised. Murder, attempted murder, kidnapping, false imprisonment, conspiracy to commit murder. They'll get the book thrown at them."

"Wasn't the death penalty ruled unconstitutional?" I asked.

"Well, it's complicated. Capital punishment's been in use in California since the 1700s, believe it or not. Even though the Supreme Court finally declared it unconstitutional, a new law reinstituted it. Lots of death sentences have been handed down, but as of last count, I think only about thirteen executions have actually taken place. Last one was in 2006."

"He's right, Julia," David offered.

"But wasn't there a movement to end it again?"

"Prop 34 would have done away with it and replaced it with life imprisonment, but that was voted down by a slim margin. Every election cycle it seems there's another effort to do away with it, but in this case it'll be up to a judge and a jury."

David shot a sideways look at me. He was aware I'd been attracted to Adam but had held his tongue. I didn't turn my head. I still felt horribly ashamed that I'd allowed Adam into my life in any way. Maybe it wasn't logical, but it was how I felt.

"We only had Karen's word that Jack was alive when she left the firm that Sunday," Sergeant Sullivan went on. "Roger Wilkinson thought he'd seen her leave, but she

431

waited around until after she was sure he'd gone. Poor bastard. Jack Harding would have had no idea what was headed his way. It was Adam who attacked Ira Walstone two nights later."

I thought of the dinner Adam and I had shared in North Beach that evening. It was unbelievable to think he had committed such an act and then calmly taken the elevator up to David's office to make dinner plans with us.

"They hadn't wanted to risk killing Suzanne Simms in the office because it would have pointed us in the direction of Schaeffer," the sergeant explained. "But they had to wait for an opportune time to get her out." He shook his head. "A mother-son duo. I gotta say, that's a new one. Maybe other cops have run into it, but it's a first for me. She had a hell of a hold on her son. Real sick relationship in my opinion."

"Adam kept pointing me in the direction of Nora Layton as a suspect. Misdirection, I guess." I turned to David. "What's happening with her?"

"I told her not to come back and offered her some severance money. I didn't want to report her to the Bar Association. I have no hard evidence about the Deklon situation anyway. Just what you've told me. But

432

Adam . . . I never saw it. Never even had an inkling."

"How could you?" Sullivan answered. "Adam Schaefer was the real deal, a licensed private investigator. A good one from all accounts. Why would you even suspect anything like that?" The sergeant closed the folder on his desk. "Well, that's it. Hopefully you'll never have any trouble at your firm again."

FORTY

The house was a one-story wood-frame cottage, very like my neighbor's post-1906 earthquake house. One of those places hastily constructed after the Big One but still solid and still standing.

Maggie had told me that Leonard O'Brien was in his early seventies, and once a cop, always a cop. In retirement, he'd felt useless and volunteered to work on cold cases. That's what Michael was now. A cold case. I shivered in the wind that came off the ocean. I wasn't sure why I was here, but just . . . unfinished business. I hoped something had turned up from the boxes of photos and negatives found in the old man's house. I heard footsteps on hard flooring and the door opened to reveal a wiry man of medium height only slightly taller than myself. "Can I help you?" he asked.

"I'm . . . my name's Julia Bonatti, and I've been told by Maggie Sefton that you're working on a hit-and-run accident that occurred a few years ago in the Sunset."

"Oh. I see. Well, you're looking for my brother, I believe."

"You're not Leonard?"

"No, I'm Matthew. Leonard's brother." Dishes clattered from the direction of the kitchen. A woman called out from the interior of the house. She came down the hall and stood next to the man who'd opened the door.

"Hello," she said with a smile.

The wiry man turned to her. "She came to see Leonard."

"Oh." Her face shifted. "I'm so sorry to give you bad news. Leonard died last week. Friday afternoon. Heart attack. It was very sudden. Are you a friend?"

My heart sank. "Died?"

"Yes, sorry to have to tell you."

"I'm . . . no, not a friend. We never actually met. I came to talk to him about a case he's working on."

"I'm so sorry. We can't really help you," the woman replied. "One of the officers from downtown stopped by and picked up the files Leonard had. Everything's been returned to headquarters."

"Oh." I sighed. "Well . . ." I trailed off. These two were obviously cleaning out the house and tying up the loose ends of Leonard O'Brien's life. He'd died on the very day that I could have been killed, the day I was pushed into oncoming traffic on Market Street. If only I'd dropped everything and come sooner.

"Maybe you could contact someone downtown. I'm sure they'd help you."

I nodded. "I'm very sorry for your loss."

"That's kind of you," the brother replied. "I think Leonard wanted to keep working because he felt so alone after his wife died. Didn't know what to do with himself."

The woman smiled. "Just couldn't stop being a cop, you know. It gets some of them like that."

I did my best to smile and hide my disappointment. "Thank you." The door was gently closed in my face.

I descended the front stairs and stood in the wind for a moment. I didn't want to go home. I couldn't bring myself to call Maggie just yet but wondered if she knew that Leonard O'Brien was dead. No, I thought. If she had known, she would have called. I'd have to be the one to break the news. I started the car and drove to the end of the street. When the lanes were clear, I crossed the Great Highway and pulled into a parking spot. A storm was threatening and the tide was so high, the waves were pounding and crashing against the barrier. Droplets of saltwater sprayed my windshield. The surfers were undaunted, paddling out to meet the waves of a raging ocean. I watched one man climb onto his board and ride a wave for several yards. Losing his balance, he dove into the roiling sea. Would we ever have any answers?

FORTY-ONE

Don Forrester pushed a generous plate of sausages, eggs, and hash browns across the Formica table top. "Eat up. I keep telling you you're too skinny."

Don, who was enjoying a day off from the *Chronicle,* and Maggie and I had grabbed a booth at the diner above Seal Rocks at Lands End, with a view of the remains of the old Sutro Baths. Down below, waves crashed against the rocks and hikers scrambled over the remaining vestiges of concrete walls now filled with sea water.

"Oh, Don, it smells great, but I can't possibly eat all this."

"What would your grandmother say?" I suspected our breakfast was Don's way of assuaging his guilt. I had insisted repeatedly that it wasn't his fault. He'd had no way of knowing, when he texted Adam's picture to me that night, that he'd be putting me in danger.

"She'd say, *'Mangia, mia cara.'* That's what she'd say. That's what she always says. She's always trying to feed me." I dipped a corner of toast into the yolk of the egg and watched it run. Then I took a bite of sausage and savored the delicious greasy taste. Maybe I would tackle all this food.

"I wish I could have known this place when it was still in existence." Maggie pressed her face against the plate-glass window, looking down at the ruins of the Baths. "I would have come here every day."

"Me too," I said. "We were all born too late." Don was attacking a plate of waffles. "You'd know, Don. When did it burn down?"

"Well . . ." He took a moment to swallow a mouthful. "After Adolph Sutro died, his heirs really tried to keep the enormous place running, but it was just too expensive. They were forced to finally give up. Then in 1966, I think, a fire destroyed what was left of the structure. I've always had my suspicions about that fire because at the time a developer was drooling over the site. Thankfully, the city shot down his plan for a luxury condominium project. Only in San Francisco. That's what I love about my city. This incredible view was far more important than allowing a developer to line his pockets."

"Can you imagine what it must have been like? Saltwater swimming pools, even an ice rink," Maggie remarked. "I've seen photos of the place and talked to older people about how wonderful it was."

"I have a framed print of the interior, an artist's rendering." I turned to Maggie. "You've seen it, I know. In fact, ask at the cash register. I'm sure they still sell them. I bought mine for five bucks."

Don was watching me carefully. "Julia, I have to ask. What the hell made you go back to Montgomery Street on Halloween night?"

"Oh . . . it was the dragon."

"Huh?" Don took a last bite of his pile of waffles before starting in on his eggs and bacon. "What dragon?"

"I was haunted by them. I kept having dreams about a dragon and its swishing tail. I couldn't figure out what it meant, but I'd wake up in a panic with my heart racing. Every place I looked I saw a dragon — at the Asia Inn where Kuan threw my grandmother's birthday dinner, at the Mystic Eye the night of the open house. I'm certain now that my unconscious was sending me a message but I couldn't decipher it." I speared a second sausage with my fork and took a bite. "I realize now it started right after I set up the charts for the people at David's firm. Karen's chart showed her Sun conjunct the South Node of the Moon. Not a good placement at all. She was easy to overlook. She was someone who always managed to blend into the background with a different face for every situation. She showed everyone what they expected to see. That's why I didn't pay enough attention to her. The only time I caught a glimpse of what might be underneath was when I questioned her about Billy, the messenger. She bit my head off. And then, with solar arc Pluto setting off that natal conjunction . . ."

"Gawd, Julia. Give me a break. In English, okay?"

Maggie laughed. "I agree. You might as well be speaking Sanskrit to us."

"Sorry, I'm speaking shorthand. I tend to forget. See, the nodes of the Moon are just points on the ecliptic, not planets at all. But the zodiac sign of those points has a lot to say about where you're supposed to be going in this life and where you've been in the past. For example, if your North Node is in Pisces, and your South Node is in Virgo, you're meant to develop a Piscean sensibility in this lifetime, develop an openness and respect for the unseen, and move away from the Virgo-type talents that your soul has already developed. You may be a brilliant accountant, but you really need to learn to appreciate music. That's a very silly, mundane example, but you get the picture."

Don nodded. "Go on."

"Well, for Karen, having her Sun sign conjunct her South Node indicated her fate to be a repetition of the past. An individual would really have to struggle to let go of the past. But nothing clicked until that night at the Mystic Eye. Someone wore a dragon costume, you know, like the things they use in Chinatown for the dragon dances. Then a lightbulb went off in my brain. I realized that given her age, Karen's solar arc Pluto would have advanced to her —"

Don groaned. "Now my eyes are really crossing, okay? I am not getting it."

"The dragon was a dream symbol for me. The North Node of the Moon is called the Dragon's Head, or the *Caput Draconis,* and the South Node is the *Cauda Draconis,* or the Dragon's Tail. Ancient nomenclature. The Dragon's Tail is a point of, and take this with a grain of salt, undoing. The point of least resistance for the soul. If someone misuses their South Node, there's resistance to moving forward. To quote one of my books, 'rigid compulsions which sow the seeds of one's own undoing.' Rather archaic way to put it, but valid nonetheless. Karen wasn't able to release the past and move toward the future. She was literally the cause of her own undoing."

"By taking revenge."

"Yes. There were times I felt I was being watched, and now I'm sure it was Karen who pushed me into traffic that day. Building security wasn't tight at first, and she must have avoided security checks by hiding out in the office all night and then appearing again in the morning. Easy enough to do; there are plenty of storerooms and closets. She didn't use her car, so it wasn't possible to pin down her movements with a parking card. Dani even made a comment once about Karen always being the first one into the office in the morning. But I was so focused on Rebecca Moulton, or Rebecca possibly being someone actually working in David's office, that I wasn't looking close enough to home. Once Adam . . ." I hesitated. Just the mention of his name brought up unresolved feelings. "Once Adam located Rebecca, I realized she couldn't possibly fit the bill. I was back to square one. Elva Karen Ward — Ward was Karen's married name — never recovered from her husband's suicide. She blamed the people who focused on the negligence of the electrical contractor, her husband. Whether he was truly negligent, I don't know, but the arson investigators thought so at least."

Don looked thoughtful. "From what I read, the electrical contractor really *was* to blame for the faulty wiring that started the fire."

"Was he?" I asked. "Or was he just a very easy scapegoat because he couldn't afford a battery of lawyers to defend himself? Maybe we'll never know."

"Well," Don said, "it doesn't change the fact that three people are dead because of this. Four if you want to count Terrence Ward. And now, two more possibly facing the death penalty." We fell silent. Don stared out the window. "I'm really bummed there aren't seals here anymore." Seal Rocks, just offshore, is a collection of black rocks named for the creatures that always used to be here, as far back as I could remember.

"They're really sea lions," Maggie replied. "Not seals." She peered out the window. "I used to love to see them hanging out on top of the rocks and barking all the time."

"I miss them too," I said. "They left years ago. I'm not really sure where they went."

"They're all downtown now, at the Embarcadero. Classier restaurants, I guess." Don placed some bills on the table. "Hey, what do you say we climb down the hill and explore the rocks? Work off some of our calories. Kathy's always on me to exercise."

"Okay, I'm game." I slipped on my jacket and grabbed my purse.

"Me too," Maggie said. "But wait for me. I'll be right back. I think I'll get one of those prints of the old Baths if they still have them." I was relieved to see her in better spirits. She'd confided that she and Harry, Michael's dog, had moved back in with her mother. She would be returning to school and finally get her degree.

Don turned to me. "Okay, Julia, you can drop the act."

"What do you mean?"

"You know what I mean. How are you feeling about that guy? Adam?"

"What can I say?" I groaned. "Awful. Stupid. Betrayed. Horrified, really. I don't understand how I could have been so attracted to him. How I couldn't have seen what he was."

"It happens. Forgive yourself. You're only human."

Maggie rushed back to our booth with a large rolled-up print of the Baths. "I got one, Julia. Just like yours!"

"Treasure it. It's important to remember what's no longer here."

We headed for the door. "Oh, Julia." Don followed me through the restaurant. "Before I forget to ask, Kathy wants you to come over for dinner next week. There's someone she'd like you to meet. She'll kill me if I forget to pin you down."

"You must be kidding." I shook my head. "No way. If it's just you two, fine. Otherwise, I don't think so."

"Why not, Julia?" Maggie said. "You should. You never know who you might meet."

"That's what I'm afraid of."

Don shrugged his shoulders. "Have it your way, but I think you'd like this guy." He held the door open as Maggie and I stepped into the brisk wind and headed toward the path to the rocks below.

I couldn't help but reflect on the choices we make. Rebecca, with the strength to carve out a new life for herself and her children. Sarah, Jack's sister, locked bitterly in the past. Elva and her path of psychosis. I'd managed to create a new and productive life . . . not without pain, but did I have Rebecca's strength? To open my heart to new risk? Right now, the answer was a resounding no.

"Tell Kathy I'll think about it," I said.

ABOUT THE AUTHOR

Connie di Marco (Los Angeles, CA) is the bestselling author of the Soup Lover's Mysteries (Penguin), which she published under the name Connie Archer. She is a member of Mystery Writers of America, International Thriller Writers, and Sisters in Crime. She has always been fascinated by astrology and is excited to combine her love of the stars with her love of writing mysteries. Visit her at conniedimarco.com, on Facebook at Connie di Marco (Author), or on Twitter: @askzodia.